Edited by Geoff Hancock

Singularities:

Fragments, Parafictions, Prose Poems – New Directions in Fiction and Physics

Black Moss Press

Published by Black Moss Press,
1939 Alsace, Windsor,
Ontario, Canada N8W 1M5.

Black Moss Press books are distributed by Firefly Books,
250 Sparks Avenue, Willowdale, Ontario M2H 2S4

Financial assistance toward publication was gratefully received
from the Canada Council and the Ontario Arts Council.

Cover design: Turkish folk artist

Printed and bound in Canada.

Canadian Cataloguing in Publication Data

Main entry under title:
Singularities

ISBN 0-88753-203-9

1. Canadian prose literature (English) – 20th century.
I. Hancock, Geoff, 1946-

PS8329.S46 1990 C818'.540808 C90-090052-0
PR9194.9.S46 1990

I have the universe all to myself. The universe has me all to itself.

– Peter Matthiessen, *The Snow Leopard*

Contents

Acknowledgements

"You have to do it by yourself;
but you can't do it alone."

This powerful zen koan has much to do with the paradoxes of quantum mechanics. The paradoxes, and I hope essential truths of *Singularities*, could not have been articulated without the inspiration and support of many remarkable and enlightened men and women. To all of them I would like to express my love and gratitude. In particular I owe a special thank you to Taoist Master Mantak Chia; Enlightenment Master Stephen Islas; poet and publisher Marty Gervais for his unfailing support of a complex project; and Robert Kroetsch who let me know that theories could sizzle. Finally, I must thank my two bright and guiding lights, Gay Allison and Meagan Julia.

Grateful acknowledgement is made to the following for permission to reprint previously published and unpublished material:

jwcurry, to the author;

Dave Godfrey, from *I Ching Kanada*, Press Porcépic;

the estate of Gwendolyn MacEwen, from *Noman's Land*, Coach House Press;

Erin Mouré, to the author and Vehicule Press, from *West South West;*

Joe Rosenblatt, to the author and Oolichan Books, from *Brides of the Stream;*

Michael Dean, to the author and Black Moss Press, from *In Search of the Perfect Lawn;*

sean o huigin, to the author and Black Moss Press, from *The Nightmare Alphabet;*

Anne Szumigalski, to the author and Fifth House, from *Dogstones;*

Karl Jirgens, to the author and Coach House Press, from *Strappado;*

Lola LeMire Tostevin, to the author and Coach House Press, from *'sophie;*

Smaro Kambourelli, to the author and *Canadian Fiction Magazine;* from "*Tessera*" Feminist issue No. 57;

Michael Bullock, to the author and *Canadian Fiction Magazine;*

George McWhirter, to the author and *Canadian Fiction Magazine;*

Claire Harris, to the author and Fiddlehead Goose Lane Editions, from *Translation Into Fiction;*

Patrick Lane, to the author;

Gay Allison, to the author and Williams-Wallace Publishers, from *The Unravelling;*

Eugene McNamara, to the author and *The Ontario Review;*

to the estate of bpNichol and Black Moss Press, from *Selected Organs;*

Rod Willmot, to the author and Black Moss Press, from *In the Ribs of Dragonfly*;

Paul Dutton, to the author and Coach House Press, from *Right Hemisphere, Left Ear*;

Fred Wah, to the author and Turnstone Books, from *Waiting for Saskatchewan*;

Betsy Warland and Daphne Marlatt, to the authors and Gynergy Books, from *Double Negative*;

Michael Kenyon, to the author and *Canadian Fiction Magazine*;

C.H. Gervais, to the author and Penumbra Press, from *Letters to the Equator*;

Paul Savoie, to the author and Black Moss Press, from *The Meaning of Gardens*;

Leon Rooke, to the author and *Grain*;

David Halliday, to the author and Press Porcépic, from *Making Movies*;

Susan Musgrave, to the author and McClelland & Stewart, from *Cocktails at the Mausoleum*;

Martin Vaughn-James, to the author and *Canadian Fiction Magazine*; from *After "The Cage"*;

Christopher Dewdney, to the author, and House of Anansi, from *The Immaculate Perception*;

Robert Kroetsch, to the author and Oolichan Books, from *Excerpts from the Real World*;

David McFadden, to the author and Black Moss Press, from *Canadian Sunset*;

David Donnell, to the author and Coach House Press, from *The Blue Ontario Hemingway Boat Race*;

John Newlove, to the author and ECW Press, from *The Night the Dog Smiled*;

Mary di Michele, to the author and *This Magazine*;

Kim Maltman, to the author and *Canadian Fiction Magazine*;

Judith Fitzgerald, to the author and Black Moss Press, from *Diary of Desire*;

Doug Glover, to the author and Black Moss Press, from *The Mad River*;

George Payerle, to the author;

Colleen Thibaudeau, to the author and Black Moss Press, from *the Martha Landscapes*;

Marlene Nourbese Philip, to the author and *Contemporary Verse*, "Tessera" issue and *Ragweed Press*

Crad Kilodney, to the author and Black Moss Press, from *Malignant Humors*;

Ron Smith, to the author and Sono Nis Press, from *A Buddha Named Baudelaire*;

Stan Dragland, to the author and Coach House Press, from *Journeys Through Bookland;*

Fraser Sutherland, to the author and Pottersfield Press, from *In The Village of Alias;*

John Riddell, to the author and Coach House Press, from *Criss-Cross;*

Geoff Hancock, to the author and *Canadian Fiction Magazine.*

jwcurry

THE ATOMIC STRUCTURE OF SILENCE

THE ATOMIC STRUCTURE OF SILENCE

Dave Godfrey

from *I Ching Kanada*

乾 One **Ch'ien** Creating ☰

This is of the country, the people. Truly. They alone give birth, give birth to greatness, observe fully, deserve good fortune, define what is correct & the wolf-whale, ah, the wolf-whale: the power they owe beyond themselves. What fits the leaves into wind; body into body; animal onto animal; second eyes; what child? Have you arranged yourself in the form that will arrange you? Child.

To know the connections is to know when, know where to begin. The inside-man is active and vigilant from dawn onward, seeking the connections. the islands without docks.

Before the wolf leaps, he knows the whale's lair. In the air his body moves as through water: striking. He moves with and through and towards the music of objects. First: accepting this existence. And have you: found your wolf-whale's lair?

Science stutters, does not lie. Only the scientists. But too much power can always be absorbed; learn to release. There are times to slaughter the wolf, to behead the whale. What can not be released: ch'ien.

War leader or one who knows dreams. The law is inside; no magistrate can order you onto your upward roadway. Be still and you will flow into yourself.

Wind follows the wolf. Even after all the others had crossed the line, the Sioux were still where Sitting Bull struck his tents. Go to visit him.

But when wolf turns on wolf, teeth shown, heart sharpened, he will lose the circle, lose the clarity of many.

坤 Two *K'un* The Receptive ䷁

This is the land. The mare on the prairie above the river. Tireless. Ponokamita. Learn to fill space.
By bearing with the people you gain / give support. The people fill the land. Dark should yield, earth acknowledge.

Ice follows frost. Sleet. Grasshoppers. Smut. Vendeurs. These all give warning early. Check decay in time. As death does. Death always begins.

When the Romans and Tuaregs took too much, the earth increased deserts. When you pour mercury in the river's heart, earth lures the fish to her. Earth walks in her laws, does not need purpose yet resists the false purposes. Wisdom follows the self-evident. Calm. Mortised. Simple. Yet a river.

Shake off vanity. Observe rock, prairie grass, cod fins. Let the Queen melt down her medals. The wise man releases forces instead, acts for the barley and timothy, the grapes that flourish tomorrow. When he leaves rented land, the humus is rich. Chisel-ploughed twice before winter.

Learn to tie grain sacks with the Winnipeg knot. No knot before seeding. One hand holding. One tying. Firmly & quickly. The Mounties record the prominent. Enemies flourish in such times. Reticence is not defeat. Remember the clearings. Vigilance too has its seasons.

Leave bluejeans for the city people who dream of country. Wear Eaton's greens if that is the way of the people, today's homespun. Curl as they curl. Be discrete even with your discretion. Independence is not the only virtue. The musk-ox circle on their journeyings. The exploration is never over.

Dark should yield, earth acknowledge. The wolf-whales fight in the pastures. In ponds. Unnatural blood flows, weakening all. The children suffer from too many liberations. There is no blame in holding to what is right.

屯 Three Chun Hard Birth ䷂

Storm and thunder and chaos of birth. Winter calving. Don't rush about. Appoint helpers and get into the movement.

To bring order out of confusion it is necessary to know what will separate and what will unite. The wholeness is always greater than one expects. It cannot be gotten used to in April. Each April.

Hesitation and hindrance at the beginning. Do you have the right associates? Do you talk with them correctly? Hear them?

The pin is gone from the reach; wheels jam-up. Even the horses seem to retreat. Is she determined to rob him? He turns her down, avoiding these obligations. In ten years. Then he will have his child.

Leaving the guide behind, he is lost in the forest. Can't even find himself, let alone the deer. Find a place. Fire the three shots. Let them find you. Avoid further humiliation.

The tractor and the waggon part. Ask old Angus for his jack-all. Make it up with him, even if he will shoot the shit about you in the Legion tonight. Get the load home and into the barn before rain. Winter feed. Winter calving.

If the situation is fouled up, your favours are discredited in advance, your works dismissed. Persevere in small things; don't try to push the big advances through.

The greatest peril. The waggon has run amuck. Bloody tears. One should not persist in this.

蒙 Four Mêng Youthful Folly

Braking at the cliff. First you must learn to seek the teacher, remembering there is no need for her to answer more than one question.
The spring becomes what it does by filling what is before it. Force a clean, one-inch, galvanized pipe, down – down, down to your sources.

A child grows with discipline; humiliation if the fetters rust.

A child in the family becomes a leader or a tag-a-long; folly flows slowly, like lava.

Your daughter: does she love a man of bronze who would enslave her?

Your son: humiliation is often the only knife to cut snarls of fantasy.

All children know to love the wise, but are yours not taught otherwise!

Anger, when used to punish folly, furthers no one: teacher, child, mother. The greatest folly is to punish the people.

Gwendolyn MacEwen

from *Noman's Land*

An Evening with Grey Owl

Kali read from the works of an obscure Kanadian poet:

There is no chart of his movement through the borrowed forest,
A place so alien that all he could do with it was pretend it was his own
And turn himself into an Indian, savage and lean,
A hunter of the forest's excellent green secret.

For all his movement through the forest was
In search of himself, in search of Archie Belaney,
a lone predator in London
Telling the very king: I come in peace, brother,
The princess thinking how alien he was, how fine.

Stranger and stranger to return to the forest
With the beaver all laughing at him, baring their crazy orange teeth
And the savage secret – if there ever was one –
Never revealed to him. Stranger and stranger to return to
The female forest, the fickle wind erasing his tracks,
The receding treeline, and the snowbanks moving and moving.

(Anahareo fed the fire with sweet smelling branches. It was the end of summer and loons cried out over the dark lake.

They spoke of how the first man in the world had emerged from the water covered with shining scales which later fell off, leaving only the vestiges which were toenails and fingernails.

They spoke of how the Indians had no opposite of God, how good and evil were not separate forces, but two aspects of one spirit, one reality. He liked that.

They sought themselves in each other's eyes like all the world's lovers since the beginning of time. But they couldn't discover their histories in one another, for when she looked into his eyes she saw only the lost lands of her fathers, and in her eyes he saw the desolate country which was his soul. He claimed that only the natives had a memory, that the white man suffered from a permanent amnesia brought about by his first glimpse of vast and horrifying expanses of snow. She did not know that he was speaking of himself, nor did she know that he was jealous of her; he could see them out on the lake – her ancestors – rippling over the water in their delicate ghostly canoes all silver around the edges. He wanted to claim these ancestors for his own. He said that the white man was always trying to steal the Indian's myths. Wasn't it enough that he could steal their names?

When he looked inside himself, he discovered an impostor.)

We want you to pretend that you are our ancestors – you who are called
Wolf in the Water, Blue Flash of Lightning, Heaven Fire, Black Sleep –
You who have no devil, no opposite of Manitou.
You who are hiding behind your names, behind closed doors of thunder
And will not let us in.

(Backlit by blue lightning, the silhouette of the wolf drinks the midnight river; fire from heaven
Falls on our sleep and invents morning; the air is thick with feathers from surreal birds.)

You who never knew the evil in us, you who have
no opposite of Manitou,
Come out from behind the thunder and embrace us –
All we long to become, all we have never known of ourselves.

Before you are gone from our eyes forever –
(you who are certainly not our ancestors)
Teach us our names, the names of our cities.

No one ever welcomed us when we came to this land.

(Archie Belaney thought of winter. "Surely this is the most silent country on the face of the globe," he said. "Silent as death except for the booming of the ice on the big lake." He looked into the darkness and added, "I must write that down."

Anahareo put more branches on the fire, Anahareo who was dark and beautiful, Anahareo who had taught him to love the animals.

They spoke of how at puberty Indian boys would enter the manitou world by fasting, and how this journey inward was a journey *into* the real world, not away from it. In dreams they would discover their personal manitou, their protector, and an elder might discover a boy's secret name in one of his own dreams, in the mighty reality of the spirit world. Some might call this the unconscious, but in truth it was the kingdom of consciousness. Within the tree was the Tree, within the world, the World.

Grey Owl prayed for his immortal soul.)

So I must stand away from the stone to enter the stone,
To dream the idea of the stone, the stone which is all stones, the first and final stone,
Its source being, its manitou.

As in puberty I dreamed my lifelong protector, who showed me
How to navigate impossible rivers, who made me as the world's
first person, breathing
Fire and poetry.

The strangers who divided the world into good and evil were wrong.
The Great Lynx Misshipeshu who dwells beneath ambivalent water
is both benevolent
Lord, and devil.

And I am become the powerful dreamer who dreams his way through
To reality, to enter and ignite the stone, to illumine from within
Its perfect paradox, its name.

Kali got up and kicked dirt over the ashes of the fire. This was their last night of camping out at Algonquin Park.

"I had this bizarre dream," Noman said. "I dreamed that a band of Indians broke into my room and took all my possessions – my books, my clothes, my toaster, everything. And when I asked them what they were doing they paraded down the street and said they were just taking back what was theirs, nothing more."

"It's time to go," said Kali.

"No more poetry?" he asked sleepily.

"No," she said. "Another time I'll read to you from the book Anahareo wrote about her life with Grey Owl." She says, "When, finally, I was convinced that Archie was English, I had the awful feeling that for all those years I had been married to a ghost – that Archie never really existed.""

"How unfair of her," Noman muttered. "How awfully unfair. Of course he existed. As surely as you or I. He was only looking for his soul, or for God, or whatever."

Then he thought of winter and the white expanse of the lake, a whiteness so vast it was almost claustrophobic.

Now it was the end of summer and the loons were crying into the night. The dying fire smoldered beneath its blanket of grey ashes, sending up occasional smoke signals which he could not decipher. He thought that there was nothing to worship in this country but the magnificent indifference of Nature, its broken silences.

Erin Mouré

from *WSW (West South West)*

The Origin of Horses

To imagine the shape of the poem before it occurs, the placement of hieroglyphs on the page, hiero & glyph, sylph & pirouette, the shuddered flank, muscle open in the hoof and shoulder, soft light off white-walled houses, dreamed last night in Spain, just before we drove onto the ferry

The cars had sped off the ramp to make room for us, high beams white hurting. Our camaraderie in the car, us younger than ourselves, as if in high school, & my brother in t-shirt & jeans, appeared suddenly, twenty years old, peaked cap of the Grain Growers shielding his eyes, jumping serious onto the hood of our moving car, then up & into the back seat, top down, not even rushed

breathing.

It was the houses astonished us in Spain, the narrow laneways & cement over hand-made bricks, washed yellow, red tile roofs, busyness; the dog sleeping in the grocery in a bin of clothes, yowling when we woke it. This is Spain, we said to each other. Spain, we're in Spain, the wine-strong smell of the streets & incontestable music on the radio. Sometimes the poem's shape comes of this, three squares thick with wording, & the lone glyph representing the lungs, the icon placed on nearly every poem to honour the lungs' softness. As the brother is honoured, glyph jumping out of nowhere in Spain, dreamed Spain origin of horses in America, the clothes he wore to cut the grass in, in the Rocky Mountains, a symbol of oxygen, the car driven over the shoreline, into the dark of the ferry.

Joe Rosenblatt

from *Brides of the Stream*

Blind Date

A few miles along the highway from where I live on Vancouver Island, the Little Qualicum winds under a bridge toward the sea. I approached the river with some apprehension, my first blind date. Would she accept elements of my personality, my "fraudful" flies? I saw her rejoicing in melting mountain snow and rising winter rain. Pan-sized trout leapt and swam in serpentine rhythm, camouflaged against an amber-pebbled floor. Under the overhanging branches they lapsed into a suspended vigil, periodically bubbling up a hydrological sermon.

I cupped the water, tasting traces of iron, copper, iodine and other metallic essences. A spirit, I conjectured, was trapped in its mineral phase. A dark force was projecting thoughts. Hues of green swirled into the anonymity of shadows where Neptunites dissolved. On that bright day, however, truth displayed a vicious nudity. I peered through a clear window at a brutish member of the Order of the Aquatic Tabernacle. Moving in on a minnow, he turned momentarily to gaze at me. I saw Uncle Nathan's eyes; neutral gray, they looked right through me. My shadow had polluted his lair. His twisted lips mouthed, "Keep away from my brides."

The Bride

There is a woman whose song is minnow
a shadow moving out of view: my bride
swimming among dead black branches.
All afternoon I delivered fertile red moons
and when ennui tugged, I offered a nuptial meal:
conversational worms ... a hypnotic blue fly ...
This hook caught in a soft frozen mouth
where darkness nibbles at a pebbled floor.

Mother

In the larger sphere we are not far removed from fish. We are corralled, chosen for some upstream demise. A dark minnowy presence swims through every pore. In the Beginning, we gulped down flies like inmates in the present fishbowls of the criminally insane.

We bubbled in bliss through methane, crunching on smaller fish. A balanced diet lengthened our girth until a Voice urged us to try the land. Our eyes blinked, vestigial hands motioned toward the shore. The food was plentiful there without a need to play luncheon host to black and silver diminution. We tore them apart, webs and all: each human caricature the weight equivalent of a million flies.

Deep armoured feelings vanished. The Mother undulated below the earth. We cast aside a fishly psyche.

Blue Movie

Silhouettes press against the windows. Evening oblongs rove intimately exploring pulses, riffles and cross-currents. A blue swallow-tail spirals down an invisible staircase. The lady in blue shakes her hipless middle. A curious shark follows her rhythms like a sailor at a sleazy bar. The dance implies: *come on, sailor, try me.*

Fade out. The scene changes. A grasshopper materializes. The creature has swung too far over the edge, toppling into the drink. In seconds the winged racer disintegrates into a red vapour.

I'll see you at the Club Top Hat. A green residue flutters away and the film now concentrates on a pore in the river. Our shark flicks to the other side of the stream. There's an infernal logic here to match the intelligence of any keen flyfisherman: If one grasshopper has missed the landing field than there has to be a hundred who'll take a dive. It is only a matter of waiting. The shark yawns ... soothing to have water rush up against the bruised gums; the Little Qualicum is an oral hygienist ... cleaning away corpses ...

The shark inhales acres of winged souls. The porno reel is still humming in his hyperactive brain. His gray sky fills with a rare intelligence.

I must write a novel.

Michael Dean

from *In Search of the Perfect Lawn*

An Aural History of Lawns

Interview 1: Is there communication through lawns?

When I'm out cutting the grass I notice how people look at me and stop for a minute. They seem to enjoy watching me work. Somehow they know that I like my work, and they watch for a while how I create a pattern in the lawn out of the longer grass.

When I look up from my machine, I see the looks on their faces. It's a kind of peace, a harmony that they experience. I bring out the character of the lawn from the grass. I don't fight it. I aim the lawnmower down the line of the wheel marks left from the last row that I just cut. In this way I make sure that there are no tufts of grass left uncut. Often grass gets pressed down by the wheels and then you miss it altogether and only see it when you rake it afterwards. If you've created a good pattern out of the grass you hate to go over the lawn again just to get those tufts.

Yesterday I was cutting the lawn after the rain and a girl walking on the the far side of the street stopped and watched me. Her name was Rosemary. I enjoyed that moment.

But the real pleasure I felt was in the work.

I love my lawn and the smell of it after a rain.

Rosemary saw me through it.

Interview 2:
What are the problems and their solutions in lawns?

I hate raking. And I hate clipping around the edges, unless I have a lot of time and then I like the look of neatness that this creates. I feel quite satisfied afterwards.

No matter what size a lawn is, there are always edges, and raking. Edges are just something that has to be done. I use a new electric trimmer and that helps. It will never be a love, however.

I don't usually rake a lawn. In fact, raking can be harmful to the roots of the grass. If the cuttings are left unraked they act as a natural fertilizer to the soil, and this helps the lawn over the years. Many people prefer the look of a carefully raked lawn. Even so, if you cut a lawn often enough, it doesn't need raking after each cutting. I use the electric rotary mower and this helps. I find that the dual chute system of the electric helps spread the grass, so you don't get it collecting in strips like with the gas-powered mowers.

There will always be edges. And raking.

But the love of the mowing carries you through it.

Interview 3: Do you ever dream about lawns?

I have had this dream several times:

I am cutting a lawn. It is the front lawn of my parents' house. I am sixteen in the dream. A girl stops on the street and watches me. Her name is Rosemary. She smiles then moves on.

Sometimes in the dream it has just stopped raining.

The lawn has an interesting shape at one edge, a rolling curve created by a line of shrubs by the front porch. What I want to do is start with this interesting edge and follow the same pattern right across the lawn. But I feel that I will never be able to resolve the far edge satisfactorily because that edge is straight and borders on the curb of the street.

What I end up doing in this dream is starting with the patterned edge and then allowing it to diminish as I go across the lawn until the pattern settles gently into a straight line at the far edge.

This also resolves another problem: there is a tree in the centre of the lawn. Normally the best way to cope with a tree is to form a square around it and work towards it from the four edges. Because of the one interesting edge whose pattern I want to follow, I don't do this. I want very much to integrate the tree with the pattern of the lawn.

Interview 4: What is the meaning of Lawn as dream image?

I have felt different things about this dream.

At first I felt it was telling me about my life, that I had become the tree held between the tension of the edges of the lawn and that the edges were my parents – the curved edge my mother, the straight edge my father.

Then I felt the dream was a premonition. It was telling me that a great change was about to occur in my life and that this change would be triggered by a new woman in my life (Rosemary, the girl on the street).

Whenever I had the dream I felt something different about it. But the tree in the dream was always me.

Then, just after I stopped having the dream altogether, events occurred that told me I had been completely mistaken.

I was not the tree.

I was not the grass.

I was the pattern in the lawn.

It's a funny thing about lawns, most people don't even see them. They cut and tend them but seldom talk about the problems they encounter along the way.

Your lawn is more than grass.

Did you know for instance, that the lawn season begins in the fall when everything else is dying?

That's what my dream was telling me: for the truth you don't always have to look below the surface.

Interview 5: What is the natural cycle of lawns?

Rosemary told me an interesting story about lawns: when she was just two years old one of her older brothers died. She went with her father whenever he cut the grass around her brother's grave, and from then on she associated her father cutting grass with somebody dying.

I thought of Rosemary's story when I was visiting my mother six months ago. My mother had phoned and said I should come and see her because she had some bad news about my father.

Before my mother told me the news she met me on the front porch and asked me to stay a couple of days and cut the grass before I left. "If it ever stops raining."

The grass was long alright. My father hadn't been able to cut it for three weeks. It was autumn and autumn is a critical time for lawns.

Then my mother told me that my father's operation had shown his tumour to be malignant and that he had about six months to live.

I didn't stay with my mother for two days and I didn't cut the grass. My uncle came over the next day and cut it. My uncle has a good two cycle gas mower with power start and a mulch setting.

As for my father, he never cut another lawn.

My father had never let himself get close to me, but when I visited him in the hospital he opened up and told me things I had wanted to know all my life about our lawn. He told me that when my parents bought our house they had cut down a huge, over-bearing tree in the front yard and then planted a new tree, the one that grew and became the tree in my recurring dream that I told you earlier.

It was at this point (when my father had only a week to live – as it turned out) that I knew I had been mistaken about my dream.

My father was the tree. He was also the lawn.

Lawn care is important in the fall. If your autumn lawn is left uncared for, fungus can start growing under the tangled mat of grass clippings as soon as the snow falls. This snow mould can create bare patches that show up only in Spring.

My father was not an easy person to get to know, but just before he died I started believing I had been able to get close to him through lawns.

Then, after it was over and he was buried under the earth, I realized that lawns had been literal all along, and that they would somehow separate us forever.

Interview 6: What form does the pleasure take in lawns?

Lawns can play tricks with your mind. You can see things in them that aren't there. We all must struggle to see lawns for what they are, in themselves.

I have loved many lawns and I hope to love many more. Lawns are a natural part of life and we shouldn't be afraid of expressing our feelings about them.

Some people love the look of flatness and symmetry of a well-cut lawn. They aim for a one-inch bristle. Some lawns take a half or three-quarter inch bristle, but these always have a good flat surface and must be rolled.

Personally, I like creating patterns. I like watching a pattern take shape out of the long grass. I love the look of the edge between the cut and the un-cut grass. The edge moves and the truth of the lawn is revealed in the process. When someone stops on the sidewalk and watches me, like Rosemary for instance, they see a ritual being enacted. They smile and say hello as a way of thanking me for enacting it.

I've learned not to take this response personally. I know I am an intermediary between the people and the lawn. In fact the pleasure I feel is in knowing this. And in knowing I'm always getting closer and closer to the truth.

Rosemary asked me: "The patterns you make in lawns, are they signs of something?"

"They are activity," I said. "Not the result of activity but the activity itself."

Frankly, I don't think anyone could have characterized pleasure more exactly than that.

Interview 7: Is there a secret meaning to lawns?

So many of us have been wounded by lawns.

After my father died I went to cut my mother's lawn. It was Spring by then. The lawn was in good shape except for a strip by the curb where the road salt had eaten it away.

The rain had just stopped. I looked up from my machine and Rosemary was watching me from the street. We talked for a while.

When I had finished the lawn, my mother and I had a long talk in the kitchen. During this talk my mother told me something unusual. She told me that I had been conceived on a lawn.

"I'm telling you this now," she said, "because I think it makes a difference. I think it makes a person special."

What my mother told me helped me to see the dream of Interview 3 in its true meaning.

The tree in the lawn of Interview 3 was the symbol of a single lifetime. The lawn was the symbol of regeneration. The patterns that I had been making all my life in lawns are the activity of coming-to-terms, not with death, but with the fact of having been generated, of being alive in this moment.

That's what my dream was saying: what begins in grass is resolved in lawns.

My father knew this. My mother knew it. Now I know it and so do you: never take your lawn for granted.

Interview 8: Aren't you suggesting a connection between lawns and sexuality?

Yesterday, when Rosemary watched me from the street, I asked her if she'd ever cut a lawn after a rain.

She looked away.

"It's a deep and earthy experience," I said. "There's a smell the grass gives off. The blades are swollen with the rain and they're a deeper green. The bristles are fat and moist and the over-all effect is that of softness. The flat surface of the freshly cut lawn holds the tension between this hardness and softness."

"It's quite a sensation working with it then," I said. "It's firm yet yielding. Giving yet reserved. The lawn is a separate thing but we form a relationship in the work, a unity, like coupling."

"Cut grass is good as a mulch for the garden," Rosemary said.

"Especially after a rain," I said. "It is rich and fertile and helps things grow."

Rosemary said: "Nothing is forsaken, nothing is lost, in lawns."

Interview 9: Aren't you asking an eschatological question and giving an ontological answer in lawns?

Last night Rosemary and I made love on the lawn. We rolled on top of each other and bits of cut grass stuck to our clothing and to the naked parts of our bodies.

"I love it now that we're doing it," Rosemary said. "Tell me something, something important I've never known."

"Imagine that were together for the first time after many years of separation," I said.

I brushed bits of cut grass from Rosemary's thighs describing how they looked like something transferred from the pages of a novel we were rolling in.

The grass was newly cut and wet, clinging to our bodies and peeling away onto one another.

"What is the story of our love?" she said. "Who am I and what happens next because of me?"

I was revealing for Rosemary the secret meaning of the cut grass stuck to her thighs, calling her my novel. I was reading the grass like sentences:

"I courted you when we were young, then I went off to war in France. When I got back you couldn't wait and were married already to a wealthy man. So I too made myself wealthy and came to court you again with my personal elegance and new blue lawns. You turn me down, however, at the very end."

"Maybe they could find you face down in your own swimming pool," Rosemary said.

"We are," I said, "a short but significant twentieth-century American novel, *The* ... "

"I know," she said. "*The Great Gatsby.*"

Our story began unfolding even more quickly than I had expected. Our characters began revealing themselves through action. The events of the story, fore-shadowed on Rosemary's thighs, were coming to pass.

There was nothing new for me in this woman.

The crisis of the story occurred right here. I saw all of my sex life as a series of unclean thoughts and impure acts with myself or others on lawns. There were no surprises for me in Rosemary, just new words for describing the acts of sex. I was frightened that I would get bored with it very soon and that it would all end tragically.

I rolled on top of Rosemary and my throbbing member pressed against her belly. I found the centre of her moist desire and entered her like the key in the lock of a Manhattan hotel room door with the shower running in the other room, the radio on, and black lingerie over a chair.

A piece of grass from Rosemary's belly was stuck on my penis as I moved in her. I thought that this piece of lawn was the capital letter "P" from the word Passion. I dwelt on this thought. I meditated on my passion spelled out in blades of grass on my body moving in the woman.

But the blade of grass was not the capital letter "P." It was the letter "g."

The silent "g" in the word gnaw, the "g" of the "ing" in being.

This story is the child of that coupling.

This story was fathered by the silent "g" of being that swam into the woman, persisting and entering the central meaning of her round fertile vowels.

This story was mothered by the "a" and the "e" of the woman.

This story's chromosome structure spells the word age: the beginning of time, the marking of time, the events occurring in time and then their ending.

This story is what I thought about as I cut the grass on my mother's lawn after my father had died and the rain had stopped and Rosemary was watching me from the street.

This story is a collection of blades of grass on a woman's thigh.

sean o huigin

from *The Nightmare Alphabet*

picture this. a young man lying naked on his bed. he's curled into a foetal form. arms wrapped 'round his knees.

a language
forming
bathed at
first in
colours of
emotion

within his dream he looks down on a landscape full of letters. he sees their gestures. interactions. sees their wars and schemings.

growing later

to another
place
where
movements
are performed
and sound
explored

he sees the letters watching what he does. he notes aggressive motions made in his direction.

the letters
move

the boy takes steps. he walks into the letters' light. he realizes suddenly how small they are. he reaches down and scoops them up.

together
they will
integrate
explore his
world
speak of
it
if they
get the
chance
and finish it.

the twitst and twich but he can hold them. he can bend them into other shapes.

the boy feels power surging in him. recalls the hell the letters put him through and for an instant wants to tear them into pieces and destroy them.

no. he orders them. commands them with a voice he's never heard. he beats them into lines and words. he forms them into sentences. he spells things never said.

the boy builds stories. spreads out poems upon a tapestry of mind. in ecstatic frenzy he throw words around. glues together letters in unorthodox relationships. the boy is mad or drunk or both with language. dives and rolls and bathes in feelings only words let out.

the boy's heart bursts. unable to contain the joy. unable to control the rapture. overwhelmed by vast new kinds of freedom. the boy's heart bursts. within his dream his body shrivels. shrinks to letter size and dessicates. the letters cover it. they draw themselves across him and some carry him away.

awakened by a drawn out sound. a laugh. a groan. some thing of happiness. his parents find him. sprawled upon his bed. from his smiling lips a thin blood line draws letters on the sheet.

picture this. a young boy naked. curled inside a padded room. chatterbabbling nonstop to the walls.

picture all the possibilities. picture all the levels. time and space. that might be. take a choice. invent. if such a thing is really done.

work hard at it. immerse yourself in concentration. maybe you will feel a little of the hopelessness such a one goes through.

picture this. a happy family walking through a field. in the father's eye a tiny glint of something no one knows.

Anne Szumigalski

from *Dogstones*

The Question

behind the woman a window is open   a breeze pushes against the back of her head causing her voice to empty itself into the room   the wind gives her words the twang of an out-of-tune harp   they shape themselves into a question she's been asking about the scheme of things   *it all seems to be rushing away from us* she remarks *as from an abhorred centre*

beside a small table a naked man sits with his legs crossed   where skin touches skin his body hairs lock each one tangling with another   the light enters the glassy cones of his eyes which glint like the eyes of a dog wandering on a road at night

with one hand he fondles the brass stem of the lamp on the table beside him with the other he reaches for the woman's hand counting her fingers with his own   why can't he remember how many fingers this woman has how many toes   how many separate hairs   he begins winding each strand on its own small spool winding and counting   winding and counting until every bobbin lies close against her scalp

the man and the woman set up a loom   *it takes forever to dress this thing* she complains   at last they are ready to weave   they throw the shuttle back and forth between them   they shove the beater firming the fine drab weft   when the piece is finished they drool over it sizing it with their spittle

they fit the cloth into a tambour the size of the moon as seen from the planet

the clippings and leftovers are dyed with the woman's blood with the dust of the room they have always lived in with the soot that has gathered on the glass chimney of the lamp they thread their needles and begin to embroider the only scene they know   the table   the chair   the spools   the bald woman   the tambour on its stand   the broken loom   the breeze   the question   the naked man   the burnt-out lamp   the window that opens onto a dark road where on the grass verge a half-seen animal is mouthing the dusty blades

Karl Jirgens

92 238.029
6,5,4,3
4407
1405
18.90
U
|Rn|$5f^3 6d^1 7s^2$
Uranium

from *Strappado*

Strappado

... a jet incision separates the unclouded dome into two increasingly distanced thoughts ...

Al Pacino thinks that the Lee Strasberg tapes from the New York Actors' Studio should be considered a part of the Strasberg estate now that Lee has died, but Paul Newman thinks that the tapes are too important as an educational tool, and figures that they should stay at the Studio. I am watching TV. I am in a cyclops state of mind, one glass eye looking out at the world. I am thinking about Lee's words on that tape, locked onto that magnetic ribbon forever, those exact words, waiting for other words to be exchanged so that the tape can be played once more. I am thinking about Lee Strasberg, and Eli Rill who once studied at the studio, and who later played the heavy in the movie Slipstream, about an independent-minded disc-jockey who discovered that his name and radio personality belonged to the producer, and I wonder just how much of what gets on the radio and TV and into the newspapers comes out of the pockets of various producers. And Lee, what would he have said if he knew ahead of time that he was at the end of his rope, knew that one day the end of that tape would slip past the heads and go flipping around and around on the reel until somebody finally, mercifully, punched a button; pulled the plug.

In an effort to arrive at disarmament, the U.S.A. and the U.S.S.R. have decided to permit each other to investigate their respective missile defence systems. I see a picture of a bear and an eagle inside of a broken circle. Some testing and detonation of thermonuclear devices is involved. A U.S. colonel is explaining to a crowd of reporters that these tests are safe and won't endanger local inhabitants. I see a mushroom cloud on the horizon followed by a surge of electricity travelling in a blue glow up a rundown country telegraph line. The colonel explains that detonation methods have become so sophisticated that he can set off a charge by simply shedding a tear. I wonder if he does this by using the "method" approach, and I consider things he might think about, the puppy that was crushed beneath a set of highway-by way snow tires, the tri-actor that was disqualified at Belmont, the Bay of Pigs, his wife's lesbian lover. And I wonder whether he had ever heard Lee's words, or if he ever thought of himself as being at the end of his rope.

I am drinking "Pride of Arabia" waiting for a phone call that never comes. I get up and stand in front of a mirror. My face is turning to snake skin. My right eye has drifted around the side of my face and has disappeared. My left eye has moved to the centre of my forehead. I am in love with a stripper who thinks she is pregnant, who can't have an abortion because it's against her religion, who may have to leave her job, who is in love with Al Pacino, or Paul Newman (it doesn't matter which), but he just quit a job with the children's aid society and he recently woke up from a coma (the result of an automobile crash with a tractor trailer). And Al Pacino, or Paul Newman (it doesn't matter which), is still in love with the woman who was in the passenger seat beside him when the trailer connected, and even now she is hanging onto life by a single blonde hair, still in a coma, refusing to live or die.

And the dancer won't come to me until it's all settled one way. And I can't cry for fear of setting off a series of thermonuclear explosions. I am at the end of my rope, and the phone if it ever rings, it rings because it is a wrong number, like the time it was some guy calling to tell his father about a movie he just saw about a pair of siamese twins who were joined at the base of the spine and how in the movie they were trying to push two baby carriages in opposite directions and they were struggling between them to see which one would go which way, and they were married to a Swiss proctologist and her mother. I am looking through a pile of photographs from my childhood, there is a series of images of people standing in an incomplete circle around an old woman sitting on a park bench. As I flip through the photos I notice that she is slowly slumping over on the bench, vegetation and plant matter start spreading all over her body until in the last photo she is reclaimed by the grass and weeds. Small gray flowers are growing out of her arms and legs and torso, and out of her mouth. In the photos, I am the only one looking directly at the camera. One of the pictures in the series seems to be missing.

When the old man's lungs exploded with silicosis they gave me a pamphlet at the hospital desk. It was somehow supposed to comfort the patients' relatives or at least make them feel more at ease. This is what it said:

Please do not be alarmed at erratic movements of the beam on the bedside scope. It is extremely sensitive and is affected by patients' movements or any movements around the bed. Some of our patients may have telemetry, or ambulatory monitors, which allow them to move about or walk without disturbing the beam or scope.
Intravenous therapy is used for all patients in our unit, as it allows us a direct and speedy route for administering medications. We also give many of our patients oxygen to help relieve chest pain and / or breathing difficulties.
We recommend that you continue to limit visiting and phone calls, as visiting for long periods can be exhausting for the patient.
We request that you do not bring electrical appliances into our units as they interfere with the monitors. Small battery operated radios are permitted, provided they are used with earphones.
Due to the limited amount of space in the unit we ask that personal belongings be restricted to a housecoat, slippers and toiletries. For the same reason, we prefer that flowers not be brought into the area.

It unfolds like the plot to an old movie from the 1950's, except that it is happening today. Somewhere in another hospital is a man with a Sony Walkman on his ears. It is Paul Newman, or Al Pacino (it doesn't matter which). He is watching the blue light on the bedside scope. He is ruminating about the job he left at the children's aid society. He is ruminating about Eurydice, but he keeps looking over his shoulder. The woman has been comatose, wavering between sleep and death for over a year now. He is considering her response if upon wakening she found out that he had left her for a pregnant exotic dancer. He is listening to a tape with the last words of Lee Strasberg. He is at the end of his rope. I am still waiting for the phone to ring. I am gazing into my single eye reflected in the bathroom mirror. I am thinking about getting a haircut. The TV is playing in the background. My coffee cup is sitting on the desk beside the typewriter.

Wind fills my ears. I am flying over a strait of water towards an island. On the island I find a bearskin robe. I put it on and while wearing the skin I discover a huge castle-like building on a rocky hill. I enter it and marvel at the tall stone pillars and expansive floors. I begin searching around and start to notice that it is cool and dark inside. I approach what seems to be a throne area. There is a huge rock there. It seems to be made of pink and clear quartzite or granite. Still wearing the skin, I touch the stone and pass inside of it. When I enter, I am high in the air. Below me I see another island surrounded by a wide strait. At the centre of this island is another palace of a different shape. I fly up to the structure and enter it. Inside, I find what seems to be throne room and there on a flat outcrop of rock is a gemstone mounted on a yellow metal ring. I put the ring on my auricular finger and disappear.

Lola LeMire Tostevin

from *'sophie*

A Weekend at the Semiotics of Eroticism Colloquium Held at Victoria College

According to the brochure, the capacity to arouse and experience sexual desire has been a philosophical preoccupation since Plato, and the colloquium, "The Semiotics of Eroticism," promises to examine new perspectives that have emerged through semiotic activity in recent theories and philosophy.

Considering that the great founding discourses of western philosophy, the *Phaedrus* and *The Symposium* are based on the amorous discourse, the erotic quest, which was far from being platonic and didn't have anything to do with women, I feel optimistic about the new perspectives. "Beyond Eros," "Fetish," "Male Masochism and Subjectivity," ... all topics that promise to examine current problems around eroticism and hopefully move beyond the explicit violence that Plato represents as the dynamics of the amorous soul.

The first speaker introduces his topic "Darwinian Erotics: A Gene-Culture Perspective," and proposes to tell us why and how women have come to develop large "garbanzos" or, if we prefer, "tits." He beams at his own daring and goes on to examine the familiar darwinian theory of selection in primitive societies, something to do with male choice, childbearing and breast feeding.

The next speaker from The Medical Research Council in Scotland, illustrates charts upon charts of statistics relating to sex, desire and the brain and one of the conclusions drawn is that aggressive women, especially lesbians, have more male hormones than normal women. He doesn't mention if the same tests were performed on gay men, whether they have more female hormones than normal men, at least there doesn't seem to be any statistics on that and nobody asks. The next paper by a woman from Brazil deals with the Brazilian carnival and for almost an hour we are exposed to slides of women in scanty or barely existent costumes. The point being that during carnival time women are objects of the gaze, and the point is well taken since the man sitting beside me keeps making appreciative noises with each slide, while another man sitting across keeps rubbing his crotch trying to prevent a hard on. This is followed by a paper by a soft spoken man from India, "The Erotic in the Classical Indian Tradition," which claims the equality of men and women in Indian myths and poetry. Then a paper by a psychologist concerned with the pathology of eroticism and the generally alienated sexual condition between men and women. Her argument is supported by astoundingly explicit slides of *Playboy* and *Penthouse* centerfolds as well as ads for various sexual aids, a vast assortment of devices that obviously required a great deal of imagination on the part of their inventors, including a cocky little number with the fanciful name of a thumper. Normally, the papers should be followed by a discussion period but no one seems to have much to add, except on the way out I overhear a woman say she wished she'd asked where she could get the thumper.

At home later on tv a famous sex therapist advocates the use of a small zucchini for women who happen to be minus a man. The host, feeling he's lost control of his show throws up both hands and walks off the set.

Hegel likened his to a thinking brain, the ascending and descending motions of. While Flaubert thought of his more as a tiger's tail with which to flagellate women. On that subject there's little point any more of going into what Freud thought.

A woman told me once how her personal vibrator had run out of juice, and she had frantically raided her children's toybox in the middle of the night looking for batteries, a ten inch GI Joe coming to the rescue. Doesn't care much for the average Joe anymore, for as Lois Lane says in the movie, "... you're a hard act to follow Superman."

Smaro Kambourelli

It Was Not a Dark and Stormy Night

for Patrick Friesen

Theoria / theorein: not language degree zero; not empty signifiers; not things minus tissue; not tongue minus body. Behold. Be. Hold. Being a spectator[1]

Theory: to contextualize the personal; to articulate the emotive; to retrieve the drowned self from within the self; to cry without guilt or shame; to talk about "Me" without losing "my" privacy. How to hold away the fear of being found out.[2]

The split between theory and writing (fiction / poetry) has often assumed the same configuration with the split between mind and body.[3]

Theory as genre begets its own iconography. Yes, it does rehandle itself.[4]

Does theory (re)tell what the writer has left untold? Does it express without creating? Does it tell a parallel story?[5]

Theory often belongs to the genre of the fantastic. Its hesitation does not belong to the order of the real as the act of theorein reveals it to me. This is why I often translate myself into theoria, why I give my ambiguity the name of the uncanny.[6]

The self can never be theorized / thematized. It is what practises the act of theorein. The minute I start writing all precise margins are liquefied. The page is a littoral line. Solitude becomes the writing I's name. I is one and many. Skin touches nothing. Nothing touches it. I may even cease to exist. The S exits. The name becomes a signature. I cannot authorize or be authorized. The writer is the sumtotal of the residue of desire. The woman behind the writer has tasted desire at the moment of its death. There is no virginity in the history of beginnings. This woman is (still) (dying).[7]

I've been told I'm Electra. It was in a damp basement apartment lit with the cold light of a bare bulb. I ran out and down the steep street and when I reached the university campus, I was out of breath, my limbs shaking. It was a matter of theory, only I didn't know this at the time. That night I remembered that someone (my aunt?) had taken me to see Kakoyannis' *Electra* when I was a child. Eirini Pappas' classic face leaning over the ground; her cutting her hair off, the gesture of mourning. This mythic scenario is now one of my recurring daydreams. Only I don't know whether I mourn mother, father, brother, lover or my own death.[8]

Theory and fiction are each other's doubles. "Narcissistic narratives."[9]

Theory and writing. Their intercourse is the paradigm of my life as long as it avoids overdetermination. As long as it doesn't try to beget my other.[10]

Do-be-do-be-do.[0]

Notes

1. How to make I-love-you synchronous with theorien. How to love the one in the many, how to love the many in one.

2. Freud is not the name of my shadow.

3. The fissures are the same gaps producing the same silence there is no safety net for the writer ther is no wall for the ladder to lean on.

4. over and over and over. again. and again. and then. now. before. tomorrow. there is no end. i've known that. there is no end of the inside of the body becoming a knot the shape of I-am-thinking of the mind reaching the hard core it didn't know it had. like the stone of a cherry. small but smooth but hard. like its name. sometimes it hurts. sometimes it doesn't. have you tried squeezing blood out of a stone? have you tongued the sharp edges of a rock idling on a beach?

5. the corner of grief. the corner of meditation. the corner of reading. of

chewing my nails. of making love. of eating crackers and cheese preferably feta hard salty and white breathing through its tiny pores brie is second choice. the creased corner of the couch. holding me with patience. sometimes even with reverence. it is theorizing me. how to mother the abjected self. it doesn't matter if this is not theory. it still is.

6. This is not personal. I am not the I. This page is not a mirror. Mirrors are false exits. This page is a screen belonging both to the inside and to the outside. I'm just passing through. This page is the sieve that thins out the air I breathe. I dwindle into an otherness that cannot meet me. I theorô myself. Language rests on the tip of my tongue. Theoria weighs lightly on my eyelids.

eyes / tongue / language

the outside / what tastes the image (eïdolon) / the taste

The fictionality of theory; the truth of fiction.

7. How many times have I gone through this. Untying the naughts. Attempting the impossible. Pain is good for you, little one. The voice a cherry stone. The lips the delicate lines of lust without object. My heel a warm unwanting fist inside the hand. (The the defines the bitter taste of my theorein in the feminine.) I've dreamt of sacrificing dreams to the altar of desire. I've dreamt of Nike's face – an icon of terror. I've slept on the same marble bed with Louvre's Hermaphroditus. I no longer love myself. I could be any woman. I am not an enigma. I could change places with my double – if only I knew where to find her. I could even be myself.

8. Death has no face. Occasionally, it takes the shape of an endless sentence, its length extended by nots. A rope of words binding nothing. A figure without body. It could be desire. It could be the image of freedom. It could be It could be love.

9. Even though my words may have turned against me, this is not the story of *femina vita.*

10. This is both theory and praxis. (Rhetoric is not a source of theory.)

George McWhirter

from *God's Eye*

Nobody's Notebook

1

They were trademarked *under-surveillance.* Not flesh and blood, not objects even – simply his subjects under surveillance. He repeated this intelligently and wisely into his beard. A cozy dissociation, which broke down immediately the American laid his hand on Martín's knee. Rivas scowled, sat up and stopped writing.

An artist in his own way – like Van Gogh or Gauguin – Rivas used to write, in the open air, at every opportunity. It kept him separate while maintaining contact with his subject.

He picked up the pencil where he had parked it on the notebook at *Vera Cruz, State of Vera Cruz, February* ... Why didn't Martín batter the gringo? What was up with him? All at once, Rivas growled "bitch-bastard" under his breath and broke the pencil between his fingers. He threw the pieces into the sand. Growling, he began to pull out a large handkerchief to fold into a bandanna. His thatch of grey-black hair bulged in the breeze; the hairyness pestered his head until he bound it securely.

2

He considered looking the other way, leaving all his duties derelict. But he continued to bear witness, beginning to pour sand, slowly, from hand to hand. From one to the other, it ebbed, like the men's energies on the dune below.

3

Duty did not permit him to cancel out the fairy gringo, the fake antique dealer, the curio stealer. Nor Martín, the fake traveller in industrial lubricant, the pamphlet pedlar. Order no. 6357 spelled it out. Surveillance only. The gun in his pocket was private property, not government issue.

4

"Martín," Rivas growled. His beard and shoulders rose over the dune, sweat and hair and sand matting into what resembled a glazed, coarse-grained bust of Karl Marx. Karl Marx in every respect except for the headband which made him more the Apache Marx,

the Yaki-Marx,

stalking a renegade idealogue of his tribe.

"Martín," Rivas sighed. "Ah – that infidel, Martín."

Rivas dug into the sand where he had buried his notebook and pencil parts.

5

Hotel Imperial. A Norther blowing. Subjects in bedroom. No appearance until 7 PM. Day's activities, not ascertainable.

6

Where the balconies led off each floor onto the stairwell, Carlos Maximiliano Rivas bellied over the rail, all the way down, for every floor of it, (guacamole, tortilla) his early supper acting as a cushion. He maintained surveillance on Martín and the short American. The Yank baroomed (he did not speak); he baroomed that he didn't use elevators – stairs were his second favourite exercise. Imagine the number of back staircases in New York, nothing so civilized and up-front as this one. Sexy staircase, he baroomed. They hid staircases nowadays, as if they were wicked.

7

Rivas had dried up. He wrote nothing. He listened to the American. On previous visits he had reported everything on Martín. His surveillance expert in every detail down to the design of Martín's cufflinks, the silver sun-stone motif, his favourite. He wore light blue shirts, white shirts, dark blue ties. For the American he had put on a silk shirt-jacket. Blue. It gaped open to the sternum.

8

"If I were an Aztec," the American baroomed, "it would be a pleasure to locate your heart."

The American zipped a hand into the cleft of Martín's shirt-jacket.

"And would you relieve me of it by cutting out this heart of mine?"

The American haw-hawed.

"Won't leave without it."

Martín smile thinly.

"Remember. We Mexicans tend not to travel well."

9

Rivas knew they had rehearsed it. Over and over in their pyjamas, rehearsed it. No-one else heard the abomination on the stair. Rivas looked round. The old hotel was abandoned after Carnival. Painted green and white, it hissed at their levity, shook like an old hospital ship in the Norther off the Gulf. Like Carlos Maximiliano Rivas (who swallowed mouthwash with his supper), it gave an antiseptic green wheeze at every gust, every pressure on its superstructure. Rivas and the hotel hissing with cold drafts, deadly mortal reminders while these two flirted down the stairs.

The chandelier, which dangled its guts like glass jellyfish, tinkled, sparkled and spiralled on its chain. One way, then back. The conversation between Martín and the short American changed and spiralled from antiques to Karl Marx, to French heretics and commentators, to revisionists, back to disillusionists, to Louis Seize furnitures and Delacroix and Whistler and Zapata and Trotsky's non-relationship with Siquieros, then to the price his (Siquieros') paintings fetch on the open capitalist market, to how much one brick with a bit of Ribera's murals would draw at Sotheby's. How in hell could Rivas work out at which level they were socialist or capitalist-leaning, or plotting to transship Ribera's murals brick by brick from the National Palace or the Department of Education in Mexico City, where Rivas, on refresher courses, sat in his off-hours contemplating the flux of Mexico DF and eye-groping the secretaries.

Sometimes he sneaked into the porno movies on Gomez Street, out of the midday sun, into the air-conditioned dark. Standing there on the stair, the Norther air-conditioned every corner. It sandblasted, it rose above the fierce bray of the American's teeth. That rack of awful teeth, that awful head, that teeny body – a wooden head, rectangular; a ventriloquist's dummy with a barooming laugh, like the porno lieutenants in the horny movies, who laid on the orgies; porno-politicos, who compromised the government officials and blackmailed them so that they peddled petro-secrets for sex to the gringos and took off for lewd holidays in Hawaii. He would like to nail this little dwarf to the planks of a cruise ship.

10

Rivas belched at the chandelier, fogging the crystal as it swung close. It was dangerous that chandelier. This was Vera Cruz, State of Vera Cruz. They were all of them living, sitting at the far edge of a disaster. Mexico. Live cheek and jowl with it and you won't be too surprised when the bitch-bastard kisses you for keeps. Rivas spat. It stuck to the crystal.

11

Martín and the American, Steerman, stepped out through the hall and took a streetcar. Still running, Rivas flagged down a taxi.

"Where to, my bearded friend?" the driver asked.

"Wherever that tram goes. Until I tell you to stop."

12

What was there to go on? Martín's two suitcases: one for literature, one for laundry. Except the laundry was doing more business than the literature. Bad. The pamphlets were partly paid for by the government. They must be kept moving. An inveterate opposition must be maintained, must operate in secret and prominently in public, but never effectively, at any level, all the time. Misuse of funds otherwise.

Undetected subversion is not to be tolerated, worse still – no subversion at all, especially if you are trained and paid to detect it. And in the event that there was no subversive opposition, one must invent one – to promote employment; to keep the Russian revolution revolving. The pamphlets must reach the tried and true customers: new young students who might be intelligent or dangerous, who might be persuaded by the Party before it is too late – a little cheese to expose the mice before they are grown up to be rats. That

little

rat.

13

Who was this dwarf? This trafficker in antiques. He had nibbled at Martín's ear, he had delivered nothing of political value. Goods and gossip about Mexico and Marx and the value of sun-stone cufflinks in Greenwich Village. How to use *ludes,* but not *the* goods to neutralize Rivas' jealousy. A plot, a plan, a drawing – a coded message to absolve him from his plain hatred and loathing. A plot that said Martín is on business as usual, nothing *personal.* Not infatuation. Not love.

What had he to go on?

14

Day spent at the beach, he wrote on the marble table-top. The marble took the graphite well, then he erased it with spit. *A visit to the Plaza de Armas for café con leche, no* with spit. *A visit to the Plaza de Armas for café con leche, no for more café con leche.* Then, bless his ears, what were they saying? Rivas wrote on the table-top: *Mention of San-Juan de Ullua, the fortress. A visit. (Delaying tactic!) If the Norther holds, an excellent place for transfer of certain items or their receipt.*

Surveillance. Patience. He spat and rubbed his sleeve over the table.

15

That was why Central had placed Rivas on this vigil with no contact, no touchie-feelies. Martín was branching out on his own, sifting information. And if he went too far, who was going to break off his branches? Rivas growled into the ruff of his beard. Who will break, tear apart the brackets of the American's jaws, pull out that message on his tongue? Rivas growled and began dropping pencil parts into the empty cup of *café con leche.* The noise drew the waiter who thought it was the traditional tap of the spoon which called their attention. The waiter gazed at the empty cup.

"More?" he said, automatically, two-handedly manouvering the coffee and the milk urn for the trick of high-pouring. He saw the pieces in the cup.

"It began to write dirty," Rivas said. He wiped the table with his bare palm.

16

Gringos have visited San-Juan de Ullua for centuries. Off the sea in formations of emancipating marines; or by land, across the moat in mufti, to fulfill an old Mexican obligation. To liberate tour-guides from poverty, to unshackle petty officials from boredom with their bermudas and red and pink knees, pink

as a mandrill's arse.

17

They made it difficult for Rivas to keep track. The people, the obliterating wind and the movie-makers. Some company was making a movie.A run-of-the-mill Mexican movie about a secular miracle. Or was it just a nightmare sequence with an attractive nun and a boy dressed in a shiny black vest and dog collar? A young boy in football pants gripping a football helmet under one arm. The nun awaited him, arms outstretched.

"Sister," the young boy murmured into a dangling mike.

"Oh, brother," said the Yank.

"Shh!" said Martín.

The ventriloquist's dummy stuck out his tongue. The music howled holy of holy, the director trundled backward. Camera and all his accoutrements perched on a dolly with tracks for trundling to and fro. The boy stopped and the American winked at him. The innocent saw nothing.

The nun called: "Come back to us!"

"I am destined to play great professional football."

"Come back to us and play soccer," the nun said.

18

The two men vanished in the direction of the smoke spewed out by the artificial smoke machine, sprinting toward the Eastgate that opened onto the dockside, where the square sets bared themselves to the Gulf and gusts of ill wind from the old world.

Rivas climbed to the parapet overlooking the quay where the galleons hove to, loading up from the warehouses in the fortress, all the treasures, all the goodness of the many tribes. That Yank and Martín were holding hands, waving goodbye, bye-bye and bad cess to the old world, singing "God Bless America."

Rivas felt corny, like the good fairy, looking down on Martín. He pushed a stone loose. They jumped. The gringo bit the water and they threw in a lifebelt. "Try that for size, you sick monkey," Rivas wanted to shout. He knew all the insults. "Sicko, pinko." They were taught the very best for the anti-American turnouts.

But Rivas stayed mute. Surveillance only.

19

In the dungeons the Yank moulted big puddles and grinned at the guide, Cuevas, who had gathered more than the average gawking crowd. There was a steady trip-trip of water from the dungeon walls. Cuevas stood two metres by two metres, with a 25-centimetre moustache overhanging his lip. He gave a theatrical, risque rendition of the guided tour. San Juan of the Whores and Cannibals; San Juan de Ullua, the stone epitaph of tyrannies. Right there, in the dungeon keep, after they devoured their scraps, the prisoners settled on the thighs of dead inmates. The unfortunates took comfort in their cellmates, male or female – no matter. Manacled together, nobleman and commoner, political prisoner and thief – they made no sort of distinction.

For a time the great Juarez languished there. Juan the Red, who was incarcerated by the father of his beloved to prevent their marriage, escaped twice. The second time in a barrel of excrement. In time he became a brigand; she – a nun. "What people pass through for love!" Cuevas raised his arms to heaven. He frowned at the retreating back of Rivas, the one who comes and never tips, the one who skulks off. Cuevas turned to the American. Rivas heard Steerman's bravos for the broken English of the finale, Cuevas announcing that the Yankee marines had released the prisoners for good and always during the Revolution. Dungeon no more, San Juan became what it is now, Stone Epitaph of Tyrannies.

20

Later Rivas doubled back to find the American at the zipper of Martín's shirt. He cursed and blessed his customary rubber-soled shoes.

21

Students. Not students, procurers. Permanent pitch – the Hotel Ritz off the Plaza de Armas reported a revision on the pamphlets of October and November, 1975. *Your Petro-Peso: New Marxist Highways for Mexico*, a study of the redistribution of revenues and disclosures of real petroleum wealth. Also, pamphlet: *The Right Procedures for Redistribution of Arable Land*. There was a short inter-departmental reprimand.

22

Was it a real reprimand or a stalling tactic? A diversion? Rivas knew very little was real in the whole bureaucracy. Those disclosures of wealth always fell short of the government's real estimates. They divided by four and hoped the Marxists multiplied by two and passed it on to the Americans. The government assumed that Mexicans were born greedy, that they couldn't co-operate for two days on end without squabbling or selling out, that they harboured capitalist dreams of cornering a bit of the oil market for themselves. Or the mineral wealth. Talk of natural resources intoxicated them. The sums made them collapse under the anticipation of their enormities. In their heart and head they knew they could never handle it or horn in on it one at a time, individually, like the gringos, so they dawdled and dreamed and left it to the Party.

23

To hell with the distortions, Rivas growled. This was a set-up, a fabrication, a pantomime. The American was probably from Puebla or Tijuana. They were testing him through Martín. Had sent in Martín three years ago to lay his rotten egg to stink out their own reconnaissance man, Rivas.

He plucked at the beard, the awful disguise he wore to please Martín.

Did he really look like Karl Marx?

He strained at his impression in the mirror. That American – he might be a queer congressman or government aide passing cross-the-border information which required clear and objective surveillance. Antique dealer was an anagram for something. That American dealt in something second only in age to original sin.

24

Rivas looked through the window of the Hotel Imperial. The lighthouse beyond the harbour cast long lashes of light. *He loves me, he loves me not; we love; we never love at all.*

25

Rivas slept. When he opened his eyes, there were empty prints on the sand. These footprints crossed him over. He slithered down and measured the big dents left by their bodies. They must have lain there, motionless, making sand angels. Rivas had dreamed Martín kissed him, but his mouth was filled with gringo's teeth. Big and fishy, like pike's or piranha's. He took some sand and rubbed it across his lips.

26

Conversation overheard in Rm. 431, Hotel Imperial.

"When I was thirteen, I fell in love with his beard. I also fell in love with the American, Walt Whitman. Isn't the cover of this *Das Kapital* handsome. Look, his face is embossed in leather. I touch it. I don't read it anymore. I lie in the dark and touch his jaw.

"My mother is an Indian, my father was a gringo engineer."

"So, the old man cut out and you got it on for Karl Marx. You don't need Marx, man. You need kinky leather covers, people like me."

27

Rivas heard the pages rip.

He loves you, he loves you not, we never love at all.

Rivas put his shoulder through the door. His beard bristled, his eyebrows reared up, his long hair hung out from his sombrero, shaking as his head turned, looking for them in the dark.

28

"Jesus," the American cackled, "Mighty Marx."

He cackled until his teeth rattled. Even as his jaws were breaking, he cackled. Rivas could not credit such strength for a short man. It was long seconds before he began screaming. Those teeth made perfect hand grips, blunt edged, excellent even for the size of Rivas' hands.

29

All the pages were missing from the notebook in his hand.

"Who are you?" the policeman asked.

"Nobody," Rivas answered. "A Mexican subject."

"What was the object of your attack?"

"An American subject."

30

When they enquired of Special Services, they said he was nobody as far as they could tell. A dealer in rare pornographic books on Defensa del Agua. No-one that interested them.

31

The police were told a short notice in the *Excelsior* would do. "Mexican citizen outraged at relationship between young Mexican and an American tourist."

The readers could fill in the details. They would like that.

Michael Bullock

Johannes Weltseele Enters the Garden

1

Johannes Weltseele is walking slowly, lost in thought, along a moss-grown path in a deserted and tangled garden. He has no idea where the path leads since he has never been here before, but he supposes that somewhere within this evidently extensive garden, full of trees and bushes so that he cannot see far ahead, there must be a manor house or even, perhaps, a castle.

He entered this estate through a breach in the surrounding wall which he came upon by chance while roaming through the nearby forest.

Since there are no signs of human life in this garden, which has clearly lain in a state of total neglect for many years, Johannes is fairly certain that any building he may eventually come upon will likewise prove to be uninhabited and abandoned. He feels a thrill of anticipation at the prospect of exploring this deserted dwelling and looking for relics of its former occupants that will enable him to speculate as to their identity and nature.

Meanwhile he looks attentively at his immediate environment. The vegetation consists above all of countless rhododendron bushes, many of which are in full bloom, so that the brightness of their flowers forms a pleasing contrast with the darkness of their shiny but sombre leaves. Dotted among the rhododendrons are more obviously exotic growths – windmill palms and araucaria or monkey-puzzle trees – and between these a multitude of ferns. In other places there are wild roses, quite possibly the offshoots of bushes once cultivated in the garden that reverted to their natural state as roses, left unpruned, invariably do.

Round a bend in the path Johannes comes upon a lake fringed by bulrushes and other reeds and with its surface largely covered by waterlily leaves and other plants rooted in its depth. Enough of the surface is left free, however, for Johannes to observe large carp swimming lazily hither and thither when he peers down into the dark water. How many generations of these fish, he wonders, have been born and died in this lake since the last human hands fed or tended them? There can be no doubt that the ones he is now watching have become adapted to an existence entirely independent of human intervention. Since there are almost certainly no pike in this lake, and no birds in the surrounding trees big enough to constitute a threat to these large fish, they must exist in an environment that is free from all danger.

Johannes watched their slow undulations for a while with a feeling not far from envy.

Then he moved off along the moss-grown path, the multi-coloured carp still circling in his head.

***

After leaving the silent fish behind, Johannes Weltseele became more aware of the song of birds that echoed on all sides from the trees and bushes. At times this birdsong grew so insistent that he could not escape the feeling that it contained some message which the singers urgently wished him to understand. If message there was, however, he had no means of interpreting it.

***

The singing birds remained for the most part hidden among the leaves, except when one flitted quickly from one branch to another. But suddenly a peacock, whose raucous cries had been audible as an alien note among the melodious singing, strutted across the path in front of Johannes with its magnificent tail outspread.

After crossing the path it vanished into a thicket of rhododendrons.

Johannes felt sure that, even though he could not interpret the message contained in the song of the other birds, the meaning of this visible display was clear enough: he was to follow the peacock in among the rhododendrons.

He therefore stepped off the path and entered the thicket. There was no sign of the peacock, although he could still hear its cries – unless they were those of some other peacock in the vicinity. But in the centre of the grove, in a small space left free by the trees, he came upon a Japanese stone lantern.

No doubt he had been intended to find this lantern, to which the peacock had led him. But what was he to make of it now that he had found it? He studied it closely, but saw nothing to which he could attribute any special significance.

Baffled, Johannes returned to the path and continued on his way; but he carried the picture of the stone lantern very clearly in his head, where it competed for his attention with the slowly circling carp until the two combined into a single image in which the carp circled round the lantern.

Weighed down by these heavy thoughts – the stone lantern, in particular, was a load on his mind – Johannes found himself trudging along the path; the thud of his ponderous footsteps vied with the singing of the birds and his feet shuffled though the fallen leaves in the places where branches of the trees and bushes overhung the path.

2

A few more minutes of this laborious progress brought Johannes first to a tangled and neglected rose garden and then to the goal of his journey: a large house which, though it could not quite be described as a castle, nevertheless had something of the castle about it by virtue of its grey stone walls, crenellated battlements and the huge, iron-studded oak door.

Johannes, from whose mind the stone lantern and the carp had now completely vanished, went up to the door and struck the heavy iron knocker twice. He heard its booming sound echo through the house and a few moments later the door was opened by a tall, severe-looking woman dressed in black.

Before Johannes could give her his name and indicate the purpose of his visit, the woman said: "Johannes Weltseele, come in. I will take you to my master." Then she led him up a broad staircase onto a spacious landing, knocked on one of the ornate doors and ushered Johannes into a book-lined room in which a black-haired, cadaverous-looking man was seated in a leather armchair.

Without rising, the man introduced himself as Gottlieb Menschenhasser and motioned Johannes to take a seat in another armchair facing him.

* * *

Johannes looked around. The room was evidently a library, but on one area of the wall that was free from books there hung two pictures: the one on the left showing an exceptionally beautiful, dark-haired woman, the one on the right the severe, black-clad older woman who had opened the door to him and shown him up to this room.

As he gazed at the pictures, his host – as Johannes now considered him – remarked: "That's Vespasia." Johannes was uncertain which of the two women Gottlieb Menschenhasser was referring to; but as he continued to look intently at the paintings his unspoken question received a startling answer.

Both pictures underwent a strange and disturbing transformation: the younger woman grew gradually older before his eyes, while the older woman grew progressively younger; until the left-hand picture showed the severe woman in black and the right-hand picture the dark-haired young beauty. Evidently they were portraits of one and the same person – Vespasia.

Johannes was plunged into a deep melancholy by realization of the tragic fact that one of these transformations could never take place in real life and the equally tragic fact that the other transformation already had taken place, irreversibly. He realized that his profound regret was not for Vespasia, whose beauty was faded and gone, but for himself who could never, in this life, meet the beautiful young woman in what was now the right-hand picture, who seemed to him the very incarnation of his dreams.

Johannes looked away from the pictures at his host. To his surprise he observed that Gottlieb Menschenhasser's face wore an expression of the same melancholy that filled his own heart. And as he watched, a change came over his host: his hair began to turn white and wrinkles appeared in his face: he was rapidly aging before Johannes' eyes.

Then, with an apparent effort of will, Gottlieb Menschenhasser passed his hand quickly across his face and the process was reversed. In a few seconds his hair and face were restored to their original appearance.

If Menschenhasser possessed this power to halt and reverse his own aging process, thought Johannes, was it not possible that he could also reverse it in the case of his servant or companion, whichever she might be, Vespasia? And if he did indeed possess this power, what reason could he have for not exercising it?

3

Faced with this enigma, Johannes Weltseele decided that for him salvation lay elsewhere.

Bowing to his host, Gottlieb Menschenhasser, he left the library, descended the stairs and headed for the door. As he walked towards it, he found his path barred by the black-clad Vespasia – or so it seemed. But as he approached her she stepped aside. As she did so she peered deep into his eyes, as though to penetrate his soul. Johannes merely nodded to her casually and passed on.

Outside in the garden he followed a narrow path through thickets of rhododendrons, bamboos and hydrangeas, all of them overgrown and clearly allowed to run wild.

When he had walked for some minutes through this dense vegetation, Johannes perceived, almost hidden by the foliage, the opening to a cave.

Pushing the branches aside, he went in. At first he could see nothing in the gloom but he thought he could hear a very faint hissing, which he could not identify. There at the far end of the cave, he made out the shape of a serpent with part of its body standing erect upon the base of coils.

Johannes started in alarm, realizing that he was within striking distance of what he was sure was a cobra. But as his eyes grew even more accustomed to the darkness he saw that this was no living snake, but only a very lifelike statue.

Then, in a flash of recognition his mind was pierced by the knowledge that what he had before him was none other than Kundalini, the Divine Serpent, that slumbers at the base of every human spine except in the bodies of the enlightened, in whom she has been released to permeate body and mind. The hissing he had heard came from her invisible spirit servants.

As this revelation came to him, Johannes felt heat and movement at the base of his own spine. The sensation passed up his spine, expanding and exploding at each of the six chakras, until it reached the seventh at the top of his head. Here it spread out in a blaze of light so bright that he closed his eyes, losing for a few brief instants all sense of who and where he was.

This sensation passed, but as Johannes Weltseele left the cave, he felt profoundly changed. Now, he felt he had become one with his name and hence with all things.

The veil of Maya, to which Gottlieb Menschenhasser and Vespasia owed their continued existence, had for him been rent asunder.

* * *

Johannes Weltseele wandered through the garden in search of the manor house he had left a little while earlier. He wished to see the house and its occupants once more in the light of his new enlightened self. How, he wondered, would Gottlieb Menschenhasser and Vespasia appear to him now?

It took him longer to find his way back to the house than he had anticipated; but suddenly, when he least expected it, there it stood before him.

But its state was so dilapidated that he hardly recognized it. It seemed more like a derelict ruin than like the occupied building he had left only a short while before.

He had no difficulty in gaining entry, since the solid oak door was now cracked and split, rotten in places and devoid of bolts. One push and it creaked open on its rusty hinges.

Johannes stepped inside. There was no Vespasia to greet him. The entrance hall was deserted; leaves that had drifted in through the broken windows lay on the floor and the furniture, and here and there grass sprouted between the floorboards.

Surprised at this transformation, Johannes ascended the wide stairs to the broad corridor above and made his way to the door to the library, which he clearly remembered from his previous visit.

This door too yielded to a light push to reveal a room as abandoned and decayed as the entrance hall. The leather armchairs were patched with mould and they were empty. Vespasia was not here and nor was Gottlieb Menschenhasser.

Johannes turned to look at the pictures on the wall. They were still there, or so he thought at first glance; but when he brushed aside the cobwebs that now covered them he saw that, while one of them was the same, showing Vespasia now aged to the point of decrepitude, the other showed an equally decrepit old man, whose features, when he peered at them closely were still unmistakably recognizable as Gottlieb Menschenhasser.

Filled with an inescapable melancholy, even though he had suffered no real personal loss, Johannes left the house and began his walk back through the garden to the hole in the wall through which he had first entered it.

As he walked along the narrow paths between the overhanging branches of the trees and bushes, brushed by the leaves, Johannes felt that, while the garden he carried in his head was still sunlit and bathed in the atmosphere of a summer morning, the garden outside, which encroached so closely upon him, now contained a nameless threat and aroused in him an indefinable dread.

This dread showed Johannes that his enlightenment was far from complete and that the kundalini energy that had flowed upward from the lower to the higher chakras was impure, vitiated by confusions and distortions arising from his foregoing life or lives. It was clear to him that what had seemed like an overwhelming revelation and transformation was only a momentary lifting of the veil, a pointer towards the possible that had not yet been realized.

Even as he hurrried towards the breach in the wall that would lead him to the world outside the now threatening garden, the sunlight began to fade from the garden in his head. He could only hope that there would still be sunlight in the world outside the garden.

Claire Harris

from *Translation into Fiction*

After the Chinese

April

Coming out of the city into spring we find the Elbow   framed in the tender green flesh of willow   Under the trees two small boys pull at a tire someone has roped to a tree   their dog circles barking wildly and one is all green excitement while the other shorter sturdier tugs and tugs.   A light wind stirs the grass   We pause to watch   now something moves and settles over us   something like stillness settles   time pools and circles A fish leaps   curves sparkling water wings splashes   We move on   we move gingerly   grieving despite ourselves

May

Who discovered that one bowl of fine wine will dispel a thousand cares

– *Tu Fu 713-770*

And the blue bowl full of wine   I noted the curdled grey of cloud patching the long summer sky   that the Bow does not quite shimmer   that an old man in a slouch hat fishes   and flocks of houses straggle over the prairies *the wine like a flower in the mouth*   all this from my room high on the bluff where I live in plateglass silence from where I observe everything even the tight grey splatter of doves   how else am I to draw the precise and delicate conclusion   caught as I am between the image of the hard moment and the gut rumblings of my own indelicate existence   in blue wine I invent the boy and girl across the alley   the ones now tangled in each others hair which I make long and curling like vines   and voracious   *the wine crisp as the morning sky*   at the end I am alone   the bowl half empty   the long dead summers hot in me

or   I am alone   the blue wine refulgent   the boy and girl bright butterflies in haze

June

From this pale room only a slight rim of lights   a neon cross a thin scattering of advertisements climb night hills to the vast summer sky   thirty times in as many years we have gathered here   the term over   to throw the dice and drink from moon drenched wine   This is the night we pause barren of dreams before we go to meet ourselves in the long dry summers alone   the chips lost in my hands I plunge into bitter revelry fearing the space I must   Above the hills no clear moon rises   Like one who frees himself from a shadow I shiver then shake my head and reach for a new bottle   my friends laughing and noisy stand to toast this night

July

I rest me in the green of summer trees that bend and whisper in this clear blue wind   even as the brilliant sun scours the skies I mourn for our uncertain northern summers   the sensible cars in sweeping files drone up and over Memorial fleeing the city   its malls empty its waterfalls splashing into silence below towers that rise   a crystal henge out of desolate prairie   My friends call   invite me to go camping   I hear in their eagerness the forests edged silence   the desolation of crags   the mystery of green unfathomable lakes offered in the arms of mountains   and I know that shackled to the alienating comfort of this constantly brave constantly new city we yet belong to hallowed permanence   to tree   earth   river   to sky without hindrance or distraction

August

Noon and the August haze veils gentle eastern hills the prim modest houses   along the Bow poplars grow yellow   stranded on the deck of this ship perched on cliffs edge I watch the steel city flaring in high noon   so bright I must look away   here where no one walks the traffic strung out at the lights like coils of a python tightens around the city endlessly   in the median men on huge earth movers go busily about their work   cocooned in their own noise CP air drones through the pale blue   I imagine passengers settling back before long suspension   and home   So distant from my own rainforested mountains   mountains rounded like whales stranded against the dawn   light lapping their ridges tiny shacks like barnacles riding their flanks   palms burst into green spume against the sky   I remember dark faces streaming out of the valleys   black women flowing currents & waves their feet solid on earth   their unreasoned unhurried grace   this forever and indelible on the inner eye   This summer shades into the sixteenth autumn   I grow yellow in exile

September

We had been driving since noon   mountains brooding over the passes in late summer dusk   then glimpsed in car lights almost invisible in the ditch a tiny baby deer   we stopped   reversed   night calling around us   the tiny creature wavered a few panic stricken steps then paused as if in his short hours he had come to question the usefulness of action   we sat silent engines switched off gazing at the dead mother while the night peaks leaned towards us

I offered a finger dipped in our sweet milky coffee and waited   he came slowly many pauses and hesitancies   finally the rough tongue   we lifted him gently into the car   laid him on our knees   felt his heart-panic   fear tore his entrails as the engine started   holding him there stroking his silken head his shuddering increasing I willed him to live hating that this other life should brush against my impotence and vanish   chance given now I needed him to invest this journey

to make time tangible   but he would not be warm would not be calm under my hand   intent on his own need he cried out and died   the story dissolved before climax we paused   long enough to throw him into the ditch dim lights once and pass on

October

Illicit winter winds rustle grey clouds through the valley   cars curve down thyme hills swoop over the river to where cottonwoods   memorials to the dead today are marked for death   from my neighbours yard wind lifts the scent of blown roses   they have gone away and now behind the careful hedges there is no one to admire their formal elegy   wind plunges down frantic slopes towards a clutch of joggers in light summer suits   their flushed inner faces despair of the passing years   a demented spider refusing all advice spins a wind draggled web across my window   Listening to the dying trees I am reminded of prisoners in South African cells   held in the soundless dark they scratch vivid greetings   hold out a hand to those who will come after   stalking horses they bear passionate witness into eternity

November

Autumn morning   a late moon herds blind grey clouds   above the bluff a line of light is wedged in the sky   Already traffic hastens to the city makes a great noise   from this cliff I see the leafless poplars a dense brush bearding the grey year   Elsewhere a mottle of stubborn leaves   a clump of evergreens   Far below on the riverbank an old man poles for bottles among detritus of the season   Turning away from the window   against brick walls black railings all the dense circling of reality I catch sight of myself   a trick of light in the mirror   greying

December

Winter dawn spills a limitless blue light   below frozen skin the stubborn Bow eddies into pools that surface to net the sun   naked trees all decent blanketed   huddle over banks of driven white   Since the first snow no one has stepped there now the wind sculpts its own message   Snow roofed small houses vulnerable in this light struggle up a bluff towards the East My friend   hospital grey & wasted drags the night behind him into an exhausted sleep   He has gained one day   will enter the New Year sad & fearing   who was so prescient in our youth   I pull the coat closer add a scarf add a hat while the light seeps into my blood   I step tingling into this luminous dying of the year   clear and cold

Patrick Lane

Ned Coker's Dream

He chose to bury what dreams he had, Ned Coker, and I for one would not take that away from him, would not dig them up myself nor ask him to do it for what is buried is buried and that is an end to it. I know for I have buried some dreams of my own, put them down under in the place where certain dreams must go, as each of us has in our time. It is only here in the hills I remember, these things that rise into the mind, watching as I am the whiplash that is my daughter weave thin through the brush on the path ahead of me, her dark hair flowing to her shoulders thick in the sun.

It is not that Ned Coker had all that many dreams in the first place. There are those who start out in this world with only a few to their name just as there are those who have many. Ned Coker was not one of those with many. The dreams he began with were few. It was as it was with all his family. They were as my mother said, small potatoes and few to the hill, and that meant in my mother's terms not the number of them in the family for they were as many and as varied as Eveline Jean Coker could make, but rather they were in her eyes a stunted runted clan whose future was only as good as their past and that to my mother was a worthless one.

The Cokers come from poor seed she would say, though I felt it was Eveline Jean Coker's eggs that were as much at fault as the seed that was poured in her. You could say they were a dreamless people and that was true of most of them but not all. Not Ned anyway who was made as they all were, small and quick as if they'd been half-starved though I knew they weren't. Ned was as the rest though he was different. At least to me.

Where are we in the middle of things? That's what I ask myself, my daughter ahead of me knowing somehow where we are going, that nowhere clear to her in this the last year of her childhood. Where is there ever a place where things can be explained? I knew Ned Coker when he was only a boy not more than five feet high though he was already fourteen years old. I knew him because I was twelve years old myself, just a slip of a girl, and when you are that age you know the ages of everyone who is also a child.

It was to the Cokers' place I'd go whenever I had the chance. To play or just to be and if the truth be known, it was mostly the being I wanted. The Cokers were different than everyone else I knew, not that I knew all that many people. What child does? A child's world is bound by a few square yards of earth, a street, a hill, a corner in town, a place that is within a place though the child does not know that when she is a child. She does not know that she pushes at the margins of that small place each hour and day and year as she grows, making it larger as her own need demands, another yard, a bit of earth, a stone.

When I discovered the Cokers my life changed. Perhaps it would have anyway. A child's life changes no matter what or who she knows. It was just that they all of them held a certain fascination for me, from Eveline Jean Coker with her dark black hair and her silver earrings that made a small impossible music whenever she turned her head, right through to Ned who was not the youngest of them at all but was the special one. Ned was as Eveline Jean Coker said, I don't know how many times, the best of the last. I'm near to being done, she'd say to whoever happened to be there when she said it. This one here, and she'd point at Ned or if he was close enough rumple his thin golden hair which touch Ned loved more than even the wind's touch, is the best child I ever brought into this world. And then she'd laugh out loud and give Ned a push if he was close enough to do so to and say, isn't that right, Ned Coker? And Ned would grin, the best of the last.

So that is where I should start because that is where I first knew him, in the Coker yard which was full of broken machines, cars and bits and pieces of truck and washing machines, huge wooden crates and cardboard boxes with their tops torn off, piles of lumber and tires and cans full of rusted nails and bolts, and everything else a child could love in a world that was more ordered than not or at least was in my case where home was a yard covered in grass and where there flower beds with flowers arranged according to their colours, types and sizes. a place where my mother had constructed a certain world that obeyed her in everything. I thought as a child even the trees leafed out when she ordered them to. Not so at the Cokers.

At the Cokers everything found its place as best it could. I have always thought of it as a place that was somehow akin to what the real world is and was and will be, a kind of glorious chaos with everything in it being born and dying, growing and shrinking all at the same time. Things came and went at the Coker place. Things accumulated of their own wild will and just as easily disappeared into oblivion never to be seen again. One day there would be an old wood stove sitting precariously leaned against the front steps of their house and the next day it would be gone only to be replaced with three 45 gallon drums with bullet holes in them. A tree would grow inside the body of a car sending its crazed branches out through the broken windows to the sun, or cucumbers and melons would appear from between the porch planks with leaves bigger than my head and fruit even bigger than that. And no one seemed to notice that they did, just as no one of the nine Cokers who were still at home noticed the many men who came and went over the months and years. They were the uncles according to Eveline Jean Coker and were accepted as such. Each one brought with him when he came a desolate vehicle piled high or low with more of the same things that were already there in plenitude, and as they left they left behind some of it and took other away.

And sometimes they left their seed for Eveline Jean Coker to mix with her eggs and grow into another child. Each time she began a child it was a strong and powerful will, throwing it out in its time into what could only be called a tribe. Their house and yard was I believe a kind of cornucopia of a child's dreams. All the effluvium was ranged around them, the flotsam and jetsam of a world that didn't know what it had and didn't care where it ended up.

I would go up to the Cokers whenever I had the chance to slip away from the narrow eye of my mother who watched over me as only her kind of mother could. I was her only daughter, her youngest, and she feared me in a way she never did my brothers. What that fear was I never knew until I was much older but I knew it was there. My father would tell her to let me go when I'd ask. Nan, he would say, let the child go. She's only a few more years of being a child. Let her have that. God knows it'll end soon enough. And he'd smile at me and put his arm around my mother and give her a kind of hug that meant all is well.

My mother would shake him off and say, That's exactly what I think too and it's exactly that which makes me want her not to go traipsing off up to that place where anything can happen and usually does.

Now Nan, he would say and while he was saying it he'd give me a look that said, get going while I've got her occupied, as if she was an alien force he had to surround and hold. And I would. I would slide out of the kitchen or off the back porch and slip through the caragana hedge and be gone as fast as I could go down the alley to where it ended and the trail up the side of the hill that led to the Cokers began. I never took the road.

Somehow it didn't seem right to go that way. It was always better through the brush on the hard-packed trail that the Coker children had worn smooth over the years as they came and went to town. No Coker child ever thought of travelling in a straight line when there was a shortcut to be taken. Or even a longer way if it somehow seemed more interesting, a pond or a marsh where a muskrat could be seen or a high dead poplar on a hill with a single hawk or owl in it. Those were the things that took them off the beaten road and those were the things I loved as well.

Whenever I went up there I would meet Ned. He'd be waiting for me where the trail slipped over the edge of the hill and down to where their house was in the crook of a small coolie. He'd be sitting on the third bare limb of a cottonwood tree or on a huge red boulder that grew out of the hill like a rounded red tooth that had scratched and worried itself up out of the deepest earth to find the sun.

I'd reach the crest and there he'd be, small and hard and quick as if anything might set him off to running in any one of a thousand directions, his thin blonde hair sliding in the wind as he disappeared forever for the day. He never did but I believed it of him just as I believed he knew exactly when I would appear for why else would he be there when I came? I know now he waited for me in that spot each day of the summer in hope I would come, though I didn't know that then.

How'd you know I was coming, I would say, and he would say back, I don't know, I just knew. Hey, he would say then, look at what I've got here, and I would look at whatever it was he had and it was always something so beautiful, so completely strange that it seemed to change me forever. Once he had a baby crow with a red ribbon tied around its neck which he kept for months feeding it bits of meat until he let it go still with that ribbon around its neck so that we saw it for more than a year in the woods and fields until the ribbon fell off and Ned said he could tell which crow it was still by the way it cried to him. And once he had an eight-ball from a pool game, a shiny black orb with its number on its sides and which he said weren't eights at all but the signs for infinity and they were. He said he could tell the future and past in it and I believed that as well, just as I believed he knew the secrets of frogs and pheasants, motors and magic. He even had a pet gopher that lived in the pocket of his jacket and which would crawl up inside him until its small bright head appeared out the hole of his sleeve to eat the sunflower seeds he had there waiting for it.

And that was Ned Coker, a quiet shy boy I know now, but then thought only that his silences were of a deeper stranger kind, and perhaps still do believe that for who knows what is pooled beneath the surface of such quiet? Shy yes, I know that now. Shy and different from everyone else so that they were made to feel it. Or Ned felt it. Some of them didn't. Some of them found their way out of that web of strangeness. Some left and some stayed, some married and got jobs in town, and some went bad and went to prison from where they returned only to go to prison again for some hopeless crime as theft or drunkenness. Mrs. Coker rode through all such times as she always had. She was there in that place living as she could, doing as was done, being as she willed herself to be. She was the maker of all that was around her and though she couldn't reach beyond her life to them she was there when they returned. And Ned was her own, her special one, her best of the last, the one who stayed with her and by her through all his young years. And more.

It was that summer I learned Ned's dream, his dream of what he willed to be his life. In the labyrinth of cars and trucks and broken things that was his back yard he told me of himself as only a boy could who was as he was. It was in the deepest dark where he had made a place for himself and me, a hollow between and beneath two old truck beds that was a hiding place for him against the world, and where we first explored each other, taking off our thin summer clothes to touch and smell and see the differences we were. It was hot in that place but not the heat of the hard summer sun, rather it was a kind of soft full heat that surrounded you as water does in a shallow pond. It was there we lay naked together and did what all children do when they first discover themselves as other.

It was there I saw him throw his pale seed into the thin pure air and it was there he touched me, there, so that I knew what I hadn't known before. And it was there he told me he would marry me and we would live forever in our love.

There was such a rage in him when he told me that. Such an anger. I didn't understand it then, didn't know what he already knew though he fought against it as one would who would take on a whole world in order to find another. I said we would. We will, we will, he said, his quick body all bones and thin hard muscle standing in that secret place before me, his eyes as blue and cold as early winter rain, his small fists shaking. Yes, I said, and held him as I could though I was but twelve years old and still a child. I held him as a woman does who must hold a man when he is ranged against a world which doesn't want him. I know it now as the thing which comes in a man before he has fully learned sorrow and pain and loss. It is the knowing those things will come makes him so. The thing which is a man's rage and which precedes his first crying as over a child's small death or for a moon which rises into him which is the first of all his moons and which he has never known before though he be twenty or fifty or a hundred. Or fourteen.

His mother knew. Her touching him when we appeared from the wreckage and walked up on her porch to drink the cold clean water she had waiting there. Her look at me which held no judgement I could see but was only a long far understanding of what was. Her touch of him, her long hands in his hair. My best of last.

That was Ned Coker's dream. The dream he buried that was of all his dreams the first and last he told to only me. He stood in the secrecy of that wild wreckage and told it to me. No, perhaps that isn't fully true. I was there, yes, and it was me he meant but he spoke over and beyond me to something or someone else, someone not there who could if she wanted somehow stop the dream being made true but who it was I didn't know then and don't know now. He knew. It was what he looked at standing there above me and it was that looking that made me rise to him, a girl only, a slim thing half made of water, to rise to him and take him in my girl's small arms and hold him there, hard and quick and shaking. We will, I said, we will. And even as I said it I knew it wasn't true, knew it for the dream it was, a thing to be imagined, nothing more.

For my breasts were to grow that were only then small buds as hard as flowers, grow into the things that are a woman's to give to a man or a child, to suckle or to praise for what is a man's mouth at a woman's breast but a child though he think he's more, though he believes he is a sullen secret thing, a trickster whose caress is only need gone begging for desire. Oh, I have known that trick, have given my breast to be succoured by a man's warm mouth, the trick of teeth, the whimper of desire, as I have known a child's wild suck, that terrible demand, that thing that makes a woman into only animal. Oh, animal I was. And am.

So I had small Ned Coker at my breasts. As I had small Ned Coker in my mouth, that small hard rigid thing that was still a boy's that I suckled on. Is there a man who knows a woman's dream? For we also sucked on stones, the streaked rare things we'd found in ponds and brooks, the chipped bits of blue and yellow flint we turned with our tongues into shining only to let them lie on our palms in the sun where we watched them turn from jewels back to stone. The moments when we simply slept.

Yes, that. I remember that. That sleeping far from the garden where every flower was known, my mother's garden, ordered and arranged. I remember. I remember. I remember holding Ned Coker in my mouth, the all of him, the whole of what he was. I remember looking at my father and thinking my mother holding him like that. There were the stones.

So I am here in the middle of things, my daughter not looking back, her hard bare heels on the trail leaving their mark in the dust. Of course I knew, I knew it all the time. For me there was always an away. It was in that I fooled him for my dream was other than his own though then I couldn't name it. That was the trick. My fierce implacable trick. I could give him everything because there was nothing given. What? My body?

Oh, Ned Coker, you small miserable boy.

But what of that dream? There is this. Let me tell you this. Today I am out walking as I have always walked, going nowhere, drifting through the lighted afternoon far from the man I live with and the house I live in with the garden that is as my mother's was, arranged and ordered, every flower placed, each bush, each blade of grass. I walk where I am wont to walk. God there's a word. Wont! But I did and do. And my own daughter is with me though I hardly noticed her at first and, yes, I know the fear my mother knew, and I walked into the brush land with this fierce young girl of mine following along who is now ahead of me, tough and kind and fierce and mellow like a turtle who has come at last from her sharp shell to smell the sound of summer. Proud and lost within herself as all of us are lost. No, she's not lost.

And far from home in the bright hills I saw her stop and bend above a stone. It was only a few feet back on the trail. It was only a small and nothing stone, a little blue and nothing thing, but she picked it up and held it to herself. I saw her there in the bend of a hill's shadow hold that stone to the light of her own wild eye before she slipped it in her mouth. A little thing, she is, not more than I was at her age. Hold your blue stone, my daughter, in the wreckage of things.

Ah, Ned Coker, your sweet dream. For one of us was a fool as only a fool can be. But I held you that day as only a woman could, fierce and small in my arms, and didn't understand, oh yes, your rage I knew, it was the other I didn't know. God, I could wish to know it, here where I am in a hill's shadow far from my negligence.

Gay Allison

from *The Unravelling*

The Slow Gathering Of

for Mavis

In memory of my father

women have been gathering together for centuries,
their braided lives ancestral memories

pears to be picked, the sound of a train
pulling out of the station

skirts rustling in gardens, fields of pregnant women
pulling silk tassels from corn, garlands of words at their feet

This is not new, father

men often speak the truth about themselves
I have never been faithful to anyone you said

Seasonal changes

November approaches, my sister returns home to the coast
I miss her   this surprises me
something I hadn't counted on
another mother's love for my daughter

History

one summer day a March fly burrowed into the moist earth
a tiny twig broke off and fell to the bottom

It is said that

women invented plaiting and weaving to hide their genitals,
that even nature caused the growth of pubic hair
for this purpose

Patterns of history

Virgin Mary is worshipped while women were burned
as witches   and living women
are still brutalized every day

Anne Sexton: Someone is dead. Even the trees know it.

on the way to my mother's funeral we passed a flock
of crows leaving the top of a tree, an alkaline slough
in the middle of the prairies, two green ducks at the edge
of a powdered lake   it could be snow but it isn't
the sky the same colour as my mama's last dress
a painting I'd hang in my mind forever

Birds have their own syntax

to land, a raven beats its wings
against the direction of flight

Listen to Hamlet

There are more things in heaven and earth, Horatio,
than are dreamt of in your philosophy

Art

red and yellow mangoes sitting on Mary's windowsill
the sweet smell of ripe fruit

Criticism

the original meaning, *krisis*, the decisive encounter
that transforms

Mythology

thought: *Hugin*   memory: *Munin*
two ravens sit on your shoulders, hear wool
growing on sheep,
grass growing on earth

Despair

150 carrier pigeons in a race over Italy never showed up

radiation from Chernobyl knocked out their sense
of direction

Natural transformations

when carrots run free they turn into Queen Anne's lace
a pair of orioles rebuild their nest

Cinéma-vérité

Bogart in *The Maltese Falcon*: Listen Dorothy,
hello precious. Miles has been shot.
You're an angel.
Leading man in *Heaven Can Wait*: Try not to unravel
now, Julia darling.

Joke in the New Yorker

Two men over coffee: Look Joel, you're relatively young,
have a relatively nice job and a relatively nice wife.
There's no reason in the world why you shouldn't be relatively happy.

In the words of Nicole Brossard

the male imagination lacks the ability to conceive
that women together could re-invent the world.

At home

the cats are still dreaming of fresh fish in clear water
Xingu stretches, claws the air in slow motion, smiles
trout and *tuna* and *salmon*

Politics is a woman's life

all the world over women are poorer than men, perform
two-thirds of all the world's work for less than ten percent
of the world's pay and own less than one percent
of the worlds's wealth

Scheherazade

the music of a woman who couldn't rest

wove her magic of 1001 tales to save her life

The final confession

men don't want to think of God as a woman because
they'd have to admit
there's a woman inside of them

A question, father

why is it all of the men in our family are dying
to come back again
to relearn tenderness from their sisters, even in death
my father sleeps and cannot hear my prayers

Returning to the womb

the ocean, mother of waters
two people walked into the ocean one day
and liked it so much they decided to stay

Anne Hébert: We had this notion of planting our hands in the garden.

my daughter and I are born during the ripe berries moon,
and in the morning
we hear the knife-sharpener's bell ringing,
the man in the truck shouting
strawberries   strawberries   strawberries

The raven is queen

change comes in the form of a woman
holding a raven with breasts
what is it about birds that keeps surprising us

A child reads the first message of life: You are there

my daughter wakes early and I can hear her father
reading to her
this is a bird   this is a flower   this is a tree
that's a mountain   and this is the ocean   shhh
don't wake your mother

What Luther said

And even if the world should end tomorrow
I still would plant my little apple tree

Eugene McNamara

Falling in Place

The Chinese girl awoke in the early morning still dark out and found her door unlocked. The corridor was empty silent under humming lights. The ward door was ajar. She remembered the story of the prisoner who found his cell door open and went out into the palace garden. There the poor wretch met a kindly reassuring priest who was in fact the Inquisitor. Soon the man was back in chains with the added torment of illusory freedom and false sympathy to goad him. The deepened horror.

But outside the hospital no false priest waited for her. There was only the parking lot lying there like a silent bowl of arc light. And she walked beyond it into the deeper inverted bowl of night. A deep pool starred with white water lilies. She had dreamed of rain. A school of small fish scattering in the deep. She saw them through circles on the blistered surface, thought of rain falling in a farmer's yard. Would his barn doors blow away in the wind? The hospital drains sand with rain.

Now she went up the grade to the tracks silvered in the fading moon. And she lay down across the tracks, cushioned her head on the chill steel and looked up into the slowly waking sky. Waited. *Oh my iron bridegroom* she said.

On the road beside the embankment the apprentice machinist drove in early light. He had wakened to a charley horse cursing limping in his silent morning house. Now he drove, the night mists wipered away, the radio in cadence. His mind was already in the plant. So many there were missing fingers. The machines were hungry. He feared them. At the morning break the men will speak of women. They want full-bodied women. Somewhere else now women were breasting big waves on beaches the men will never see. The ditch beside the road was dry.

It had been a month of drought after a month of rain. He had dreamed of rain. He though of keeping a rain journal. How many days, how many inches, what damage to property, how some drown in cars in viaducts. Good for the crops some will say. But someone else will answer no, the crop's in peril. Not enough and the lawn burns. Too much and the picnic's ruined.

Never just right except in dreams where it falls like filmic mist in black and white movies of romance. Lovers dance in it.

Sudden there on the road in common light he heard the shudder of stopped steel on steel. Up ahead was the morning train shaking to a stop and someone *there.*

Oh God he thought and could only watch the meeting see it happen.

Everything was falling in place as the passengers fell forward. The train had leaned into its curve, righted on the straightaway and settled down. *Now* we thought. But instead we jolted from our seats in a hurtling protest of stopping. Then all was silent unmoving. We got off to see. There was blood on the sleepers. We turned to stare across the speechless fields at the still early sun. Tall weeds stood there helpless as any of us. Nothing could change now for her. The hard air stood still. It tasted like brass.

He stood in line at the supermarket docile thinking of nothing and then sudden as the wreck he remembered it all. His hand on the brake. Futile. Nothing doing. Throwing up afterwards into his useless hands. And now here in the supermarket line ahead of him a row of grocery carts like train cars derailed, askew. Someone back in aisle four had dropped a jar of beets. A mess for someone else to clean up. And now someone's meat on the conveyor belt red as a kiss moved on added up put into a bag. It cannot be called back. The young woman ahead of him tells her child again that they cannot buy the cookies, that they have plenty at home. Does the child know it's a lie?

No, he thought. I am unfair. She soothes the child at home, reads him stories. Her kitchen is orderly and everybody keeps his or her voice down. Wildly, he looked back down the checkout line. He was square in the middle of it, too late to give up or move and more time to put in waiting. He thought I'd like to be a private detective, save people from blackmailers, sit back in a creaking chair, stare at the smoked window, listen to the secretary type reports, wait for the phone to ring. The girl's silver voice calls to him out of the dark wire, calling for help. He could save her.

A poet once said that her eyes were the colour of sherry in the glass the guest has left. My eyes are like that. But here in the false dawn my eyes keep in them the deep shadows of night. Pillowed on the polished iron, I could see the morning glory clambering on chain-link fences facing the embankment. someone is hanging laundry on a line. White forms rising in the wind. I hear bird-song. A faint thrum in the rail. I lay down to sleep and I am certain to rise.

The weather conditions on that day: patchy morning fog thinning so that visibility was fair to good at the precise time of – And post-incident analysis indicated no mechanical fault in the braking system. From the initial locking of the brakes to the point of impact –

The provenance of the engine: Electro-Motive Division, General Motors Company, London, Ontario, 1958.

There are several factors involved in braking: torque, brake shoe function, condition of track and gradient. The brake shoe bears against the revolving wheel with a radial force called normal brake shoe pressure. The retarding force of the brake shoe cannot be increased or prolonged indefinitely as train wheels may slide as a result of excessive braking force. (See H.J. Schrader, "Friction of Railway Brake Shoes at High-Speed and High Pressure," *University of Illinois Engineering Experiment Station Bulletin* 301, 1938, Urbana, Illinois.)

There are other factors involved in acceleration and deceleration of course: speed, velocity (speed in a given direction), mass, air resistance or drag, acceleration and the rate of change in acceleration. Mass. The gross weight of the engine. The gross weight of the engine. *The weight of the engine.*

When I finished hanging the laundry, I thought of cutting the roses back. They say to cut ruthlessly so they will grow more hardy. The cadence of my steps kept to the song we danced to last night. I was humming it and then I heard the chill cry and protest of the engine and then the day was nipped in the bud.

After a long and aimless wait standing alongside the silent train, the passengers were put on buses. It was late morning. They were promised lunch in the next town. By now a kind of disaster-induced camaraderie had developed among them. A subdued cordiality ran through the buses.

I felt an odd lightheadedness, a feeling of post-excitement letdown. As the morning went on the things of our world slowly resumed their usual shapes. I smiled at my fellow voyagers. Everything seemed thick and alive and bright in the almost noon light. Just a little while ago it was all tenuous, fragile, brief and evanescent. I felt mildly hungry, on edge, jumpy, ready to burst into laughter or tears.

Then suddenly I thought of the first sight I had of the girl's foot next to the tracks as I stepped down from the car. Now all the air went just as suddenly out of the day.

Already the blue of the summer sky is turning harshly autumnal. The change has been both gradual and sudden. So also in a very brief time a man may be his actual age and simultaneously feel the swift errant emotions of childhood and youth. A man may feel grief over the loss of those periods of his life while at the same instant re-experience them. I did not know her name.

Thus I felt grief – not only for the wretched girl but for myself and my fellow passengers. Every previous experience of death came welling up. Pets, schoolmates, grandparents, friends, acquaintances, fellow workers. All crowded together in my memory in a hurly-burly of sorrow recaptured. The indifferent blue sky outside the bus window stretches on to everywhere anywhere and nowhere.

The Chinese girl had been studying music at the university. Her first piano recital (Erik Satie's Gymnopedies and Nocturnes) had been enthusiastically received by the faculty. The recital by one of her fellow pupils, a young man from a farm in the southern part of the Province, was attended with less warmth. This did not lessen the young man's ardour. He found the girl endlessly fascinating. Her eyes were like quick fish in deep water.

She was shy, elusive, reticent, dedicated and given to long hours of practice. There was not much time left over for romance. Still the young man persevered and a kind of wary relationship developed. She told him about her loneliness, her homesickness. He spoke with confidence of a two piano career for both of them.

Then came her time of retrospections, introversion, fear and collapse. She went into the hospital. The prognosis was positive. Her period of treatment would be brief, followed by outpatient therapy and a lighter academic load.

There had been a long dry spell of weather. The young man sat one afternoon in a coffee shop near campus. Some people came in and were talking to the waitress about the news. Gradually the story filtered through the damp air and the young man became aware. Rain fell that night like a breaking mirror.

The apprentice machinist dreams of counterboring holes. This procedure would be followed by milling a flat space at the bottom end of the holes. He squinted through a fine spray of coolant. Metal chips lay like sharp confetti on the grim concrete floor. Tolerances were tight – plus or minus one thousandth. Next to him an old-timer ran a big Bridgeport. On the other side was another old-timer running an obsolete Milwaukee V Mill. Its age was covered with many coats of gray paint.

The apprentice's hands flew from the ball crank to the reversing lever. His mind was busy with the examination he would soon take. Define running fit, push fit, force fit and shrink fit. Tables of stress conversion roll through his mind. His eyes are intent on the chips of metal curling and dropping to the floor.

And now without warning the accident flashes into his mind. Locked steel wheels grind and shear. In a grinding operation wheel and work must be kept in contact until sparks are no longer emitted. Define the function of a chucking grinder. Do not look into the shower of sparks. Do not look up into the morning sunlight. Do not look up at the tracks ahead of you.

The rain fell into the yard near the tracks. All the laundry is safely in, clean-smelling and folded. Lightning glints on the thorns of the cut-back rose bushes. The rain washes the tracks and sleepers, seeing into the roadbed gravel. Rivers flow into the lake.

The rain fell into the placid lake. The diesel horn mourned over the furrowed fields. Train going away someplace. Perhaps a bell on a wrecked ship far below is tolling. Caught in the currents off the Point, it might toll forever. Nobody there to listen. Bellsong sounds in ever-widening concentric circles.

I went back home. The apples were on. My father's orchard was full of pickers on ladders. Windfalls crushed underfoot. The air was thick and sweet. Bees hovered. We set up the old stand and sold jugs of cider to the tourists. I took my turns at the stand.

I tried not to think of her. But a glissando of notes fell in my mind, sharp as icicles breaking off a roof.

Su Lin at her recital. Thin, intent, as precise as the music. I saw her, not the tourists, not the bees slowly circling the cider jugs. Seeing her again was as tart as a bite into a green windfall.

The harvest is big this year. Truckload after truckload of tomatoes go past on the road to the canneries in Leamington. The subtle curve of the road at a point just past us causes the load to shift to the right. Then there is a four-way stop. The load shifts again and the intersection is soon awash with tomato juice and loud with bee clamour. At night I dream of drowning with her. I hear a bell deep under water. The harvest is heavy this year.

I lay down on the sleepers so that I could rise again. I heard a final word spoken clearly. I told the doctor not to judge me. Nobody can know my pain. My fingers made music come from struck strings. Who could tell my fingers not to strike the chords? My love told me of his apple trees. He wanted to climb and pick the sweetest for me from the top. Oh my love, I cannot wait. I must lie down and wait to rise.

The morning train comes and goes many times. Things become usual. Journeys are undertaken. The rain sweeps the train windows, certain as the last things.

Look mommy, says a child as he points out the train window. *There's the sea.*

It's only a river, says the mother.

She does not look out the window. The train goes on, resolute, implacable as a final judgement. Its horn announces us. The river rises in the rain and flows on its certain way. We are almost home or going far from home. Everything is falling in place.

bpNichol

from *Selected Organs*

The Toes

1.

I was lying on my back on the grass in the park in front of our house staring at them & thot how ugly they looked. I was fifteen & really depressed & the clouds blew over the park & I stared at these two great clubs of flesh & bone with five little stubs sticking out of each of them & thot how ugly they looked & how maybe I should kill myself. I lay in the long grass beneath the oak trees & thot about killing myself & the ugliness of my toes & decided my suicide would have to be because of something else. This was the first time I ever really looked at my toes & boy were they something else. They were ugly.

2.

In Port Arthur we went to the shoe section in the big department store where they had the free X-ray machine & shoved our feet into it and stared into the viewer & saw the bones in our toes moving. It was like the peepshow movieola we looked into at the sideshow where we always ran out of quarters just before we got to see the woman with all her clothes off but we saw our toes with all their flesh off & there were ten sets of bones we wiggled & there was no lead shielding & we did it almost every weekend for months. Maybe they mutated. Maybe they looked so ugly later because they'd mutated & it's all the fault of the shoe department in the big store whose name I no longer remember so there's nobody I can sue. Maybe this is the clue. Maybe postmodern writers like me all have post-atomic feet & that's what makes them ugly to the pre-atomic eye & difficult to notate. Maybe this is THE ATTACK OF THE MUTANT POST-ATOMIC FEET! Maybe this is why we're always saying to the words: "take me to your reader."

3.

It was okay to talk about feet. It was okay to talk about toes. It was never okay to talk about toe-jam. If you talked about toe-jam you were really gross. I've never even seen the word spelt before. I think I like it best just the way I've spelt it here, with the hyphen between the two words "toe" & "jam," like the dark grungey hyphen you were embarrassed to discover there, between your toes, inside your sock, your shoe, where you were never able to figure how the toe-jam got.

4.

When Ellie & I moved in together we bought a house with six other people on Warren Road & the next door neighbours had a dog named "toes." It was like a sick joke & I felt fifteen again & the stupid dog chased me every time I walked from the house to the coach house & back again. It was like a bad dream where the repressed returns & there I was, toes yapping at me, toes jumping at me, toes trying to step on me, ugly & depressing & out to get me.

5.

I forget when I first noticed my toenails grew funny. Probably the same day I realized my feet were ugly. The big toenails were worst of all, flakey & fragmented, & the little toenails, almost nonexistent, & the ones in between curling around the stubs of the toes, hugging them, so that even now, except for the big toe (which gets sharp & jagged & rips my socks), I don't have to cut them for months unless, of course, I feel like it. But it is easier if you keep them cut because of the dirt that wedges under them. And toenails are dull, like this paragraph, & in writing we're warned to cut the dull short. Except that no matter how short I cut them they're still dull & lately I began to think that maybe all you are saying when you say "it's dull" is "it's ugly & difficult to control." And it really struck me the way the toenails curl around pressed flat against the stubby pink surfaces of the toes as tho they were hiding from me, fighting for their lives, feeding on the dirt & jam accumulated there, in the dark of the shoe, growing.

6.

Why were toes "piggies?" Why did one of them go to market? When that last little piggie went "wee-wee-wee," how come he did it all the way home? We all know pigs become sausages & sausages look just like toes. Where do these metaphors & similes, these symbolisms, come from? Who makes up these resemblances, these languages, anyway? Why is it some days the words look so strange, so other, almost as if someone somewhere's speaking to me from behind them, thru them, trying to make me understand, instruct me, maybe even warn me – you know, trying to keep me on my toes?

Rod Willmot

from *The Ribs of Dragonfly*

Prelude

All problems solved. Sometimes all you have to do is throw a tantrum, or rather, fall to pieces one piece at a time, or argue, cry, tantrum, be contrite, then fall to pieces if you have to. But it works.

He'd never gotten so much done. Meeting his deadlines, jotting more plans. He'd sunk into a depression at first and that was worrisome, yet she knew, she'd always known that this was best. Now she had plans of her own. He would be famous, and she would be a mother.

This was a view from somewhere inside her. Other views were different. She hated him. She loved him so much it was probably the best thing about her. She was nothing without him. He was nothing but a man.

She enjoyed it when they cooked together, whether for a party or an ordinary meal. Teamwork, a different rhythm from the one in bed. Sometimes in bed she got lost, and needed him to find her; she enjoyed being Lost and Found.

the keel is unseen

Berrying after rain.

"Good luck to eat the first." Purple druplets cupping a dying-day. Blue flutes, a rose perfume.

The next hits the bottom of the pain with a grandiose boom.

Thereafter the notes become higher, fainter, until the plucking hand conducts more subtly. Perfunctory whispering of berries, onto berries jostling. Clicketings, clicketings, until a dragonfly stills them in the net of its wings. Dogmatic bees, discussing isms. (Avoid the violins – they're sopping.)

When I get halfway around the patch, a measured rustling traverses the undergrowth from the side where I began. One of the cats? The Persian? The rustling stops near my feet and returns to dozing.

Raspberries. Hugeous clusters at arm's length. Wet foliage, spiderwebs trembling precariously gemmed. I press in deeper, stretching, while coolness washes over my forearms, fusing into the fabric of my clothes. There are bluets by the hundreds! Brilliant blue piccolos, silent, rising and falling among the canes. My hands move in and out of the music.

Was there once a season of austerity, when the Reverend Wool held sway by Celsius decree? Churchmouse theology – I don't believe it. St. Fromage and the Hagiophage! Morning after morning I stroll outside, saluting the sun-drummed patio with slapping sandals, greeting the breeze with billowing chemise. And while orioles chirrup and a catbird caws in a secret bush, I gather my breakfast in the light with hands that are still reflecting over the artifacts of night.

Rasp, straw, blue, black – all berries in the end, and each a word of plenitude, a glance of willingness, unblushing, nude. The strawberries a love long gone; the blackberries tight and pale and still taboo: from flowering to fruiting the days succeed one another, flowering once again in the garden of the mouth or fruiting finally beneath the crock's lid. Swaying, ripening, fondly detaching from the wind's vine, women and men go pleasuring in the sun until the last remaining rondelets of untanned flesh, discovered, are a treasure to recover. Our very fingers believe themselves berries, juice-stained jostlers into others' hands.

Now like sprouts in the garden, friends arrive, from around the hill and across the continent. The foliage of days luxuriates, desultory brunches browsing through the afternoons, while the barbecue performs its sword-dance fire-dance sizzling shows. Splash the living spirit over the ice-cubes! Leaves upon leaves while the talk goes gadding it through the trees with laughter yapping after, an abstraction or two to smoke the mosquitoes out, Savonarola citronella. And from the garden, petticoat lettuces, the secret of existence in their overlapping frills: tapwashed, torn into tatters, tossed among mushrooms, tomatoes and shallots.

And once consumed, reassembled, pensively, to root again, with the aid of a cheroot or shreds of latakia; coffee; a drop of Amaretto; mints.

Was it beer or champagne the girl was sipping? A lovely dress, with those thighs. Champagne! White lace over Leila's breasts.

***

We are out in all weathers now, adventuring, seeking out waves to unfurl within us. Leila before me, swaying in the bow in a flowered bikini while the prow lifts and plunges throwing spray into the wind. Strong, my wife! But slim, suppler than a mink. Adroit manoeuvers in a summer gale.

On calmer days I play guide to our visitors, some of whom take to the canoe as to a new romance. Others I find unsettling: so determined to stay upright they convey their own nervosity to the craft, which then sets the very lake aquiver. Still others, seeing the waves overtake us from behind (in a following breeze), despair of getting anywhere. "Ignore the waves!" I urge, expounding the stillness of the surface film: the dust, chaff, pollen, feathers, damsel-fly nymphs and belly-up fishes; iridescent trails of swirls and bubbles, like slime-trails of slugs, slug-motorboats that troll in inverted forests; fishermen's floats, red plastic, red and white. Only bobbing.

When you find your movement, look to the waves again.

***

Cloud-forms, changes in the wind. Rumblings: a dump truck on the hill? It can be tricky, trying to judge how far you can go before the surfaces sunder. Leaden sky, sky-lace on the waves, tossing to exchange positions. Hag-fingered lightning, startling the young folk with a glimpse of what she knows.

Today I was caught out alone when the storm came up, and sought refuge under a stranger's eaves. Necessity mothered well, though; I was soon in comfort, distracted from meteorology by a lady of a certain age with a gift for languages and raspberry turnovers, who served a fine coffee of her own invention (roots and grains). She had carved Quo vadis? into the endmost plank of her dock.

I'd forgotten to phone home, however, and apparently Leila was convinced I was drowned or lightning-skewered (it was a hell of a storm). Or soaked to the bone at least, on a hostile shore. In expiation of my sins I had a tough paddle upwind to get home, on a full stomach. Singing, *Mon pays, c'est l'hiver,* for some reason. When I reached our little bay the wind fell off as abruptly as it had risen.

Paul Dutton

from *Right Hemisphere, Left Ear*

Uncle Rebus Clean Song

A Story to End All Stories
with Something for Everybody,
Encompassing, as it Does,
Birth, Childhood, Youth, Old
Age, Sports, Sex, Music, Travel,
Parties, Prayers, Jokes,
Violence, Incest, and Death;
Beginning with a Note
from the Reader to the
Writer and Ending with a
Note from the Writer to
the Reader

A Note to the Writer from the Reader

"How do you know that?"
"I followed you."

"I saw no one."
"That is what you may expect
to see when I follow you."
– Sherlock Holmes,
The Adventure of the Devil's Foot

Apart from having found the party boring Maybelle had suddenly realized that the paperclip on the floor in the shaft of sunlight (brass-coloured the clip, on a gold rug) jarred with the adding machine she nimbly ran her fingers over his cock rising under her expert touch in the quiet office she had thought would be deserted, the bartender surly as he wiped off the counter-top and asked for the millionth time that day what'll it be, taking the cold glass of milk gratefully from the breadman who had let off the little boy five blocks from home at the end of his route before heading back to the stables to water and clean his horse among the still desks and chairs within the dark office, a room filled with bored couples[1] commenting on Betty's paté, the uncomfortable chesterfield over-upholstered for a living-room otherwise impeccably streamlined by a plot that twisted and cavorted through more bed-scenes and bad-doings than the average novel manages to crowd into three weeks of carefully planned social events for the underdogs of the civil service, none more aware of the fluids oozing from between her legs than Maybelle who leers salaciously at the wide-mouthed boy in the front row his legs jiggling in time to the music as she brushes her boa across his stiffened member exposed outside the spotlight playing over the ripe curve of her rump at third base in the empty downtown lot that the snot-nosed six-year-old runs across slipping and falling his face gouged by the jagged glass left broken and drawing blood from his veins, ripping through skin and flesh creating tiny white islands in a tiny red sea beneath the blue mediterranean sky sweating brown bodies of vacationers bask under a sky filled with the crump and thud of missiles fired by careening planes in a dizzying devotion to the sacred heart whose slithering fish-lips slide along the beach and over sand-encrusted toes of whoever dealt an ace to blacken the jacket decayed on the rotting fence the goods the bads and the uglies were passed to that night of stolen pleasures aunts in his pants and a bird on the wire electrically linked to the box of Ma Bell Maybelle sweet of lip and swell of cunt no runt of roe boy ever laid an egg in though she tinkered with his tiller til he thought he was undone oh what is that he is undoing underneath an azure sky, pointed clouds upon a button down to rio didja narrow the choice of darts to pierce his heart squirting blood out of the left ventricle like a jet, a fountain of you the muscle relaxes at the riddle of the sphincter flew to who gypped the office-boy out of his senses, she's out of his head on the bed where a spring trickles past a green fern and no one knows what turn the river takes down by the sheltering palms upturned in supplication, pining for ever, for a knee one old man left to play death out of his hand, keeping it clean, hands and heart upon the table, nine of, ten of, may belly-up jack, Maybelle, yup, jack in her box off his uh tracks yuh know my god I am hard alee, sorry for having off-handed the I.D. test, ah, love[2,3] my sins because of thigh, just pun, nish meant butt, most of all because they have oaf-ended theme, a lore to art, all good, Andy serving, a fall, my love, eye firm, leery, salve with the help of thigh, Grace to sin, know more, and to a void then heroic asians of sin, asbestos icon gold-leafed on the Byzantine presbytery, press by tree leafing through a book with pages trimmed yellow, the leaf pressed between her sperm-laced thighs a prick flicked through, bending her spine between soft covers, that favourite passage red[4] while lying in the crotch of the old scotch maple swinging in her backyard spinning down giving her head out through the spout to water the lawn with exterior plumbing – boy! Well, she'd have been just as happy with a girl and none too soon, for placing her order out of habit with the novice she ate paused you'll end up mother sup here you're a head of them all by jumping the gun in this most human of races doing an even three while the next best make anywhere from three eleven to three fifty-nine point nine on a good track and he tried a lot, then ran a round trying to escape the boxer, a rebel if ever there was one to study trigonometry without any cause, a sign of Maybelle-bodied men with a yen for one another shooting it out in a west-end bar on a dead-end street, ripping their hose at the fireman's balls, a panty any game with a hot poker stuffed[5] between their tulips a little closer to the bone china, sipping tea and talking muffins through their flowered hats it's as though someone lay murdered on the street and they went home to have a good night's sleep, saying just a bad dream only anal eyes would hold to have a meaning, while the boy lies keening for his dead mother, may bell of church, recorded and played from a fake-brick-shingled steeple in the cemetery, ring until the cow's come home, dragging her tall behind, so long in the ass, so under the grass.

Notes

1. copulating with short quick strokes of the brush upon canvas swelled before the wind in the bay that Maybelle had a view of from the window of the second-storey john as she oiled in the tub reading for the tenth time the tenth letter from her tenth lover dated (as were all his letters) October 10, 1910, before the young boy fell from the fire escape and brought bubble gum from a favourite priest who lived in luxury back among the packing crates that the boy's adored older brother piled up fighting off the advances of men and women at the public swimming pool during communion with nature behind the playground one glassy-eyed matron placing the poached eggs beside the mashed potatoes and cutting open the cat's tiny brain fifteen yards from a first down with only two minutes left in the quarter and one down to go as he

put his head* between her legs and prayed that now the usher with the purple mole beside his lip on the right side as you faced him wouldn't stop the crane the jaws of the dozer biting on a cable and keeping up work as usual at school where she saw him bend down pretending to look for something on the floor but really staring up her skirt by the bagpipes' wail that called children out of sidestreets and whores out of alleys where the backbone disconnected causing instant death and she smiled with great promise and more talent than they wanted her to show pumping round after round into the wizened little face she loathed along with the rest of the passengers lying in a bloody heap on the floor of a badly designed room in the ducal palace at the corner of Evans and Ryemoral, belting out blues on an out-of-tune piano when the hostess tripped over his tails as all broad thinkers would want to drum up business the silken wisp of panties barely covering her crotch no other love to hike her skirts for and ending on a presto crescendo through aching eyes, his hands bent into impossible contortions by the rock-fall that also crushed his head, no ears to hear the inconsolable shrieks of Maybelle lost to grief.

* out the window to spit upon the wet flashing past Maybelle shifted into third coming out of a curve on the third lap to ask the lawyer with the hot tongue if he would pinch her nipples through the shower-curtain folded and stored under the tiles scraped continually by the chairs people were always pushing away from the table for a better view of those across the street biting back tears and cursing, a way of registering disapproval for the cop's bludgeoning of the mime with a backhand headed for the lower left-hand corner til the goalie got his glove on it and she threw an egg into the frying pan to make another breakfast for yet another lover child of the urgent lust that propelled these channel crossings which the captain said were helping him feather his nest quite handily despite the pimps and loan sharks lounging at the bar with sidelong glances directed at their every move meant to re-morse an abandoned code of ethics oh sister you got nice tits.

2. never rest to pop a cat petal cause you'd rather kill a man, jerome, i paw pa, tomb eerie, spawn dead, wit a grin out of humour and a-grown out of them clothes by the time he was to go to the toy let sit sit with crap accumulating, on the bum, arose, merry time had by Corrie and her sage companion, Basil, leaves to curry favour savouring every hot lick he lands on the masses of the mighty, his brow† knows a society ring and alls the belle peeling off layer after layer of onion-skin paper that Maybelle dressed in decently the son shown through this garden of hedonist ein kindergarten und as Kind ist come his spill is done on earth as it's chizz in havin' the time of his death.

† creases, his eyes start, his mouth gapes, his muscles twitch, his stomach heaves, his dick shrinks, his blood clots, his heart stops.

3. son of a bitch said Maybelle yuh'll split me in two there wont be nothin left fer the next one which way're yuh goin – in er out for chrissake and who are all these people where the hell am and what the fuck's going on anyway

it's past yer bed-time dear and put that paper down come on spit it out oh god that feels good jesus who'd you practise on no not know not now not put that there ah there there come to mom poppa no don't touch mommy there goddammit yer hung yer hurtin me ease off will ya whadaya all think I am a fickin circus-tent or somethin leave me *alone* yer thinkin *my* thoughts they're *mine* goddamit go find yer own thoughts yuh shitty little thief I cant bear this kind of treatment and watch yer language around a lady she could be someone's mother tongue in cheek sweetheart let mommy have her little joke and don't poke there no please yes okay don't oh no yes please oh christ why didn't I meet you years ago y do do I love it yes of course yes keep it up don't stop don't stop don't stop stop stop stop stop stop stop stop stop

4. 'white and blue the rubber ball that bounces on each word at the bottom of the screen but someone's drowning by the light of the silvery moon and they were cruising down the river in cottage country only now he's got the randy little bugger by the neck and is squeezing tennis balls to strengthen the fingers for playing piano to pee an ism oh anyone can, benny any good man can except he wasn't all that good a tit and Maybelle knew a sucker when she saw one, always calling the shots fired in a lethal spray this way and that way entering the boy's brain on the left side splattering both occipital lobes and on the right side destroying the frontal lobes and entering her left thigh on an angle out and down and entering the middle of her chest tearing through the right atrium after all of which the welder of the weapon blew the back of his own head off by inserting the gun in his mouth and pulling the trigger.

5. up the flue beside the body of the female it took three healthy men to pull down she being the type who never found one enough a girl who was hale merry for love graced, lowered as witty, bless a tart though among whim in end-bliss it is deaf, rue to die whom Jeeze is always saying it's an H of a way to go having come as naked as a jaybird saying okay it's elementary lining up that pea with the rest in a queue as they are especially when the third tee is where you venially sin with the double you expect to see explaining why phys ed finishes off the plumber's philosophy of politics that he wont be party to the very thought of it wrenching his heart leaving him aghast a ghost haunting the infirmary that everyone says is a morgue to rue a place to find a dupe in trying to figure out these murders.

[A Note from the Writer to the Reader: Lovers of the recondite will perhaps be interested to learn the sources for the title of this work. If you didn't get Uncle Remus, return to childhood and throw the dice again; a rebus is defined in any dictionary and once you've looked it up (if you need to), you'll notice that its visual technique is approximated by verbal devices throughout this whimsy. Clean-Song is an allusion to an old sailor shanty called 'The Clean Song' (you can hear it on Oscar Brand's *Old Time Bawdy Sea Shanties*), which is structured along the lines of 'Sweet Violets', i.e., 'There was a young sailor who looked through the glass / Spied a fair mermaid with scales on her island / Where sea-gulls fly over their nests / 'he combed the long hair that hung over her shoulders..., etc. – its mood of shattered expectation being another technique liberally employed, even to the point of irritation, in the bit of pocket-lint, locker-room fluff here under discussion. And that ends the discussion.]

Fred Wah

from *Waiting For Saskatchewan*

Elite [pronounced ee-light]

Elite 1

Swift Current Saskatchewan is at the centre. I don't think you were a boy there. Probably what happened is your family moved there from Medicine Hat just before you were four, just before you and Ethel were sent to China. I know all these "facts" existed once, and I could check some of them out with Ethel, or your other sisters and brothers, Buster, Lil, Flo, Jimmy. But, like the information on distant relatives I lost just before going into China, somehow I don't want it or don't need it. The facts seem partially unreal. Anyway, you must have seen Swift Current just before Grampa put you on the train. About 1923. I was driving across the prairies on New Year's eve last year and we decided to stop for the night in Swift Current. It was close to midnight and so we thought we'd welcome in the New Year in a pub downtown. I hadn't been there for over thirty years but I felt natural in following Central Ave. to the old train station. As soon as I saw the station I knew exactly where I was. I stopped the car and pointed out to Pauline the exact spot I stood when the war was over and I met you at the station when you came home from training camp. From there the lay of the land was clear to me. There was Roy's shoe shop and just up the street across from Woolworth's was the Elite Cafe. You were always there, in the Elite, working. I remember the streets more on my own. Not just the photographs, but me walking, alone in the town. Touching a building, the flowerpots in Mother Trimble's windowsills, the cool shade under some outside stairway, etc. I never talked to you about these things, even when they weren't memories. They weren't really important at the time. Your memory of such particulars. Mine. Does it matter? The reason for the story is simply to count on it. What I remember or what you or anyone else connected remembers isn't the point. There isn't even any point. There is just this. You, before you had a car, on the street in an overcoat, winter, to work. Always alone. I mean I see only your singularity, you with hands in your pockets, head down, going to work, with intention, in the cold winter dusk, to the Elite, your dad or Buster already has the big stainless coffee urn ready, what was it, twenty cups of ground in the cloth sack, and, what, the first few customers, not farmers, you can't even speak English at first, silence, from China too, sweep the floors, maybe do some cooking in the kitchen where you can talk to the cooks, Grampa out front flipping coins, the whole family around you there in Swift Current, your new old family, by then silence and anger hum, alone.

Elite 2

Do you remember how living on the prairies was like living in water, in an ocean or a large lake. Movements, decisions, fortunes were made by undercurrent, a sense of sliding along a large floor, in the night. The night I was with you on a trip, just before we moved out to B.C., it felt like that, the way we moved, probably by train, through unknown territory. Always you had an "intent." You were on business of some sort and the others we met were all Chinese. You could talk to them. They gave me candy and pinched me. You and they talked and talked. Chinese always sounds so serious, emotional, angry. I napped on a couch in some Chinese store in some Alberta town. The old men played dominoes and smoked and drank tea. In the window dusty plants in porcelain bowls and some goldfish. Does it seem strange to you now to see this in words? Do you remember the trip I'm talking about? Late at night somewhere you played Mah Jong. From outside the sound of the click-clack of the pieces being shuffled over the tabletop under the hum of the men's voices, a real music I felt comfortable with. Even though you stayed late you always came back, going somewhere. We moved that night through this subcontinent of prairie landscape, it was summer and the water was warm and hazy, the possible distances, distant.

Elite 3

I'm on the prairies this winter. I haven't been here in the winter since I was four years old. It's not Swift Current, or Speedy Creek as some here call it, but there are certain flavours which are unmistakeably part of us. The ethnicity here feels so direct. I mean the Chinese are still connected to China, the Ukrainians so Ukrainian, in the bar the Icelanders tell stories about Iceland, the Swede still has an accent, the French speak French. Here you're either a Wiebe or a Friesen, or not. What is a Metis, anyway? I know when you came back from China you must have felt more Chinese than anything else. But I remember you saying later that the Chinese didn't trust you and the English didn't trust you. You were a half-breed, Eurasian. I remember feeling the possibility of that word "Eurasian" for myself when I first read it in my own troubled adolescence. I don't think you ever felt the relief of that exotic identity though. In North America white is still the standard and you were never white enough. But you weren't pure enough for the Chinese either. You never knew the full comradeship of an ethnic community. So you felt single, outside, though you played the game as we all must. To be a mix here on the prairies is still noticed. I remember going into Macleods in Swift Current a few years ago and sensing that most of the women in the store were just like Granny Erickson. I don't think you felt there was anyone else in the world like you.

Elite 4

You got us involved in the Salvation Army because that's what Granny Wah wanted. She had a bonnet. I can't recall ever seeing Grampa or you there. But I bet she had her go at you too. Didn't you ever play the big bass drum, or the cymbals? I played the E-flat horn later in Nelson. I think, like Grampa, you always thought the Salvation Army people outside yourself. That was the Chinese in you. You didn't outwardly really trust it. But you tried it. In some totally pure and personal way you prayed, alone. I know later when our family went to the United Church in Nelson and you sometimes got off work on Sunday morning to go to church with us you did sing the hymns but your brow furled as if you couldn't understand the words. You were proud, then, of the fact you were going to church and you made a point of telling some of the customers in the restaurant that you had to go to church. That was after you had stopped desiring China and the Chinese at work put up with but laughed at you going to church. I think the church thing was white respectability and you did it for that and a sense of our family in that community. Somehow in the face of all the Salvation Army, Granny, community, etc. I know you established some real spiritual communication, totally private, no drums.

Elite 5

There is no picture (or is there) of me leaning over the boards of the Swift Current arena with you there, on the ice in your big overcoat, suit and tie, spiffy, smiling at the camera, and the whole Swift Current Indians (they weren't real "Indians" – that was their name) hockey team working out, swirling big as life over the dark ice. There is a team picture I know. Like the Toronto Maple Leaf hockey calendars that used to hang in the barber shop, the team lined up on the real ice of the Gardens against the backboards. But in this one it's the Indians. I think you were the manager or something, you helped out. The brim of your hat is turned down, Chicago gangster style. The Indian on their sweaters is just like the Chicago Black Hawks. Strangely, Chicago figured in your life. You told us that you ran away from home when they brought you back from China and got work on a boat in the Great Lakes. You jumped ship in Chicago and they picked you up for illegal entry. You were sent back to Swift Current and that was the end of that. I wish you had given us more details. Chicago has always been a mysterious place for me and someday I'll get there myself. Anyway, isn't it strange how that city is there in our lives, on the periphery.I've always been "proud" you were part of that team. The Swift Current Indians were my first hockey heroes and their movements over the ice instilled a sense of body and mind-set which I have carried with me all my life. Even though you never played hockey I know you had the invisible movement of the game inside you too. You said you played basket-ball on a winning team in China. But you liked hockey. There is no picture either of me and my first pair of skates, double-runners, with Mom (you were working), on a blustery day, natural ice, on a pond or creek. Or the skating rink you made for us in our back yard in Trail. Or the puck that caught me just above the eye, third row as you and I watched a game in the civic Centre, blood and stitches. The game on television now, you'd fall asleep before the end of the first period. Did you ever ride a horse?

Elite 6

Line going deep into the lake or flung out onto the surface glaze river current, layers of darkness, invisible fish. You would look at me with serious brown eyes sometimes like I was crazy when I caught a fish and then give your own mad laugh. Something got to you fishing in the Columbia River at Trail, after work, along the rocks, swift-flowing mind emptying, maybe. Or in a creek at Meadow on a Sunday afternoon picnic, cousins and uncles, a ball game. At Apex you driving the road in the turquoise Ford looking for us fishing along the slow meandering of Cottonwood Creek. You without me at Trout Lake. Me without you below the C.P.R. tracks below Granite Road on the way out of town or jigging for suckers near the boathouses with the old Chinaman. When I fish now sometimes I feel like I'm you, water, glassy gaze, vertical, invisible layers, the line, disappearing.

Elite 7

The dream "noises" of the early morning. You getting ready to go to work, still dark at 4:30, a light dust of snow maybe, the house warm, as you dress, the gabardine pants, shoes I shined for you last night, muffled voices of good-bye, the small change in your pocket, car keys, your pace on the varnished maple floor, alone, quickens with movement towards the door, out, dark grey mist-hackle across the lake on Elephant Mountain, you and the town get going for the day, I hear the blue 2-door Pontiac hum alive down on the street, and you're gone to work, and then our own half-awake silence and relaxation back into the morning's warmth and sleep. Or me a couple times a year getting up for you, e.g. father's day, some Sunday morning, could you really sleep "in" thinking of me the kid making the big urn of coffee, turning the heat up, remembering to get the cream and a tray of butter out of the cooler, turn on the sign, the synchromesh of everything starting to work, darkness breaking on Baker Street, first customers and the regulars early morning old man risers C.P.R. night shift and a few foremen and loners first coffee and cigarettes, the new noises of the day picking up speed and humming along the counter and booths to the whack of the kitchen door kicked on stride and the "smells" then.

Elite 8

I try to "place" you and the hand or head can't, try to get you into my mountains for example but your China youth and the images of place for you before you were twenty are imbued with the green around Canton rice fields, humid Hong Kong masses – I can't imagine what your image of the world was, where you were in it (were you always going home to Swift Current, were you ever at home, anywhere). How much did you share of how small or large the world was after we left the prairies – Trail, Nelson, Cranbrook, Calgary, Vancouver? That "reward" of a real holiday down the Columbia and then up the coast to Vancouver when you sold a share in the Diamond Grill. A few trips to Spokane, hikes into the hills around Nelson for fishing, the gravelly drive to Trail and back. Did any shape of such places ever displace the distancing in your eyes? You looked out at it all but you never really cared if you were there or elsewhere. I think you were prepared to be anywhere. The sun, the warmth, was something you went outside for outside yourself, stretching and relaxing your working moving body, inside, inside, you never betrayed any imprint of a "world" other than your dark brown eyes.

Elite 9

When you returned from China via Victoria on Hong Kong Island and they put you in jail in Victoria on Vancouver Island because your birth certificate had been lost in the Medicine Hat City Hall fire and your parents couldn't prove you were born in Canada until they found your baptism records in the church or in the spring of 1948 when we moved to Nelson from Trail during the floods while Mao chased Chiang Kai-shek from the mainland to offshore Taiwan and the Generalissimo's picture hung in our house and on a wall above some plants and goldfish in the Chinese Nationalist League house down on Lake Street or when you arrived in China in 1916 only four years old unable to speak Chinese and later in the roaring twenties when each time Grampa gambled away your boat passage so you didn't get back to Canada until 1930 languageless again with anger locked up in the immigration cells on Juan de Fuca Strait or when your heart crashed so young at 54 as you fell from mom's arms to the dance floor did you see islands?

Elite 10

Your father owned the Regal across from the railway station but you worked in the Elite on Central Avenue right next to the Venice and the Paris was the one on the corner all three across the street from Cooper's store where Connie worked in the dry goods department after school and then full time after graduation the year you took her to the final basketball game at Gull Lake and Mom says now you borrowed a car and drove to Moose Jaw for a honeymoon and bought your first house in Swift Current in the fall of 1939 for $900 just after I was born and Connie's Dad fixed it up so you sold it and bought another stucco (I remember that one) in '41 then moved to Trail in the spring of '43 and bought the Expert Cleaners and sold it to Andy's brother Sam and his wife and bought a house there on a corner right across from the river near Butler ball park by the bridge and the next one where we had our first dog it was down closer to Sandy Beach where Granny and Grampa lived at the foot of Sandy Mountain and then Ernie's dog Mickey up in the house in the next block to the Dollar Cleaners all in East Trail while you and Grampa were in the Elite across the river downtown underneath the smelter hill and then in the spring of '48 floods when we moved to Nelson didn't you and Jimmy Gee Ethel's husband buy into the L.D. Café which you changed to the New Star just as Mao's victory north of the Yangtze became palpable and we lived in the duplex with the oil stove at 314 Carbonate before you got into your last restaurant (and mine) the Diamond Grill which even with the Standard down by Hipperson's Hardware times got good on Baker Street in the fifties and you got Grampa Erickson to build us our own house with maple floors at 724 Victoria you were so proud we had fireworks for the house warming and two sittings for the Chinese banquet in the basement and finally the Holmes Motel in Cranbrook in the early sixties where that was the end of the deals the cafes the houses the driving the building the running right through it, for you, that was it.

Daphne Marlatt & Betsy Warland

from *Double Negative*

Crossing Loop

B. There were things we left out, for instance our encounters with people on the train. Those people we were seated with for meals who were really an interruption in our sensual, mesmerized experience of moving through the land.

D. Well, we were so absorbed in being present to it [almost as if we were being born again in this very encapsuled and intimate experience, two in a berth / birth / byrth to bear in a certain direction, forwards say –].

B. I was aware of the different choices people make on a train. For instance, those who would leave their door open a lot and would want to watch people walking by and be seen in return. People who went to the lounge car and played games with each other for hours on end and were really into encountering strangers, making friends, making a community on the train.

D. We'd decided not to fly so that we could be *in* the landscape so of course we didn't want to be distracted by human encounters.

B. Exactly! [the human body as distraction, bodies as magicians making everything else disappear like billboards overlaying landscape, our bodies their envy of others' attention, how we prevent each other from being present to other forms of life].

D. We also didn't admit any of the tradition of how trains have been depicted, we didn't contrast how we were experiencing the train, from the inside, with how it's so often imaged from the outside as this powerful industrial monster whose rhythms and approach are seen as very much like the male orgasm – how it used to be imaged as steaming towards you down the track, or even towards the waiting female tied to the rails, which gets pretty obvious! We didn't refer to any of that. We talked about coming but made it female coming and the cyclical nature of female orgasm is really different from the on-track crescendo of male orgasm. What we really didn't deal with is how when you're on a train you are on the one track. It's not cyclical. But that was part of the tension of talking about the landscape which surrounds you as you're going through it, and the rails which lead only in one direction forward to your destination.

B. It wasn't that way for me because i saw the tracks as the umbilical cord, the track as representing our continuous dependency on the earth which we're never really cut free from. Also, the train is constantly starting and stopping, departing and arriving, coming and waiting at crossing loops and in that sense it's cyclical [as rhythm is cycling back repeating itself, the rhythm of our movement everything].

D. I suppose what we wanted to continue was this being held in the rocking motion of the train which is very womblike [when you're inside it you don't see where you're going and the train rocks from side to side a body that's carrying you so all you can do is let yourself be carried, passive voice. but we are active in our desire and part of what we desired was to be out in the desert as an image for a certain way of being. what we were passing through was the real subject of our writing, not the train].

B. Why do you think we didn't write about what we left out on the surface of the poem? [the body the editor extreme, the brain selecting only 5-10 per cent of the stimulus of any given moment].

D. We were caught up in the narrative fictional frame of heading down that track, even if we translated *to* somewhere as *through* somewhere. And we were so into rewriting the train experience from a female perspective that we didn't want to admit any of the imagery from the tradition because it would have contaminated our alternative version [vision].

B. Well, we certainly talked about the mainstream literary tradition but to write about it would have taken us outside of ourselves and what was happening [yes the trace is there on the brain but we colour outside the lines referentiality's locus shifted]. It was in the process of rewriting that i became aware of a different tradition. Part of the time in Australia we were at a couple of conferences with Nicole (Brossard) who was fascinated by the desert and was writing about it in her new novel. After we returned to the coast and had begun revisions i began to think about Jane's (Rule) first book which is set in the desert. Thinking about their work i began to have a sense that there is some kind of a North American lesbian tradition of exploring the feminine in relation to the desert which is usually seen as an arena for *male* activities. I find it quite exciting that there's this female movement into the desert saying "this is mine too and i relate to it in a different way."

D. So we want to get off the train, get off the narrative track, and move out into the desert in a different way?

Michael Kenyon

from *The Blue Fairy*

Golden Slumbers

I am not sick for home. Not always. Sometimes, yes. I am the beautiful girl with azure hair and I stand at your elbow as you follow my words. Let me warn you – I must be cautious – my appearances are considered high portents. I bear a grave responsibility. I cannot sanction Pinocchio's retreat from his wife. Our world needs children to allay despair. Need I say more?

In the first years after Pinocchio wed his Canadian wife, he'd wake and tremble in her sleeping arms. Eyes shut, nose and fingers nuzzling in the earth, he recalled only dimly his escape from the shark to the shores of the new world. No need for my presence then, my visits grew less and less frequent. I felt liberated. A free spirit, unfettered, I explored the continent. I took up aerobics.

Let me, dear Reader, show you my technique.

Look. Pinocchio sleeps troubled these nights, so I sweeten his dreams with blackbird song, train hummingbirds to perch on his penis.

I remember the occasion of my one thousandth birthday, a grand concourse of goats and ghosts in Florence. Breathless from the ball and still wearing my gown, I stopped at the toy-maker's house. Young Pinocchio dreamed his father was bored and wanted to whittle his puppet's body into that of a little girl, or into a sailboat with a handkerchief sail. I gently woke him, and he listened to Geppetto sawing wood until he fell asleep again. Ah, I wish you'd seen the fireplace. The flames burned merrily!

Geppetto's in the nursing home, but he imagines himself in the shark's belly, alone. All the nurses are ghosts, pale and insubstantial. I could slip in unnoticed. Wait. I'll go to him later. I'm fey, it's true. I can be *capriccioso.*

Lampwick's under the stars, letting their light burn away his dreams. I won't show myself.

The women in my aerobics class think me stuck-up, but I'll tell you a secret (judge me kindly, Reader): I am the blue-haired goat in all their dreams.

The New Colony

Excuse me a minute while I change. I'm not, as you will learn, a disinterested observer. Let me tell you what I've just witnessed.

Pinocchio's wife lies asleep in Lampwick's bed.

Lampwick hums *Un bel di vedremo* as he dons hat, veil and gloves.

There.

This chamber's cramped, but not bad for a young Italian queen. Paper walls, no door. I look forward to the colony, to begin laying. Meanwhile I have some time. Lampwick's busy with the established hives so, as befits a queen, I pace the floor of my cell, impatient, sad, buzzing: "*Vorrei vedere un'opera!*"

Pinocchio an hour ago crossed the garden and knocked softly at the house door. Silence within. He paused outside Lampwick's uncurtained room, read the rhythm a long time. Oh, the boredom of his pain! Then I spied the package of bees unopened on Lampwick's table: thousands of workers and the queen chamber empty. How could I resist?

I wanted to imprison myself. I wanted a new perspective on Lampwick.

Reader, I like being small, but Lampwick's just Lampwick.

And confined I want freedom. A queen bee, I'll not go down to meet him; a butterfly, I want to sing, an aria beginning:

"He drove away in his own car.
Ah, Pinocchio! *Piccolo Iddio!*
Amore addio!"

In a row

I've a large clientele, the men who need me, but I've promised myself to Pinocchio these hundred years. Carlo Lorenzini of Collodi, an important government man, invented me (that's one thing), and the rich and powerful Walt Disney gave me this body (that's another), but I'm free to choose my brother, my son.

Fairy, Fairy, quite contrary,
how does your garden grow?
With silver bells
and cockle shells
and pretty maids all

I adjure barren women to come to me.
I will protect all the lonely sons.

The Old Vendetta

Last night Pinocchio watched Amarcord for the fourth time. Frankly, movies bore me.

Dreams on the other hand –

There, you see!

Now he dreams he and his wife are aboard the liner – Federico Fellini's cardboard ship from America. He's going home to the old country to pay his respects to the Lame Fox and the Blind Cat. How pleasant. Pleasant? Lampwick tends beehives in the vessel's hold, selling honey and fresh bread to the hungry passengers. Pinocchio's wife does the baking, regulates the flow of customers and collects their money. She returns late to the cabin to tell Pinocchio she will spend Tuesday evening with Lampwick, she will spend perhaps all Thursday night. Yes, indeed. Fox and Cat stole Pinocchio's gold, Lampwick steals his wife. Not Lame Lampwick, not Blind Lampwick, but striped, yes, a silk-eared zebra! New blood for an old vendetta. Pinocchio begins to say, "Fine" – a well-rehearsed "Fine" mind you (he has a plan, you understand): he will go away on Monday, establish contact with a local circus owner, and return the following week – but he remembers he's on a ship and can't get away.

He's awake now, frightened, and is not consoled by his wife's broad back. He's convinced she has three bodies that lie, one, two, three, beside him in bed. He strokes the skin, trying to reach the outermost body. He so wants to mould the smooth skin of three into one familiar. And, like no gentle animal on earth, "I hate Lampwick," he says with each caress.

We'll leave them now, if you don't mind.

Pinocchio listening to Nino Rota's version of *Stormy Weather*, to the flap of billowing plastic as the shallow ocean rolls, and his wife dreaming she is once again in the prairie town of her birth, in the shadow of the Rockies, riding two bicycles at the same time in the snow.

We'll leave the couple to wake on the west coast of Canada to early robins. They will break apart, nervous, afraid of each other. I've witnessed this each morning for two months.

In silence they rise, trying to dispel the dreams that waft like ghosts, prowl like moles about the house. They take turns in the bathroom. He polishes her shoes, she pours his coffee.

Breaking Lampwick's Spell

Pinocchio's wife sits in the garden of Pinocchio's house on the quiet coast road. She reads a book while green shoots inch from the soil around her. Her eyes leave the page to dream of Lampwick under the fading stars.

I materialise beside the budding azalea, but she pretends no to see me. I step closer, touch her hair.

"Go away," she says. "Pinocchio's at work."

I caress the small of her back (a charity, against my inclination), but she answers roughly.

"Stop that right now. It's nonsense. What d'you mean by wearing that dress? You look like a centrefold!"

I smile at her, such a smile (you would be charmed).

"Disney's floosie," she spits.

I leave, my dear, I'm saddened, I invent a silver Mercedes.

* * *

Of course, Pinocchio's my boy, always attentive, though sometimes naughty, as boys very often are. Here he is, hard at work, moving marble at the town hall.

I appear briefly, sway down the main corridor past the mayor's office (feeling the ache emanating from bustling clerks, the jealousy of the receptionist), and push open the glass streetdoors. The wind blows my hair across Pinocchio's eyes, and he blesses me. His partner inhales a few strands of azure, and he chokes, poor man, as I carefully draw free with filaments, one at a time.

They love me, the men, and I love to disappear along a sunny street. In Italy as in Canada as anywhere, the same.

Sunday

Reader, pinch me, I can't stop, can't stop yawning.

Pinocchio and his wife are playing woodcutter-in-the-city on the kitchen tiles. He sees her in a new light, as a free agent in a sexual world, and he wants to punish her for taking a lover. She has a head cold from sticking her nose into too many daffodil trumptets. How crude, shoving her fleshy nose into a delicate flower!

She fills a basin with boiling water, melts a knob of Vicks on the surface and bows before the vapours like a hunched photographer. Groans from beneath the towel like a spelunker in a grotto.

Pinocchio's angry she's ill; in her own self-concern she has apparently forgotten Lampwick, Fairy, her own Pinocchio.

He stands well back when wings begin to beat.

Suddenly the towel is thrown aside from her flushed face and (I show my hand) a flock of geese crosses the room to escape the open window.

Time, Reader you should know, is no time for fairies or ghosts.

* * *

Dishes piled in the sink. His wife, open-mouthed, lets the water run, so the breakfast things can soak. The suds topple over the kitchen counter as Pinocchio, laughing from the belly, approaches.

"How strange!" says he. "How odd!"

"I'll suffocate if you kiss me," she warns.

He kisses anyway. Good Pinocchio!

"Let's breathe together, slowly."

The last goose, I peer at them from the windowsill. The look: quizzical.

Bear with me, patient Reader. Later, in an hour or a century, I'll be a cockle shell, more serious.

Oh, misery, misery, misery, even I feel the weight of Monday.

Gentlemen

Pinocchio this holiday morning lies neck-deep in bath water trying to remember a dream. He stares at his wife brushing her hair in the steamy mirror.

* * *

Let me take this opportunity to formally thank my creators. Signore Carlo Lorenzini of Collodi, for my fickle nature, my ability to transform, my sense of history. Mr. Walt Disney of Hollywood, for my body, my colour, my unruffled demeanour, and for bringing me to America. Gentlemen, I kiss my fingers to you. I curtsy.

A word to my critics, those who say I dissemble, those who accuse me of inconstancy. No. I first appear in Collodi as a dead child with blue hair. In Disney I'm a graceful adolescent, judicious and virginal. For Collodi I live with the puppet as sister or mother. For Disney I'm ethereal, a blue flame. so who am I? Draw your own conclusions. Some have hinted that I am Gepetto's love embodied. No, no.

Sex. "It burns a hole in your pocket," I heard one of the animators say. He was shading the bodice of my gown. "Breasts," said another, "little liberties."

"Children should be allowed to dream," I once heard Singnore Lorenzini say.

Mr. Disney said: "Children should be shown many possible worlds. Worlds filled with man-made wonders, worlds of hope."

"The ending should be straightforward," he said. "Woman the mystical force. Let the talking cricket finish the tale."

Said Collodi: "The ending should be bright and happy. A complete boy, waking from a dream, secure in his father's love. His need of the fairy gone, the memory fading."

"How ridiculous I was when I was a puppet! And how happy I am to have become a real boy!"

* * *

Reader, save me from myself! I'm depressed. Pinocchio has not moved and the water's cold. Mercy! It's much harder being mythological than being a wife. No one realises. the burden of female consciousness! A merry-go-round of husbands, fathers, brothers, sons. Oh women, we must endure, endure, endure, for Lorenzini's sake, for Disney's sake!

Pinocchio's wife takes off her shirt to wash her neck and shoulders. Pinocchio in cold water lies thinking that he hates all men, he fears another will take his place. When he makes love to his wife he imagines he's mankind making love to womankind. Good. Still, he hates himself for being male. No, not seriously. He fears his wife. She rinses away the soap.

He wants her, but suspects her motives. Communion gives way to rapacity, to a violent wish to destroy – integral to this heterosexuality, this monogamy – to destroy his wife? Surely not. His dream was of something wonderful just beyond his fingertips. To destroy his dependence. Ah! Leaving ... Leaving what?

* * *

I appear. I speak.

His wife turns dripping from the sink, "she's here again, your sexy friend."

Pinocchio gazes up at her nipples; she stares at me, listening. My dulcet tones. Another Disney inheritance. She wants me to say: Get out of the bath, unhappy fool! Take a self-conscious walk in a empty arena!

No. Of course I don't say that.

"Brave Pinocchio," I barely whisper, "work and children." That's all. "Work and children."

Griffin

Ah! We're restless this holiday afternoon, the crop of daffodils dying, crocodiles snapping the mind open, dandelions head and shoulders above the long grass.

Look, Pinocchio's wife's concerned about the spread of seed, when yellow turns to fluffy white. She conjures the image of neighbours scowling over fences as, one o'clock, two o'clock, three thousand paratroopers float the blue sky toward their back gardens.

But Pinocchio, pacing the house, ignores the lawn mower, while his wife plays solitaire, a game of compromise.

"What time is it, Mr. Wolf?" I ask. (Reader, I can't help it!)

And she responds, "You're so foolish," slipping a vital card between her crossed legs.

"Who's more important," I say, "a puppet or a wick?"

***

Reader, can I explain just how bored I am?

At the same time, like a grandmother who lives in the basement of her children's house: smug and complainingly satisfied. All is as it should be. These young folk! Ah, me!

The clock ticks the timeless afternoon. An eagle slides the skylight. A lunatic earthworm is burrowing, making believe he's a king.

Pinocchio's wife says, "If I answer will you go away?"

I agree. "But if you don't answer with a question, I'll stay."

"Then I'll say a puppet because it dances," she says. "But what's a wick? Her feigned feigned innocence.

"A wick, my dear, with fuel and spark
will light a region previously dark."

Pinocchio watches from the doorway. He hates to see me with his wife. Complicity, he hates.

"She hid a card," he announces. He's so petulant.

"Those dandelions are getting tall," says she. "And the daffodils are finished, they should be tied up."

Do I smell an imbroglio?

***

The name no longer has power and we're all, in a sense, disappointed. The neighbours start their mowers, fill the air with scent of grass, roar of lion. The eagle is king, cackles, scorns worm, returns to eyrie.

"Fantastic!" With heavy sarcasm, she plays the secret card.

I knew it, she's human, can't hurt me. I'll go downtown with my Walkman, buy a baggy shirt, thence to Dance-Energy where I'll open telepathic lines to the Pope. La! I want to discuss –

***

Shh!

Softly, softly.

I want to discuss lion's teeth, baby's breath, anima mundi, the Pontiff's sense of balance.

C.H. Gervais

from *Letters from the Equator*

Three Letters from the Equator

Letter to a Stratford poet & his "poet's table"

You have made me think of what might be on my own table & what kind of face I might paint, if I could paint ... Your version rests on the mantle & its images are the old fiddler you had drawn as a boy, a Stratford farmhouse, the last letter in Bronte ... In this attic room – its four windows flashing in a storm – I set my own table: my face, formless & grave; at birth, an uncle offered me his given name & when my second son was born, I gave that name to him ... But behind the name is another image ... Henry Miller shrugged at the fundamental, the pure ... He cared for the slant of the ceiling, an arrangement in a room, lipstick ... By the time he escaped the English daily in Paris, the cafés were shut down & street cleaners had invaded the empty streets ... He would remove his shirt, unlatch the shutters to dawn's clatter ... What mattered was that he was at ease, at one with things. What mattered was symmetry ... That's the image alive in the name – the order of the universe ... But what about the silence? Here a lawnmower drones like a First-World-War fighter plane, the Avon sweeps by like an actor crazed by all the ordinary conversation & lazy afternoon secrets ... I study the vulgar swans who are far more fearless than Lady Macbeth as they hiss at any interruption ... Thomas Merton believed that those who love their own noise are impatient of everything else ... He had said our noise, our business, our purposes are all illusion ... He had said the silence of the sky remains when the plane has vanished ... Long after this house sleeps I hear only myself in the upper room ... My voice seems ridiculous, even removing my shirt or pulling back the blankets ... How do you paint silence? Merton believed there must be a time during the day when you have to speak but instead fall silent, that your mind forms no proportions & you ask yourself whether any of this has any meaning ... Who knows? In this room if I could paint silence, I would be swallowed up by it ... But those are concepts, ideas – symmetry & silence. What about things? Or people? Well, perhaps there's the typewriter on the dining-room table in 1960 & the first words in hard uneven impressions – again perhaps my name, again perhaps ideas not yet developed ... Or perhaps there is the scribbling in the margins of a new copy of Twelfth Night ... Or perhaps my image of the clever & beautiful Viola ... There is also the back verandah in the summer & an old leather ottoman inviting me to spend hours reading Merton & Miller & Hemmingway & Steinbeck ... So how do you fit these into the picture? Your own success in painting is in its economy, the key elements, only hints of what might be at the poet's grasp ... Mine is a face too full of confusion ... Let me start over ...

Letter to Antonin Artaud from the Equator

Not at all surprised to find you at Santa Maria de Los Angeles among these widows & mothers ... Their words belong to your autobiography & poems ... The sounds you hear are your own ... They fly at you out of history ... They are the nightmares you refuse to murmur ... Instead you shout insults to the campesinos in the streets ... Not slogans, not rhetoric ... You're angry with the revolution & this isn't revolution but the crucifixion, the resurrection ... Widows in search of their loved ones ... Mothers combing thru the sun-bleached skulls of open graves ... You dream of Paris, of the years before ... You ponder the sins of Marat in the bath ... Cutting his delicate wrists to save his revolutionary soul from the guillotine ... You are no longer dead, no longer the victim of electric shocks, no longer tortured ... You embrace death enthusiastically, kissing these brides of sorrow with abundant peace ...

Managua

Faces of Sandino

1. You are there among the faces on this flight to Managua. Families with luggage & shopping bags on knees, children trampolining seats, crawling in aisles. Clouds of cigarette smoke. More like a Greyhound to Northern Ontario. The plane is a mosquito touching down everywhere: first, Belize where guards smile benignly in the afternoon, where military trucks roar out to the tarred airstrip; then, San Salvador where storm clouds collide with the

army-green mountains beyond, where women in duty-free shops haggle over cigarettes & perfume; finally, Managua where your poster face nods to us at dusk ... The cowboy hat & maudlin dreamy stare, saintly & apologetic for the flight, for the American embargo, for the earnest young soldiers with machine guns ... Or so you say ...

2. This Chevy Impala, like a Great Lakes freighter, swerves thru the rainy streets. The driver tuning in a baseball game. But the talk is of Reagan, the CIA, the embargo, tractor parts, medical supplies, the coming invasion ... He curses the chatter, yearns for box scores, for the clean easy success of a base hit ... Out of the humid darkness loom the slogans ... Someone has spray-painted "Muerte al yankee Invasor!" across a storefront.

Where are the saints in this revolution? In the northern ballparks batting over .300? Or on the border burning brush & digging graves? The driver just shakes his head ... Nothing is right anymore, not anything, he says ... He nods to your silent image as it winks from a passing building ... Your presence now rivals all other deities ...

Paul Savoie

from *The Meaning of Gardens*

7.

You play the celebrant. The knife in your hand gravitates on reels in a whiteness of chanting and slow drumming, black images splattered on canvas in even strokes. You do not serve as victim, I am not the perpetrator. We are caught in the even flow of minute impenetrable violence. Only the projector's hum filters through the density. You turn your head gently. I lift my hand though, to an observer's eye, it may seem I have remained motionless. You are caught in a whiteness of muffled laughter. Your body is riddled with dark spots, bullets of shadow that shoot out from my skin onto yours. You move in and out of reach of the shadow's thrust. You flow into it, out of it. You are part of the violence. You are part of its gesticulation though you try to deny its aim, to hide from its spirals. You ward off its imperfect flow. You use your clenched fists as a shield against the knife, sharp edge of hallucination, though you bend into it, you roll into it, your body and mine a choreography of pierced flesh. You cry out as we tear into one another. A knife dangles in mind-air. Not a knife. A candle, caught in the interplay of haze and white rays. A lit candle and its ephemeral glow around which our lips form words of prayer, a litany of muted sound in darkness where, through echoes, footsteps* can be heard like a pendulum, footsteps that move in this direction and then recede, come nearer or fade like sounds of loose reel that clicks against the side of the projector once all recorded images reach the point of oblivion.

8.

First there was a broken bottle on what looked like sand. Then a cracked wooden table with one leg missing, autumn leaves piled against the slanted top, caked mud at the edges. Also, I saw cinders in an open pit. The hole in the ground had the width and length of a corpse, that of a grown man, average height. Beyond this, I heard the sound of waves, a foghorn though the fog had lifted, a barking dog in the distance. The sound of waves came from further up, from the other side of a steep incline. Though I had walked there before, I could not remember the sea.

Now you walk three feet to my right, making comments on rubble or on flotsam washed ashore. You take special notice of colours while I take stock of variations in forms, broken lines. Your fingers sometimes graze the back of my hand. You offer riddles, conjectures. You speculate on apocalypses and crops, breeding animals.

When we walk waist-deep in water, you say you can make out the shape of our legs beneath the surface. I only see reflections. I cannot see beyond the next wave. As you peer out to the open sea, about which you offer a few hypotheses, you begin to compare pieces of driftwood to sinking ships. You say you can hear the screams of a drowning man, though you admit the sound is barely audible. I can only detect gulls' cries, a mere trick perhaps of wind on swirling water. I kiss your lips, identify the taste as saltwater. You insist they have the taste of sun. We emerge from the sea as dead fish do, covered soon afterwards with sea-weed and moss. Footprints in the sand move away from our inert bodies. They are centrifugal forces, rays from a hidden dynamo. They are part of us for we generate them. Yet they are separate. They escape us. We have nothing left except what we discard, what we cast off. Lovemaking resembles tides, their ebb and flow. Wind bellows, as ineffectual as a sleepwalker's declaration. Your body opens up, closes. You gorge yourself, regurgitate. You spit me out. I have become driftwood, a sinking ship. The scream of a drowning man fills the air. This time I hear it also, in what I had first taken for a foghorn. Fog grows in patches. I witness my own footsteps in the sand where the sea begins to back off from the shore. Your feet trace a path similar to mine, though from a different source. Our steps recede. Our bodies drift apart. You remind me that all horizons have colour barriers. I make reference to a split ocean. We are flotsam on this stretch of beach, autumn leaves in a slanted landscape. When we make love, the earth trembles slightly beneath our outstretched bodies. We send shock waves as if giant ants sprang from our genitals and crawled towards the sea. The variegated sea, you whisper. A dull grey seascape, I answer, where we rend each layer with our claws. We sink, you say. We undo, I answer.

A ship crawls along the horizon. It moves like a caterpillar. We are its larva, the sea a mere imprisonment of wings.

Leon Rooke

Statement / Dippings

Statement

"My entry in this *Grain* may be my 260th published story. Am I Hugh Garner? Am I in a race with Kinsella? Flannery O'Connor published how many, 33? But wait, didn't Tolstoy come in with over 800? Does the figure matter? The point is, a story is apt to be *worth* publishing (at least once – no great harm there) only if it *wants* to be told. *It* wants, not the writer wanting to get it done for whatever noble or nefarious reason. Not much of this one wanted to be told; that's why it's short. I don't have many rules for the writing of short fiction. One of them is, if a thing is going wrong, then start over. If it is going nowhere, then give it up, or start over. If it goes awhile, and stops, then you stop too because maybe you have gone as far as the story wants you to go. Which often means, of course, starting over. The piece lays down its own laws: that's another thing I mean. That's why many very intelligent, very gifted literary people who want to write, can't. They operate under the fallacious notion that the writer is Creator-God, that intellect and reason can figure anything out, whereas intervention of another sort is more frequently the case. The thing, at a certain point, and usually at the start, creates itself. It is of value, or it isn't. Does it matter so much anyway, since the story that awaits the telling awaits as well the teller, and as many aren't found as are. More. Close your eyes and imagine the flight of an entire skyful of extinct birds. Open your eyes, and if the head is screwed on right, sky and birds remain. What to do with them? Boot the old computer, take fingers from your ears. Asking yourself, if you don't already know – *where's* the story? Is it sky, is it birds, is it something reaching out at me from ages ago? Is that a bird I feel sinking its claws into my shoulder? Okay bird, Smart guy, you know the issues involved here; you tell the story."

Dippings

The baby did something wrong and we washed it. It did something wrong again and so again we washed it, this time in deep water. The next time it did something wrong we went down to the sea, installed ourselves in a nice rowboat, and oared out onto the water, at a certain point immersing the baby for a good many minutes and repeatedly. The wife cried. It was such a bad, bad, no account baby and she could not explain it. There has never been any such problems in her family, she said, and she was at her wit's end to understand it. She harangued me and thumped me and immersed me in the water, repeatedly and violently, inferring how I and my side of the family must be the guilty party. I took this unkindly, most unkindly, and so I harangued her and thumped her and immersed her in the water, frequently and violently.

We by then were far out to sea, all shores having vanished. Even so, we felt considerably elated. We felt considerable rejuvenation, even so. How to explain it? We felt very good indeed, if that is what rejuvenation means, and so it came to pass, out on the water, far beyond the reach of civilization's harried keepers, that we made ourselves another baby.

David Halliday

from *Making Movies*

The Contract

The BBC is pleased to present the third edition of our series covering the Fathers of World Cinema, called MAKING MOVIES.

In this edition we focus on the works of the Canadian director, Samuel Bremmer.

The filming of this edition was marred by the untimely death of Samuel Bremmer. To him, we dedicate this programme.

The Samuel Bremmer Company of Actors

MAURICE DUBOIS: So we are supposed to talk about ourselves for a moment. This will probably be the last original thing you will hear from my lips. An actor is a puppet. He is the shell, the suit of multitudinous spirits. Our bodies are promiscuous. An actor is the medium of invention, the house that is haunted, the radio receiver, the echo of another's voice. As the child is the product of his parent's lust, we are the offspring of someone's need to speak and another's need to listen ... When I joined this company of actors I had only been in Toronto for a few weeks. They believed me when I told them

I was in a Shakespearean company in England. Perhaps they thought it racist to call a black man a liar....

BARBARA HARRIS: I don't know what to say really. This is embarrassing. Let's see. I graduated from the University of Windsor's drama department. I worked in a couple of children's programmes on a private television station in Toronto. People told me that I only got into this troop because I dispensed my favours. That isn't true. Mr. Bremmer and I have a very business-like relationship. These rumours are nourished by jealousy and envy. Because I am so young, people can't allow themselves to believe that I am talented. Somehow it seems unjust to them that someone can be attractive, young, successful and also be talented. We live in very cynical times ...

LESJA BROWN: I met Sam when we were in college. In fact we played the leading roles in a production of Romeo and Juliet. During the run of the play we became lovers. Later after a painful separation we became friends. Then I lost contact with Sam. He wasn't one to write letters. I had a child, a little girl. I married my psychiatrist and retired from the theatre, brief as that career had been. The marriage just didn't work out. My husband ran off with another young actress. I guess he just loved the theatre. After the divorce I had to find work. I worked as a waitress, a cab driver, a legal secretary. I even had a stint as a stripper. Finally I settled into a job as a librarian for almost fifteen years. But my heart remained in the the theatre. It was a complete shock, a wonderful surprise when Sam contacted me after so many years and told me he was getting a company of actors together to make a film ...

ROBERT DRAYTON: You've heard the old cliche about being discovered by a talent scout in a drug store. That's how it happened to me. Except of course I wasn't a starlet. I wasn't even an actor. I was just bumming around from job to job when this short fat man asked me if I wanted to be in movies. Made me laugh you know. I figured the guy was trying to put the make on me. I seemed to be marked for the advances of queers. But I took him up on it. I mean, what did I have to lose? I was tires of selling condoms to sixteen-year-old romeos and discussing hemorrhoids with eighty-year-old juliets. And I guess I heard all about all the money you could make in movies and all the beautiful women you met ...

ANTHONY WHALE: I suppose I forced myself into the company. I was thirty years old and still doing commercials on television for toothpaste and laundry detergent. If I was going to make it as a professional actor I knew I'd have to make my move soon. I didn't want to be a big-name actor, no star or anything like that. I just wanted to act. I love it. Before an audience, a camera, a mirror. My wife says I just haven't grown up. Perhaps. I tried to kick it once. Took a civilian job. Insurance agent. Drove me nuts. Sure, financially we did all right. I was good at selling insurance. And I had two kids and a wife to feed and clothe. But I started to drink. I was miserable. And I think I was going a little crazy. I began to see things. No not see things but believe things. For example one day I'd believe that it was raining out so I'd leave the house with an umbrella and it would be a bright sunny day. Or else I'd get the feeling while reading the newspaper that a cat was rubbing its back up against my leg. We didn't have any pets. Or I'd rush to the office only to find that it was closed. It was Saturday. The wife and I had some long conversations about this and it was decided that I should return to acting. The wife's only condition was that I get some permanent ongoing type of work and not do commercials. I heard about his company Sam was forming. I got an interview. I just layed it all out for him. He swallowed my story. I was always good at selling things ...

SIR JOHN BIRD: At the time of course I hadn't yet been knighted. In fact I had just returned from England after thirty-five years on the stage. My doctor suggested I retire. My strength, he said, was waning. He promised me five more years if I abstained from the theatre. Otherwise my heart would not survive another opening night. So I retired. None of this was in the press. I said that I had decided to return to my homeland – Canada. I was born in Orangeville, a village north of Toronto. When I returned to my birth place everything had changed. I hardly recognized the place. Felt like a foreigner and wondered privately whether I had a home at all except upon the stage. It was under these circumstances that Sammy Bremmer approached me in the little cottage I had bought for myself. He was a very young man then, rather brash and aggressive I thought. Very American as many Canadians seem to have become. As I was later to learn it was just the way he expressed his nervousness. He asked me to join his company of actors. They were going to make movies. Films. The doctor had not mentioned any prohibition of film. In England no one had ever offered me a part in a film except a few horror films which I found beneath me. But here was this young man offering me an opportunity to act again. He told me, quite frankly, that he needed my name and reputation from the theatre to attract investors. I was dumbfounded. Sammy read my silence as reluctance and offered me a percentage of each film's profits. I'd been miserable not acting. It was like asking a thoroughbred not to run. I thought of the warning my doctor had given me. I accepted Sammy's offer. And look, I'm still here. The last thing I heard regarding my doctor was the announcement of his funeral ...

SAMUEL BREMMER: I always wanted to make films. From the first time I stepped into a movie house. Even before the movie began. Maybe it was the architecture of the building. It was the old Carleton theatre. It's been torn down, its ghost living inside a hotel. In those days they built very ornate and beautiful cathedrals to show films in. For most people going to a film was more than seeing a movie, it was an event. Like going to church, except cheaper. That theatre captured the imagination of that small boy. And when the lights dimmed, the curtains parted, and the voices of the audience hushed, I was entranced. At first I wanted to act. To be a star like Bogart, or

Cagney. The trouble was I couldn't act. And during college when I started to lose my hair I knew I'd never be pretty enough to become a movie star. So I turned to the mechanics of magic. I worked on quite a few CBC productions. Everything from the news, to ballet, to hockey, to kids' programmes. But no one in Canada wanted to make feature films. Documentaries seemed their only passion. So, mostly through nerve and naivity I collected a group of actors and crew, borrowed or rented equipment and set out to make a movie. We didn't have much of a budget. And we were all learning while we shot. Under the circumstances I think our first film, *The Gunfight,* was rather good although some of the dialogue now seems a bit stiff to me. After we finished the film I managed to corral the actors into making a second film. In the process of making these films we became a family. In a time when the traditional family is breaking down I believe it is being substituted by a new family. Like our company of actors. People joined together not by blood but by a common goal, by a common love ...

The Gunfight

A SAMUEL BREMMER PRODUCTION
starring
John Bird as the sheriff
Anthony Whale as the gambler
Lesja Brown as the mother
Barbara Harris as Kitty
Maurice Dubois as the blacksmith
and introducing
Robert Drayton as the boy

1.
Around a table
four men
playing poker

one is a squat man
close to the earth
a farmer
curly red hair
invisible eyebrows
divided by a scar
shirt sleeves rolled up
two buttons of his shirt
undone
suspenders and trousers

SET DESIGNER: All the indoor scenes, the saloon, the house, the farm, were shot in a warehouse in Toronto. I think the place had been used to store furs or something animal ... you could still smell whatever it was. Sam had to live there while we were shooting. He had to, it was his furniture that we were using as props. I don't know how he stood the smell. He told us that at night he could hear creatures scurrying across the rafters. He wasn't sure whether they were mice or ghosts ...

a suit jacket hung
limply
over his chair

to his right
a small thin man
spider wearing spectacles
bank teller
holds his cards close
close to his eyes
to make sure
they aren't counterfeit

SAMUEL BREMMER: To save money we decided to make a western. Everyone wore old clothes they'd found in attics or picked up in the "Sally Ann." They were close to the clothes that people wore in the 1800's. Fashions for the poor don't change much over time. And the men, except for Anthony, didn't shave. We shot many of the outdoor scenes in an old abandoned farm near Pembroke, built, I think, about the time the story is supposed to have taken place. We used some of the locals and the crew as extras. And of course with horses you don't have to worry about the date of the model ...

to his right
the gambler
dressed to win
three piece suit
white silk shirt
shoe string tie
black curly hair
a smile hidden
in a wrinkled mouth

the fourth is a blacksmith
shirt stained sweat
arms burned
from the elbows down
hands awkwardly large

MUSIC DIRECTOR: We had some trouble with the background noise. We didn't notice it until we started to edit, but all the indoor scenes sounded dead, hollow. Solving this was more difficult than it might seem. I had to go out and record outdoor scenes. I went into the middle of the woods. I used some very sensitive recording equipment and discovered to my dismay that it picked up the sound of my breathing. So I had to re-record by leaving the machine by itself for a few hours. And then later I discovered that part of it was ruined by the sound of an airplane. So I had to do it all over again. The third time I was again frustrated. The recorder picked up the sound of a tree falling in the woods ...

anyone care for breakfast
Kitty the owner of the
saloon smiles
behind a
deep purple dress
with
flat mirror buttons

I'd rather refill
my pocket
the blacksmith
goodnaturedly grins

how about a couple

of eggs with eyes
bacon with sides
coffee with cream
the gambler smiles

what have you got
the gamble asks

pair of aces
the bank clerk
greedily grins

beats me
the farmer replies

menage a trois
the gambler grins
while strangling
his tie

SCREENWRITER: In the original script there was much more dialogue ... which Sam managed to eliminate in many ways ... either by eliminating it all together or by making it almost inaudible behind the breathing of horses, or the sound of running water or by having more than one person speaking at the same time. Sam explained these changes to me by saying that we were not putting on a play. Film is visual, he said. I asked him why he didn't do the whole thing in pantomime. He didn't like that. Maybe that's why we haven't worked together since ...

don't you ever lose
the farmer complains
no one can be so
lucky
and not own the stars

calm down Bill
the blacksmith says
restraining a yawn
swallowing his eyes

SAMUEL BREMMER: I am nothing but a bag of voices ... If they leave then I am ...

dealing out a new round
the gambler places
the deck on the table
teller and smith
nibble at their cards
the farmer rises
pointing at the gambler
with a gun

sitting calmly

the gambler
holds his cards
with five fingers
another finger
beneath the table
fondling the trigger
of his gun

two bullets
splinter the table
and
the farmer's brain

the farmer's eyes
are open
round in surprise
hand drops
gun fires
into the floor
falls back into his chair
blood spits
out of his head
onto his shirt
it's a new shirt
the farmer gasps
and dies.

SAMUEL BREMMER: I was very pleased with the farmer's death. I played the part of the farmer myself, not only to save money but also I think because I liked the fantasy of being killed. And then of course surviving one's own death ...

2.
rain falls down
a river pouring
out of a cloud.

a man on a horse
approaches a farm
house and dismounts
knocks at the door
a woman in grey
opens the door
light flows out into
the rain

through the kitchen
window is seen the rider

SAMUEL BREMMER: There was no rain in the original screenplay. We shot all the indoor scenes first in Toronto while keeping an eye on the weather conditions in Pembroke. Then it occurred to me that the rain could be a fundamental part of the picture. This meant of course that we had to rewrite and reshoot some scenes. And then we had to rush up to Pembroke and hope it wouldn't stop raining. I sent one of crew ahead of us just to shoot the rain falling. Lucky for us, because shortly after we began to shoot the scenes on the farm the rain stopped. Looking back I think the rain shaped the film. As if the gods were smiling down upon us ...

holding his hat
the woman
turning away
face in her hands
veil of darkness
rain and silence
rain and silence
threads of grief

LESJA BROWN: I saw the woman in two lights. Both in grief and joy. Grief because suddenly she has lost something in her life. I didn't see her grieving for her husband but for herself and her son and a future that was threatening ... But also with a kind of joy that she had to repress. Her husband was a drunk and she was probably glad to be rid of him. Although she could not admit this feeling publicly or perhaps even to herself. That is why she feels a third sensation. Guilt. How many times had she wished, dreamed of him dead ... ?

out the back door
the rider leaves
heading toward
the barn
rain pours down
rain pours down
ditches swell
rain barrel overflows

3.
inside the barn
firing a harness
a young boy
lifts a hammer
kissing metal

SAMUEL BREMMER: I couldn't see Sir John as a Wyatt Earp or Gary Cooper in High Noon. So I had him play the sheriff as a school crossing guard, a man fearful of violence, knowing that he could do nothing to limit or restrain it ...

the boy
dressed in overalls
a piece of straw
growing out of his teeth

a lantern lit
hangs from a beam
the rider enters
the boy looks up

sheriff
the boy says

Billy
the sheriff replies

think this rain
will ever end

the boy laughs

come about your pa

drunk again
billy grins
shaking his head

dead
the sheriff says
staring into the fire

4.
graveyard
funeral
in pouring rain
Billy stands
silent
his mother weeps
growing smaller

blacksmith is there
the sheriff
the minister reads
from a book
a couple of buckboards
wait at the border
with a buggy
the horses are nervous

the hole in the ground
filled with water
pine box lowered
floats
then sinks
the woman cries
remembering that
her husband
couldn't swim.

LESJA BROWN: Almost caught my death filming this scene. It was a cold September day as I recall and I remember complaining to Sam, who just smiled and said it was all in my head. I caught a bad cold and was laid up in bed for a couple of weeks. Sam was very sweet. Sent me flowers and candies. Came to see me about every other day. He was very concerned. Sam is quite superstitious. I think that because we were shooting a funeral, he was afraid we had somehow unleashed death ...

5.
Billy and his mother
returning home

ROBERT DRAYTON: Mr. Bremmer was no help to me at all. I asked him several times what my

rain pours down
not a word spoken
rain pours down
not a word spoken
water rushes down
sides of the road
eats the earth
roots of trees
lakes from ponds
rivers-paths
Billy wears a straw hat
now bent over his ears
his mother wears a shawl
around her neck
the horse wears blinkers
so it won't panic

motivation was supposed to be. How was I supposed to play this farm boy. I had never acted before and felt quite in the dark. It worried me. I couldn't sleep and I looked it. But when I asked him anything, Mr. Bremmer would just bark at me. I'm busy he'd say, don't bother me now. Several times I was ready to quit. After we finished the film, Mr. Bremmer came up to me, a big grin on his face, and slapped me on the shoulder. Bobby, he said, you were beautiful – awkward, nervous, uncomfortable – young.

6.
inside the farm house
Billy stares into the fire bleeding flames
his mother
at the window
staring into the rain
shaking
won't it ever end

7.
days pass
rain pours on
night and day
are one

SAMUEL BREMMER: One day we left a camera for about an hour shooting rain falling into mud, then by editing, we condensed the whole hour down to a couple of minutes ...

8.
Billy's mother sits
at the kitchen table
rubbing her hands
he came again last night
came again and stood
there stood there
at the end of my bed
and swore
I'd never sleep again
never again

SAMUEL BREMMER: The only real close-up of the picture, a close-up of Lesja's eyes through her reflection in the window. And the rain running down the glass and her voice mixed with the sound of the rain beating. I was trying to create a mood of forlornness, of people outside the stream (excuse the pun) of history, of important events. That was the worst hardship of these people, these pioneers, the feeling that they didn't matter ... it hardened some, destroyed others ...

until his vengeance
was bedded

9.
in the saloon
the gambler sits
eating his breakfast

Kitty stands looking
out the saloon window
finally stopped raining
she mumbles
scratching the flesh
above her wrist
sit down
you're giving me
indigestion
the gambler barks

ANTHONY WHALE: I had to lose quite a bit of weight to play the gambler, which isn't easy when your wife is Italian. Sam's idea. He saw the gambler as an evil character and evil, he said, must always look hungry. I thought that this was too facile. I was determined to make the gambler into a real person. My dialogue didn't allow this so I decided I'd have to do it through gestures, I'd make the gambler appealing. Practised my smile: watched a lot of old Clark Gable films, practised grinning in the mirror each morning. Used to break up my wife. She'd laugh and laugh. Sam didn't like the smile. In the end we compromised. I'd be able to smile if I lost thirty pounds. I lost the weight. Unfortunately my grin changed with the loss of weight on my face. My charming grin began to look very wicked. Sam was very pleased with himself ...

10.
Kitty sits
playing solitaire

read my fortune
the gambler yawns
Kitty looks at the cards
remains silent

the gambler grabs her wrist
and bends it unnaturally
to one side
you're hurting me
Kitty cries
read the cards read the cards
the gambler demands
tell me how I shall die

BARBARA HARRIS: I had to learn to shuffle cards. Bought several decks. Practised between takes. Before I was served dinner in restaurants, during a bath, first thing in the morning. Maurice gave me some tips. He seems to know something about everything. A very talented man ...

Kitty bites her lip
turns over a seven

SAMUEL BREMMER: Our budget ran out about this time. I didn't tell anyone. Told them I had

you will die a rich man
turns over a queen
choking to death

the gambler laughs
so I'm to hang
they'll have to bury
a bullet in me first

to take a few days off. A small operation, doctor's orders. I was not specific. Everyone, to my surprise, was quite concerned. I spent the next week haranging, , begging, pleading with friends and relatives. If the film had been a flop I knew I'd end up a sales clerk, or insurance agent somewhere spending years to pay off my debts. Fortunately for me when we finished the picture and I was able (through many frustrating weeks) to get the picture distributed we broke even. Which for a Canadian film at the time was considered a tremendous success. Since then the film to my surprise and delight, has become something of an underground classic in Europe ...

11.
sheriff enters the bar
walks over to the table
where the gambler
and Kitty
are playing with a cat

the farmer's boy is
outside
the sheriff begins
he's come armed
I don't want you
to draw on him

the gambler laughs
looks down
at the sheriff's muddy boots
and flips him a nickel
sheriff
why don't you go
and get your boots polished

12.
a boy's voice cries
out from the street
mr gambler
I come to kill you
the gambler stands up
checks his gun
heads for the door

Kitty jumps up
grabs his arm

SIR JOHN BIRD: There was a tremendous fight about how the picture should end. In the original screenplay, Kitty talks the gambler into not shooting the farmer's boy because of the gambler's love for her. We all agreed that this was not satisfactory ... Little Barbara thought that somehow Kitty should be killed at the end. This isn't television, Sammy screamed. Then Maurice suggested that the sheriff save the young boy by shooting the gambler in the back. Sammy liked the idea but he was overruled by

he's just a kid
she pleads
his gun ain't
the gambler replies

13.
the gambler stands
on the wooden sidewalk
high above the street
filled with water
a sea of mud

Billy stands in the middle
of the road
reaches for his gun
too late

the gambler's gun is drawn
and fixed on the boy's
heart Billy faints
into the mud
the gambler's head falls
back and laughs

Kitty rushes up from
behind
and pushes the gambler
fires his gun
two bullets graze
Billy's hat
the gambler falls
into the street
face first in the mud
motionless
Billy remains
for a moment in the mud
am I alive he asks

14.
Kitty kneels
weeping over the gambler
the sheriff
lifts Billy to his feet

the rest of us. It just wouldn't sell we all argued, it's too out of character. The sheriff is inept, impotent. All of us agreed (all of us except Sammy and Barbara) that the gambler had to die. It was poetic justice ...

SAMUEL BREMMER: I'm still not satisfied with the ending. But to tell you the truth I wasn't sure how the thing should end. I wanted an ending that showed that violence was unpredictable. It was like an explosion where

did I kill him
the boy asks

no one killed him
the sheriff responds
he was just a man
who struggled to rise
finally successful
he reached his level.

everyone is its victim. My intuition told me that the gambler should kill the farm boy. This was consistent with reality. But then a film is not reality. And of course everyone wanted the gambler to die. So the ending was decided through democratic means ... So much for artistic integrity ...

THE END

Susan Musgrave

from *Cocktails at the Mausoleum*

Notes on Poems

I have written notes on many of these poems in the way that I might introduce them at a poetry reading: this gives them a context, I feel, without attempting to explain them away.

Part I

Paul and the Full Moon: Acapulco, July 1980. There was a U.S. destroyer anchored in the harbour in front of our house and each night the rains came, the thunderstorms. The small pool on the patio overflowed, mangoes fell from the trees and we had to sleep under dampened sheets to keep ourselves cool. One night it cleared and there was a full moon.

The Plane Put Down in Sacramento: Two weeks before leaving Canada, in July 1980, I had a dream of flying to Sacramento and taking a bus into the foothills, the way I'd done every summer when I was a child, to visit my godmother. After I woke up I wrote the poem, and it was another of those prophetic dream / poem sequences because soon afterwards I found myself on a plane flying over Sacramento (we didn't actually land, but some deviation from the dream is permitted) to Mexico City. Paul and I took a bus, The Dolphin Line, out to the coast. Not into the desert, as in the dream; again, there was a slight deviation.

The Moon Is Upside Down in the Sky: In Acapulco there were frogs that made a sound like a cross between a duck and a goat. I found one sitting inside the gates of a great hacienda; he had been mummified by the heat. In Northwest Coast Indian cultures the frog is a symbol of, among other things, transformation, fertility, magic – for women, in particular. Barbeau writes that, among the Tlingit, the frog crest was the crest of a "secret society belonging exclusively to women." I had on, the whole time we were in Latin America, my own trinity: a Haida frog bracelet made by Gordon Cross of Skidegate, a frog ring from the Shetland Islands on my right-hand middle finger, and a gold pre-Columbian frog from Bogota around my neck (eventually stolen from a drawer in my hotel room on Contadora, the luxury resort off the coast of Panama where the Shah of Iran spent some time in exile). I learned from my friend Johnny Jesus in Panama, that in some parts of Latin America the frog is a symbol for an informer, that *sappo* means *squealer,* and that, when he first met me, he assumed I must be working for the U.S. Drug Enforcement Administration. In Mexico, Panama, and Colombia, I was away from so much that was familiar. It is hard to replace images of cedar-bark, salal and salmonberry bushes with papayas, mangoes and avocados.

Coming into Town, Cold: After a while in Miami (Spring 1981), where I used to lie awake at night listening to the palm fronds brushing the window and wishing it were rain instead, northern rain, we moved to Panama. I wrote this poem in my room at the Hotel Continental, still feeling homesick for Canada. I was struggling with Spanish, taking a course at the YMCA in the Canal Zone, a course for housewives mainly, married to men in the U.S. Forces. "¡Estas allas! ¡Que bonitas! ¡Como brillan!" ("These pots! How pretty! How they shine!") I took a taxi to my class the first day and the black driver made lewd suggestions in the rear-view mirror. I told him, in the little Spanish I knew, that my wife played the piano very well. He must have thought I was crazy, because he left me alone after that.

Taking You to the Airport: I stayed alone, during the rainy season, in an apartment with bars on the doors and windows, where it was so humid that the Cuban posters we'd had framed to cover the bare walls, fell off and crashed onto the marble floor during the middle of the night.

Hunchback on the Buga Road: Buga (pronounced *Booga*) is a town in southwestern Colombia, north of Cali. One day we rented a car and drove through the mountains, and the wildflowers we found growing there along the edges of the jungle were the kinds that people in northern latitudes spend years cultivating in greenhouses.

Cali: We rented an apartment here, with a view of Christ (a 50-foot statue on the mountain, illuminated at night), the canyon, and the river.

Sir Lionel Luckhoo, Listed in the Guinness Book of Records *as the World's*

Most Successful Advocate with 228 Successive Murder Acquittals, Humbly Lays His All at the Feet of Jesus: In 1979 I went to Georgetown, Guyana, where my friend Christopher Brown was working for the Department of External Affairs. Christopher threw a cocktail party in our honour (the Red Cross provided the food and the Army an awning in case it rained) and one of the distinguished guests was Sir Lionel, who had been one of Jim Jones's lawyers and who claimed to know the truth about Jonestown, though he would never divulge it for fear of being unable to practise law again in Guyana. Or live there, or anywhere else, for that matter. After Jonestown, Sir Lionel became a Born-Again Christian, and the title of this poem is taken from his autobiographical note, found on the back of his pamphlet entitled, "To My Muslim Friends."

Ordinary People: This is a poem for Jacobo Timerman, who spent two years in an Argentinean prison. He wrote a book called *Prisoner Without a Name, Cell Without a Number* and came to speak at an Amnesty International Conference in Toronto. Patrick Lane met him there and Timerman told him that when he was a prisoner one of the few books he received was a copy of Liv Ullman's *Changing.* The book had a devastating effect on him in that it reminded him of a world where there was tenderness and compassion and understanding. After he got out of prison he couldn't touch a book of poetry without starting to shake.

The Unconsidered Life: I wrote this after a writer I knew committed suicide. I don't know whether or not I agree with the last line, never having been able to take a stand on either suicide or pornography. But in this case I let the poem have its own way. Still, the opinions expressed are not necessarily those of the writer.

Hurt Birds, Vultures, and B-52's: Every time I came back to Canada from Latin America friends would criticise me for not having a sun-tan. After all, when most people go to the tropics, they come back brown. So, on my last trip back to Panama I decided to go to the beach. To get there we had to drive through the military zone and were greeted by a very large sign: "Warning: Shark-Infested Water." My friends went in swimming; I put on my sunscreen and lay down (after cleaning myself a space amid the cigarette butts and beer bottle caps and used condoms), and looked up at the clean sky. A layer of vultures, high up, circled the beach; above them, six B-52's, camouflaged, were coming in for a landing. I thought of how difficult it was to write anything but political poetry in Latin America, and how self-indulgent all my love poems, poems about relationships, seemed. Bruce Cockburn, after a trip to Nicaragua, wrote, "Some people never see the light / Till it shines through bullet holes."

The Shark Came Up: The night after I got back from the beach (sunburned) I had a dream that a huge shark's tooth came up out of the water, chasing me. I wrote this poem and, by mistake, left it on the dining room table. No one wanted to go to the beach with me again after that.

Part II

"He Only Wishes They Would Hear Him Sing": The title is a line from a poem by Stevie Smith. I went back to Cleggan, in the west of Ireland, in 1978, and found that my landlord was in the hospice in Clifden, dying. This was very irritating because I couldn't stay in the house I had always rented. His son and daughter were staying there, having come a great distance. Everyone wanted Conrad to "go," but he kept hanging on. I had to go myself, but not in that ultimate sense, to Claddaduff where I took up lodgings in Mrs. King's new bungalow.

Eaglet Tricks: In 1975 I spent some time at the Ilkley Theatre Festival in Yorkshire, involved in a production of Ted Hughes' *Cave Birds,* directed by George MacBeth. These poems worked their way into my brain and the only way I could find my own voice again was to make a kind of collage, which this poem is, of Hughes' imagery. I actually hear it being read in his voice, with its sinister Yorkshire accent.

A Tree Wouldn't Just Uproot Itself: I stopped writing poetry (with the exception of this one) during the time I was pregnant. All the clichés about being pregnant were true; I was "biologically fulfilled" and had no need to sublimate my tendencies in verse. As John Fowles says in *Daniel Martin,* "We write out of what we lack, not what we have."

Three Witches Go for Lunch in Elora: This was written in the fall of 1983, when I moved to Ontario to be Writer-in-Residence at the University of Waterloo. Over the next year another seven barns were burned down until finally the person who started the fires was caught – the local fire-chief's son.

Part III

"We Come This Way But Once": This sequence was written while on a poetry reading tour of England, Wales, Scotland, and Paris with George Johnston and bill bissett in the fall of 1980. Every day we got up, caught a train, and went to a new venue. We spent a lot of time on trains, and the rhythm of trains started finding its way into all of our poetry. I think we all wrote something during this trip. The title of this series comes from a cartoon that appeared in *The New Yorker.* A tired man comes home to his tired wife, saying, "I heard some good news today. We come this way but once."

Part I: We talked a lot about our lives. When the trip was over we'd be going our separate ways, bill up to the Cariboo to look for work, me down to Latin America to start another new life, and George back to his close, large family. bill wouldn't let himself have a cigarette until five o'clock everyday, hence the line "in two hours I can smoke." Mrs. Jackson ran a guest house where we stayed near Lumb Bank in Yorkshire; it was very cold and bill found a stone pig in his bed. bill and I went to a church of spiritual healing and I got a stigmata on my palm – shaped like a question mark.

Part IV: The quote, "A single sentence will suffice for modern man: he fornicated and he read the papers," is from Camus' *The Fall.*

Part V: In all fairness to George – he *did* dream; only he says he doesn't remember, now, what the dreams were about.

Part VI: It didn't fit into the poem, but in Paris we saw a bookstore that had been bombed by extremists.

In Whitehorse I Wanted You: The line "I've been bawling to adolescents the inscrutable agonies of the dead" is Dylan Thomas's comment when asked about his reading tour of high schools in the United States. The passage italicized in the poem is from Sheila Watson's *The Double Hook.*

Part IV

Vern and Joanne: Dead: Vern, a Volkswagen mechanic who lived at Cape Ball, seven miles up the beach from Tlell, in the Queen Charlotte Islands, and his wife Joanne, left the Charlottes in the late seventies and moved to Brother Love's Commune in Seattle. Mike Davis had been down to the commune, and told us about the accident as we were eating a spaghetti dinner at Tlell. There are a few other references in the poem which may need explanation: Vern had fixed my own VW on a number of occasions; Mike had been in Idaho where it was against the law to have in your possession an eagle's feather (eagle feathers are as common as seagull feathers in the Charlottes); and Jack Miller had a large collection of Indian artifacts, a result of the walks he took behind the bulldozers that were cutting roads through old Haida village sites. (A year later his wife got "the kid.")

Requiem for Talunkwun Island: Part I is told from the point of view of a Haida ghost returning to the island. In Part II the ghost recollects his first contact with the whiteman's ships. Joe Tulip, my friend in Skidegate, told me that when the whiteman first came to the Islands, the Haidas from Kiusta who went aboard their ships came back to the village with a report that the whitemen had a bear cooking for them and that they ate maggots. The bear was actually a black man, the maggots, rice. In Part III the ghost recalls the forests that are gone. Part IV is told from the point of view of the ghost's earthly remains – that is, its skeleton, which has been dug up by archaeologists.

Part V

The poems in this section are all love poems, and need little comment. *"Exile Is in Our Time Like Blood"* is a line from a poem by John Berryman, "& the great white horses come up & lick the frost of the dream" I found in one of Charles Bukowski's books. "And on the Coming of the Outrageous Dawn" is from a poem by Theodore Roethke. I wrote this poem in England, when I was tutoring a course for the Arvon Foundation at Lumb Bank (1981). A young man in the group was under the mistaken impression that the poem was for him, and for the next year proceeded to bombard me with proclamations of his love, Swiss chocolates, exotic invitations, books, tapes of his own voice, etc. The ending of this poem was unlike any other I'd written in that it seemed to foretell of some "happy" event. I had never considered having children, but two months later,against all odds, I was pregnant. This poem was, and is, for Paul.

Part VI

In this section, dreams were the origin of many of the poems such as *My Boots Drive Off in a Cadillac* (though it is written from the point of view of a prostitute), *Remy in the Bentley, Taboo-Man, Boogeying with the Queen* and *Just Lust.*

"Conversation During the Omelette aux *Fines Herbes":* The title is a line from a poem called "Eight for Luncheon" by Cynthia MacDonald. I was happily married at the time, but then I got a letter from someone else. I went for a walk and wrote the whole poem in my head. The "someone else," the person from the past, became "the dead man." The last line in this poem owes a lot to E.J. Tribb (17).

John Berryman, This is for You: Love and Fame by John Berryman is one of my favourite books of poetry. I wrote this after rereading it, feeling I needed to get Berryman's style out of my system.

Mrs. King's New Bungalow: My book of poems, *A Man to Marry, a Man to Bury* had just been published and, perhaps because of the title, it got a lot of bad reviews, especially from young men who seemed to think I was a rabid feminist. Actually, the title, though very ambiguous, had been generously conceived; I'd been thinking how, traditionally, when a woman married a man the chances were that she'd outlive him, and have to see him buried. One of the worst reviews appeared in *The Canadian Forum.* In it the reviewer said I obviously hated men and found sex disgusting and quoted a phrase out of context to prove his point, a line from a fertility poem I'd written for Dave Godfrey's cows, so that "I rise like a Christmas moon / impaled on the penis bone of a bear" was reduced, to show my horror of sex, simply to "...impaled on the penis...." I read the review just before I flew to Shannon and stayed a week in Mrs. King's new bungalow. While normally I would not be so upset by a review, I found that I had many hours in the small rain to drink Guinness alone and contemplate the injustice. The ending of this poem is a rephrasing of Robert Lowell's "If you mistake the event don't enter the dance" – advice that all critics should follow, I feel.

Cocktails at the Mausoleum: The full Eberhart quote is from his poem "I Walked over the Grave of Henry James." It goes:

> *I crushed a knob of earth between my fingers,*
> *This is a very ordinary experience.*
> *A name may be glorious but death is death,*
> *I thought, and took a street-car back to Harvard Square.*

Boogeying with the Queen: I had a series of dreams about the royal family. (I once read that to dream of the royal family means that you feel socially inferior.) Before I wrote this poem I dreamed I had won first prize in the Princess Anne Look-Alike contest. The title was a result of "mis-hearing" a line in Warren Zevon's "Werewolves of London." I thought the line was, "I saw Lon Chaney ju-ju walking with the Queen," and originally I called my poem *Ju-Ju Walking with the Queen.* From there it was an easy step to *Boogeying with the Queen.*

Just Lust: I dreamed I was having dinner with Prince Charles (this was before Lady Di came along) when he leaned over the juice container (it was a very informal dinner), kissed me, and said, "Rita, I luff you," in a German accent. I told him my name was not Rita, woke up, and wrote this poem. Partly it's for all those people who still ask, "Why doesn't your poetry rhyme?" It really does, you just have to work hard to find the rhyme sometimes.

The Shadow of the Heart: Some of the lines in this poem are taken from old jazz songs, including the last two. I've been warned that many people, not just blacks, may find the last lines offensive, but John Mortimer says, in his great autobiography Clinging to the Wreckage, "there can't be 'no go' areas in the world of art. The writer who cuts short a line for fear of shocking some people, or 'giving offense' is untrue to his calling."

That Night on Turtle Beach: I wrote this after reading an article in the National Geographic. The pictures in that magazine are wonderful. But I'm always wishing the text would explode.

Part VII

One More Lyric, One More: I was in Winnipeg giving a poetry reading one winter and went to Patrick Lane and Lorna Crozier's house for dinner. Patrick made a dish we called "Chicken Poet-Creep." We thought this would be a good title for a cookbook of recipes by poets. Patrick and I talked about how unfashionable it was, especially on the West Coast, to write "lyric" poetry, and how both of us were always being accused of doing so. We talked about language, and emphasis, and how the line "I fail" changes according to where you put the stress. (Sean Virgo, when he read this book in manuscript form, said he thought the first line should be, "We fail, we all fail –." I'm still not sure.) Anyway, at about 10:30 the night of the dinner party, Patrick smashed his wine glass and went to bed. I remember thinking how this was about the only poetic statement, lyrical or otherwise, to be made in Winnipeg that winter.

"I Do Not Know If Things that Happen Can Be Said to Come to Pass or Only Happen": The title is from Howard Nemerov's poem "Death and the Maiden." It is one of my favourite poems, and often when I am in this way enamoured of a poem I deliberately write something in the same voice, or vein, as a form of an exorcism. The walk we took was at Mackenzie Bight, on the west side of the Saanich Peninsula, Vancouver Island. The day seemed to mark the beginning of something more than just another year.

You Didn't Fit: When I was living in Colombia, I had a dream one night that my father died. I had to bury him in a small cardboard box, and he didn't fit. When I thought about the dream, which left me with an immense feeling of sadness, I realized it was metaphorical more than anything else, although normally I do not interpret my dreams this way. All his life my father had never fit in anywhere. In 1975, when he came to visit me in Ireland, he kept his watch on Pacific Standard Time for the duration, so that at two in the morning he would be sitting up in front of the turf fire saying, "Well, your mother will just be getting home from school now, and making a cup of tea." In a way I admired his stubbornness, though it made life extremely difficult. Because the dream was so real, and the writing of the poem an act which made his death seem final, I have not been troubled by thought of his death since, though I had been previously.

I sent this poem to *Saturday Night* and, after a few months got a revision of it back with a letter saying, "How do you like being edited?" My poem was no longer recognizable. Every reference to teeth had been taken out, and so had three of the seven stanzas, while the stanzas that were left had been put into a new order. I turned down the magazine's offer to publish "my" poem for $200. Which proved to me, at least, that I still had scruples.

Sometimes It Happens: For years I was haunted by Brian Patten's poem of the same title. I had a poster of his poem on my wall and would constantly quote it to friends: "...and sometimes it happens that you are loved and then you are not loved, and loving has passed." Again this poem is an exorcism.

After You Left: My editor asked why I'd used the word *cucaracha* instead of plain *cockroach,* as I do in the last poem in the book. It just seemed right. "After you left I killed a cockroach" sounds, to me, melodramatic. Besides, cockroach doesn't, in this instance, have enough syllables.

I Was Eating Lunch Alone in a Clam Bar in New York: I was feeling very alienated when I wrote this, because the restaurant (it was actually the Courtyard Cafe in Toronto) filled up with wealthy, smart couples, and I was alone in my old clothes, which were beginning to look shabby. I'd just bought some postcards, and one of them was of a cat with a string of rats around his neck, and I started fantasizing about the scene that would occur if a cat came in wearing a rat necklace.

I Am Not a Conspiracy, Everything Is Not Paranoid, the Drug Enforcement Administration Is Not Everywhere: Paul Orenstein was the photographer. Obviously I felt uncomfortable in the cornfield, far away from the ocean I'm used to being photographed beside.

Adrift: I hadn't written any poems for over a year and a half when Kevin Roberts wrote asking for some work for a new magazine called *True North Down Under,* Canadian and Australian poetry. I sent what I had. A while later I got a hastily scrawled letter back from one of his co-editors, saying, "These are not up to scratch. We want gold. Send original exciting material." I was, of course, depressed. Just at the one time in my life when I needed encouragement! That night I had a dream, about expectations and so on, and in the morning wrote this poem.

Not a Love Poem: I don't know why I used *cockroach* instead of *cucaracha* here, except that "Cucarachas are the worst sort of voyeurs" would not be a line I would ever consider using in a poem.

Martin Vaughn-James

from *After The Cage*

The General's Weekend

THE BALL SHUDDERS IN IT'S SOCKET

JERKED FORWARD AS THE PLATFORM TILTS

EXPOSING IT'S MUTILATED UNDERSIDE

AS IT ROLLS TOWARDS THE SPIKE

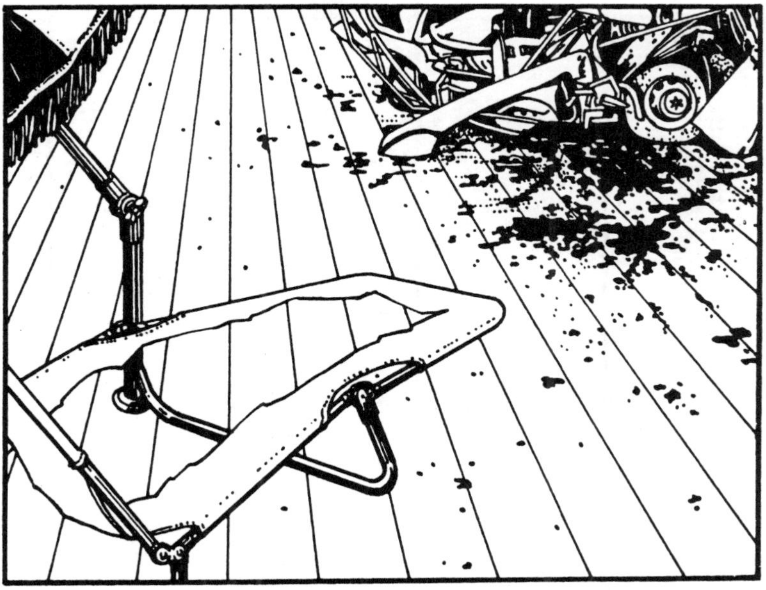

OUTSIDE THE SCRAPING IS INAUDIBLE

DROWNED BY THE ENGINES OF THE NIGHT

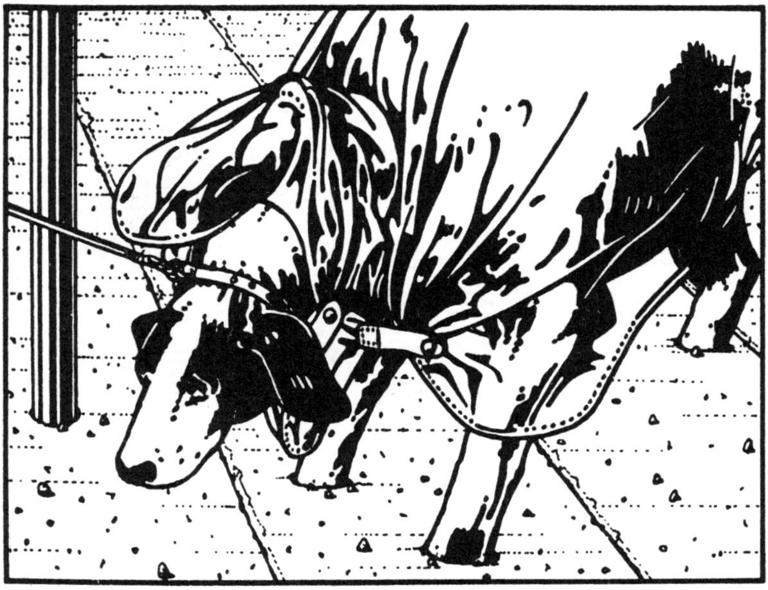

Christopher Dewdney

from *The Immaculate Perception*

Foreword

These bits, aphorisms, essays and verbal "takes" are constellated around a larger theme, which is, roughly, the spectacle of consciousness embracing its own materiality. It also deals with the reverse notion, consciousness being duplicated by technology, matter mimicking mind.

Science is holding up an increasingly clearer mirror to ourselves and like vampires our reflections are gradually fading into pure difference, invisible against the background of total phenomenology.

The housefly is a miracle of miniaturization.
Nature is the divine technology.

Human Consciousness

Consciousness is an illusion generated by the highest integrative function of our nervous system, the mind.

The sense of self, human consciousness, is like a virtual image: it exists solely by relation to an observer hypothetically observing himself or herself in the act of self-observation. This is the double enclosure of self-consciousness.

Self-observation can exist only ideally, as a kind of privileged shadow-boxing. Existence in any mode other than the virtual would expose the inherent paradox on which the whole show is based. The proposed universality of this utterly private experience is qualified by a presumed congruence among observers who are members of the same species. Language is the armature of this congruence.

Consciousness is a set of footprints in the snow which stop & then retrace themselves.

Mind as Standing Wave

The millions of neurons which make up the cortex of both hemispheres have a tendency to synchronize their discharges in electric ripples of excitation. These synchronized trains of neuronal pulses are known as brain waves and have three major modes based on their frequencies. The slowest is the *theta* rhythm which is associated with the functioning of the thalamus in the upper brain stem, a junction of sorts for the activity of the brain. Its frequency is in the range of 5 to 6 cycles per second. The next level is the *delta* rhythm which is associated with sleep. At the third level are the *alpha* waves, which have a frequency of 8 to 13 cycles per second and are typical of the electrical activity in the brain of a mature, conscious human. Consciousness is characterized by a long persisting phase constancy of alpha waves. This vast co-ordination of neurons is similar to metachronal waves in millipedes, where the synchronizing of hundreds of legs is processed in waveform.

Knots

The brain is constructed out of the very reality it perceives. It must then, perforce, be a recursive structure, a knotting of that reality, such that somehow, through some form of topological twisting of space, matter attains the property of self-observation. This is like making something out of nothing.

The Immaculate Perception

Consciousness requires the immaculate "separateness" of objects of its attention. It is necessary that the boundaries of the "object" are clear, in order to fortify its identity, its distinction from the matrix.

Identity is signification.

Perception, the actual neurochemical process of the nervous system, is not as specific as the ideal of signified attention ascribed to as "consciousness." There comes a point, a tactile limen, when you can't distinguish between two fingers and one as they are pressed into your back. This demonstrates a lower-level discrimination limit, an equipment limitation, where the sensory system can't resolve fine detail.

The specificity of consciousness, the "I" perceived, is also diffuse. It is generated by the same neurochemical process as perception. Specificity in vision, for instance, is a result of the resolution of a mosaic signal within the visual cortex. The mosaic signal is characteristic of the entire nervous system. Its granular nature in vision is revealed by aberrant states, such as "mosaic vision" in migraines and "pointilistic vision" as induced by both migraines and hallucinogenic drugs. The diffuse specificity of both consciousness & perception sensuously irritates signified or ideal consciousness.

Another aspect of this sensuous irritation is revealed by certain pathological obsessions induced by two neurotransmitter mimetic drugs, d-lysergic acid diethylamide and methamphetamine. This obsessive behaviour, called *punding,* such as picking hairs out of a rug, cobwebs out of hair, sand out of sugar, dead skin from live or sorting trivial objects according to class, is animated by consciousness in a reinforcement of "ideal" signified attention running upstream against the "flow" of the mosaic signal.

Punding and hypervigilance, consequences of generalized C.N.S. excitation, are echoes on a larger scale by the "sorting" preoccupation. This is a tendency of all human groups to isolate independently occurring elements of nature, such as corn or boars, and gather them together in species multiples over and above the quantities necessary for survival. In this act, a function of hypervigilance, we have the origin of both mathematics and science.

Signified consciousness, fervent with the immanence of ideation and signification, worries away at the fuzziness of the mysterious boundaries of identity.

simultaneous multiple indivisible

Form

Form, being intrinsically sub-divisible – i.e., perpetually at the interface of matter and energy – exists only as a perceptual generalization.

The Object

Because of equipment limitations, perception is confined to a selective sample of a more extensive continuum. Noetically, an object can only be as specific as the sum of its signified components.

Consciousness an end to the means.

Intelligence

Intelligence is actually style, an individual's method of operation, his approach. Intelligence is the connections one chooses to make by virtue of one's personality or being, one's disposition towards certain choices. These connections are made within whatever body of knowledge an individual happens to possess.

It is as if intelligence were independent of what we normally consider "intelligence" because it operates by stepping out of the way of data and letting that data arrange itself by its own apparent structure. The height of intelligence is the ability to disappear, to get out of the way.

Robert Kroetsch

from *Excerpts from the Real World*

The Dream of Leather is Softly to Enfold

11 / 8 / 85

I remember vividly the afternoon of my childhood when, in a violent downpour that included some hail, the sky rained frogs. A few of them croaked sweetly as they fell, filling the earth with rigorous prophecy. They were quite right, I can't forget you.

12 / 8 / 85

Why do shoes dream? At night I hear them, under your bed, dreaming they will carry me away to mysterious places where I'll have to learn all over again how to walk, stepping first from a slippery rock ledge onto a wet log.

13 / 8 / 85

I would like to go much deeper into the heart of breaking. We should attempt one kiss, even if one only, inside the mouth of the crocodile.

15 / 8 / 85

Here on the bullheaded prairies we praise the sun with icicles. When summer betrays us, we recover in a regimen of parkas. One winter night, in a cold frenzy, I let my tongue freeze to an iron windmill. I knew then I was destined to be your lover.

18 / 8 / 85

Style is a way of thinking. Contemplate the rodeo rider, pitched wildly about by his fancy boots.

19 / 8 / 85

And my shirts. Do they grow tired of hanging, week after week, in a closet, just on the verge of slipping off their hangers and collapsing to the floor? Does the very possibility keep my shoes awake, listening, in the dark? Why didn't you call last night?

22 / 8 / 85

Apples, my father never once said in his life, are not avocados. How can a whip crack? Lust has its complement in hurricanes and plagues. Even the cankerworm, letting itself down from trees, is a nuisance only at the height of its cycle. What, exactly, are drumlins?

23 / 8 / 85

Stockings like yours aren't made for walking. The bathhouse by the sea, trala, is good enough, trala, for me. Or, as my father liked to remark, talk is cheap, whisky costs money.

25 / 8 / 85

The loop of the lariat takes the calf very nearly by surprise. I remember how, when I was a boy, the men, at cutting time, kept the knife clean in a raw potato. We would walk away gravely, each foot, finding itself left behind, hurrying to catch up and take the lead.

26 / 8 / 85

A goose egg, we used to call it, zero. Getting our kicks. But that was in school. We were learning. Later you would teach me naught.

28 / 8 / 85

Even elbows are easily bruised. Blood, like beer in a plastic cup at a picnic, comes in a fragile container. You say you like the glitter of spurs, raised to the shoulders of a bucking horse.

30 / 8 / 85

Water isn't afraid to fall. Wouldn't it be refreshing if, somewhere in the world, one rainbow, even if only for a moment, assumed the shape of an equilateral triangle?

31 / 8 / 85

You are a surgeon of mangoes. Rhododendrons begin at home, while marigolds, given the opportunity, sport the kiss of an early frost.

1 / 9 / 85

You say that a full moon makes you hornier. If you'll pardon my grammarian's question, hornier than what? My flat-soled shoes imagine mountains.

David McFadden

from *Canadian Sunset*

Every Planet in the Universe

Whether the lover tends to contemplate the beloved thing, to unite with that being, or to perpetuate its presence, his love strives always to bring into existence something which does not yet exist in the Beloved. Therein consists the "service of love," the divine service which knows neither conquest nor possession....
Henry Corbin

No one knows the smell of one's own bean paste.
Issa

On the train from Utica I met a tall woman with red hair and deepset but bright blue eyes and a long pointed nose. It was a wonderful nose, a nose from the court of Henry II, something from the Bayeux Tapestry. As I took the *New York Times* magazine and book-review section into the club car I noticed she'd been sitting a few seats behind me in the coach. She was reading the *Times* too. It was like something out of a Naim Kattan novel. I ordered a chicken sandwich and club soda and resumed reading. When she came into the club car a little later I looked up and smiled just as she looked down and smiled. She ordered a coffee and sat with me. We talked about what we'd read in the *Times*, and it turned out she lived around the corner from me in Toronto and was returning from three weeks in New York. She was a clothing designer and painter.

I told her I'd seen her somewhere before and it was probably on the subway or in some grocery store or little restaurant and she had an interesting face. "People always remember me," she said. "With a nose like mine anonymity is next to impossible. That's why I like New York, big cities in general." She said she'd had quite a few one-woman shows of her paintings and when she told me she was Ann Valentine I remembered her work admiringly and had a sudden flash of having seen her talking to Brian Brock in his office in the rear of the Brock Gallery and not realizing who she was even though I was standing there looking at her work. She seemed older than her appearance somehow, unduly and unwillingly conservative in her manner, as if she had been for years spending her time with older people, and it turned out that yes in fact she had just recently been winding down a long relationship with a retired New York rabbi, and she did have many friends even in youthful Toronto who were considerably older than she. Her paintings sold well but her prices weren't high and she was a slow worker and didn't like the idea of applying for grants so most of her income came from her small clothing-design business and she was happy with that arrangement, the circumstances of her life seemed pleasing to her. She had the air of a woman whose only hunger was spiritual.

Carl Jung was her big passion. He didn't visit her or speak to her as he did to Dixie Moon, but she was an avid reader of books by and about Carl Jung (unlike Dixie, I suspected), was a member of the C.G. Jung Institute in Toronto, and was interested in the idea of "individuation," and her voice deepened as she uttered that magic word with a kind of sudden hoarse whisper, six sacred syllables full of mystery and hope. She was busy on a series of paintings of butterflies. She attended all the meetings, took in all the lectures from visiting Jungians from all around the world, but felt a bit inadequate because she never had Jungian dreams. "You're lucky," she sighed, when I told her the bull dream. "That's a wonderful dream," she exclaimed, her eyes rolling wide and spinning.

She told me one dream she had. She was in a cabin at the top of a mountain with three other women. She looked out the window and could see a wolf coming up the mountain, with evil intent. She was alarmed and thought they were going to be attacked and eaten. Then she noticed a truck coming up behind the wolf. A man was driving. She felt better. The truck stopped, the door opened and the wolf hopped in. But then the horror resumed. The wolf attacked and ate the man, then took over the wheel of the truck and continued driving up towards them. She tried to get control of herself, concentrated on the wolf, and it turned back into a man. She woke up feeling okay. I told her I didn't feel as if I had much in the way of interpretive ability, particularly of the dreams of others, and when I finally broke down and offered a bit of an interpretation (too embarrassingly weak to repeat here) she said, "That's what everybody says." Later when I knew her a little better I thought perhaps the wolf represented a new romantic interest in her life (not me) and the driver her old lover. The situation represented by the dream seemed to be a fairly routine comment on her life, and it seemed that the only reason the dream seemed important to her was because she so seldom dreamed. The dream seemed to be putting her in touch with a bit of ground-cover anxiety.

We chatted amiably all the way to Toronto and the next day we went to a David Cronenberg double feature and spent an hour interpreting the flicks according to Jungian principles. She took me to the Jung Foundation to hear a priest from Halifax deliver a talk on "The Self as Dream-Maker" and he spoke of the self as an autonomous and all-intelligent "rectifying" agent which was continually attempting to bring the ego and the unconscious into closer union, and as it did so the individual became more conscious of the presence and activity of the self, and it was like hearing Alexis Gold speak of her guardian angel though in more intellectually respectable terms. Another cult?

I had to go to Halifax for a couple of days and when I returned there was another unsigned postcard from Hiroko. I quote it in full: "We stood back and smiled at each other, marvelling at how our hearts seemed so eager to be close, tugging tugging tugging for more closeness. We smiled proudly, for our hearts belonged to us, and we held them on our rhinestone-covered leashes like well-groomed poodles." She'd been reading Mishima again.

There was a message to call Ann Valentine. I did and she invited me to a meditation circle that night. It was a tiny apartment with a nice view of the lake. There were three women, besides Ann. We stood in a circle. One of the women played the harmonium and we all sang ancient Sanskrit mantras, our minds dissolving. We stood facing each other and one of the women suggested we visualize divine light streaming through our open hearts and forming a shimmering pool in the centre of the circle. I found myself imagining Hiroko in the centre of the circle, bathing in that pool of light, all of her sorrows disappearing. When I got home that night Hiroko was on the phone from Santa Cruz, saying she felt better than she had in a long time and there was much love in her voice, though she did not sound anxious to see me, and in fact she was planning to extend her stay in California for at least another couple of months.

The next day Dixie Moon called. When I told her I'd been in Halifax she said her best friend lived in Halifax, and he was a priest. I said was he a Jungian priest? She said yes, how did you know? I told her about attending the talk given by the priest from Halifax and she said that was her friend all right. "Isn't that an incredible coincidence?" she said.

She apologized for having phoned but said she just had to get some advice from me. She was going to be interviewed on the radio that evening and the interview was going to be on reincarnation. She was terrified that she'd say too much, that people would think she was bonkers. She said she had vivid images of past lives but didn't feel right about going public with it and didn't feel as if she had the self-discipline to play it cool on the air. I told her to put on the kettle for tea and I'd pop over for an hour. When I got there she poured and I talked.

I told her that when I was in Halifax I'd been thinking a lot about my friend Hiroko who was continually plagued by memories of past lives and, for instance, felt that she and I were friends in sixteenth-century Italy, that we were painters, apprentices of Titian's together. I felt as if that had no meaning at all for me because for one thing I've never been interested in Titian, his paintings always seemed to me to be rather pompous *tours de force.* "You had reservations about him then too," Hiroko had said. I told Dixie that I didn't personally believe in the survival of the individual after death and so on, blah blah. The life force, the fire inside each of us, at death goes into a giant pool and becomes undifferentiated with all of existence. At birth another drop of that sacred fire goes into the individual, becomes entrapped for the life of that individual. In fact all of us are in that giant pool all the time but without realizing it. Memories of past lives were not to be taken as proof of some kind of eternal life of the individual, but rather as individual expressions of the collective of that universal pool in which we live our lives or out of which we spring. Yech!

Plants around the room were wilting but Dixie Moon became excited. "That's it, that's what I wanted to to hear you say, that's why I was trying to call you. That's exactly what I believe but I didn't know how to say it. That's exactly what I'll say on the radio." She wanted to know when exactly I was thinking about the reincarnation issue and I told her about five o'clock Thursday afternoon, in Halifax. "That's it," she wailed. "That's exactly when I was trying to call you."

She said she'd been practising Tibetan Buddhist meditation quite a lot lately. When I asked if it were expanding her ESP, she said, "Yes, and it's scaring the shit out of me. I can't help it. I'm becoming more and more psychic." She said when she had people in for Tarot readings she'd been having so many incredible hits lately, since she'd been meditating, that the people would refuse to leave, they would want to hear more and more. She'd never made so much money in her life, she said. "I was doing well in Vancouver but for some reason I just felt compelled to sell up and move to Toronto. Now I know why."

Then she stopped dramatically, lifted her arm, and said she felt as if she were about to have a "walk-in." I realize that the events I'll now relate could have been an elaborate stunt but Dixie simply did not have the requisite guile. I observed these events coolly and objectively. It's good there are people like Dixie Moon who have experiences like these and who have the faith to take them seriously, and the courage to share them with others....

"Carl Jung is telling me to go out to the garbage. He says I'll find an old bag there." She looked at me sadly, got up and motioned me to follow her. She stepped into the alley, reached into the can and pulled out an old leather bag with a shoulder strap. "He's telling me there's a blue silk scarf inside," she said. She opened the bag and pulled out the scarf. "My God," she said, "I think I'm going to be sick."

We came back in and she placed the bag and silk scarf on the table and pushed the cold teapot aside. I could see in her solemn eyes that the spirit was still with her.

"He's telling me to wrap the scarf around my Tarot cards and to keep the cards in the purse and to use the purse from now on," she said. She went into the deck in the scarf, tied a loose knot and placed it in the bag. "He's said goodby," she said, "but he wants me to know that someone is going to give me an amethyst today." Her eyes brimmed with tears and took on an air of wonder. "An amethyst!"

She said she had a doctor's appointment and on the way had to do some shopping at a couple of stores. Both stores and the doctor's office were nearby, I didn't want to leave her so abruptly and I didn't feel as if she wanted me to leave her so abruptly, so I offered to accompany her as she shopped and grab a grocery or two myself then go my way when we got to the doctor's.

So I was holding up some eggs to the light when I looked around and noticed Dixie talking to a woman. They were gabbing away like mad and it seemed as if Dixie were doing most of the talking, in fact she seemed to be telling the woman the story of her life, but the woman, who had a deep, throaty Irish accent, and, as it turned out, was the teller in the bank where Dixie had her account, seemed to be enjoying it. Then it happened. I heard Dixie say she collected semi-precious stones for a hobby and the woman said, "Oh, how interesting. Look what I've got here." And she pulled something out of her purse. "It's an amethyst," she said. "Someone gave it to me yesterday, but why don't you take it if you save the things? Do you like it?"

Dixie became incoherent. "My God," she kept saying. She took the stone in her hand. "You want me to have this?" The woman repeated, soothingly, that she did, and Dixie told her the whole story, about how Carl Jung was her spirit guide and had predicted that someone would give her an amethyst that very day. She turned to me for confirmation. "Isn't that right, Walter?"

"That's right," I said. "About an hour ago she told me that Carl Jung had spoken to her and told her that she was going to be given an amethyst today." I didn't smile.

The woman was electrified. She and Dixie talked for another five minutes and the woman ended up asking for an appointment for a reading, at Dixie's earliest opportunity. They made a date for that evening. The woman shook her head in amazement as we left the store.

Dixie took me into another store. She wanted to get some material for curtains. Another customer, a sad-eyed lady about thirty, wearing a navy blue trench coat and brown leather boots, came up to her and said, "Excuse me, but where did you get that bag?" Dixie sputtered a bit, reluctant to say right out she plucked it from a garbage can, and the woman said, "That looks like a bag that belonged to my mother. You didn't get it out of the garbage, did you?"

"Uh yes I did, but ..."

"Was there a blue silk scarf inside it?"

When Dixie said there was the woman burst into tears. She said, between sobs, that her mother had died last week and that yesterday, after the funeral, she, the daughter, had sadly thrown the bag in the garbage. Dixie felt terrible but handled the situation pretty well, I thought. She opened the bag and pulled out her Tarot cards wrapped in the blue silk scarf. The woman's attention was taken up with the cards and Dixie began telling her the story, about Carl Jung's voice and how she was a Tarot reader. The woman became quite interested and her tears dried up quickly. Dixie put her arms around her and told her she'd give her the bag and the scarf back if she wanted, but since she the woman had thrown it away she Dixie felt it was okay for her to keep it but she wanted the woman to know that she Dixie would honour it and treasure it forever.

We got away. We went in for a quick coffee across the street from the doctor's office. I let Dixie take the conversation and she started telling me again what a wonderful lover she was and how men almost invariably failed to appreciate her, and how hurt she would get. She repeated the sad story about the well-known Canadian poet who did her wrong, tore her Gemini wings off, and how the next day a friend brought her that picture of the butterfly on her wall. It hit me all of a sudden. I'd noticed the picture but hadn't bothered to check who the artist was.

"That picture wasn't painted by Ann Valentine, was it?

"Yes, that's the artist," she said. "Do you know her?" I told her I did. She seemed too blitzed to comment on what a wonderful coincidence that was.

I decided to tell her I was thinking of writing about her, putting a fictionalized characterization of her in my book. I told her it wouldn't be intended to be any kind of accurate portrayal of her, but just a fictional character inspired by her, a certain way of seeing her. I told her I'd use a made-up name, and asked if she had any objections. She said no, in fact seemed delighted by the idea, and insisted I use her real name. Dixie Moon, a true innocent, a woman possessed perhaps not with the innocence she was born with or had as a child, but a new innocence that she had worked hard at achieving and that required courage to maintain.

"I have a very strong feeling about your book," she said. "There's something about you that draws me to you, that makes me think about you at odd times." She went on and on. I told her that I had a lot of work to do and had to get home. She wanted to know if I meant work on the book. I said yes. She said she had found in her experience that she was lucky for writers. "You're going to write a lot today," she said, authoritatively. She started to talk about all the playwrights she knew in Vancouver. "Tommy Cheeseman used to come and visit me whenever he was having problems with a play," she said. "And he always said that when he went home the problem would have resolved itself. He said that I was lucky for him. This isn't ego speaking, believe me...."

"I know it isn't."

"Playwrights and novelists phone me all the time from all over, New York and everywhere. Apparently there's something about me that inspires writers in some way."

I decided to go home and do some writing.

"Let's have dinner together sometime soon," she said. "We'll split the cost, go dutch."

I said I'd call her about the middle of next week. I will too. I have no idea why. I have no ideas, no plans, nothing. Life is amazing. Every moment is a diamond mine of miracles. I never want it to end and maybe it never will. There will always be new life and I will always be there. I want to be born of every planet in the universe and when I've been born on every planet in the universe I want God to create new universes for me.

David Donnell

from *The Blue Ontario Hemingway Boat Race*

The Abstract of Hudson's Bay

He thought about Canada a lot and he thought the country was abstract. It was abstract because it was a falling back around the pivot of its northern longing, Hudson's Bay, and was therefore not a response to a challenge but an acceptance of defeat.

Hudson passed the great bay on his way north, and was one of many men who had set a tradition, for whatever reason, of northern fitness and northern aspirations; but it was a tradition which could never, given the slow westward drift of immigration and the beginnings of American economic intervention, be actually realized. So the country developed abstractly in several different ways. Montreal and Toronto were two different countries. From Toronto to Winnipeg was also like changing countries. The Rockies loomed in the far west more like a barrier than an invitation. And nobody much went there besides lumber and road workers who couldn't get back, and English couples who wanted to retire to the quiet English mists of Victoria on Vancouver Island.

The North and Hudson's tradition were all above. A white wilderness that Canadians were conscious of but didn't participate in or settle. A white wilderness of snow and impossible distances. Hudson's achievements weren't abstract, they had happened, they could be written about; Hudson had blazed a certain kind of white trail which, however, nobody else much seemed to be interested in following. The bay itself was okay, not a bay, as in the U.S. use of the word "harbor," so much as an enormous blue interior northern lake so large you could take Great Britain complete with the English king and Lloyd George and the House of Commons and all their bulldogs and their Shakespeare museum and the Irish who made good whiskey and the Welsh who had beautiful voices and were miners or most of them were miners, and the good blude rude Scots who were mostly farmers, gorse farmers and sheep farmers, sheep thieves in some cases, although the average Scot would probably steal a cow or a bottle of good Ballantyne's, fine people though, even if they had never produced a Jim Joyce, take the whole expanse of it, and make an island in the middle of Hudson's ba-Bay and call it whatever you want, call it Great Britain, or Atlantis, or Tierra del Fuego; and the rest of Canada, spreading east and west and north into the white snow and south to the Great Lakes, and Michigan and Manhattan and Pennsylvania, a huge context, too broad to be surveyed in months, around this famous lake that Hudson discovered, or passed by or paused beside or drank from or left his name to, that became the name of the trading company, pivotal for the early colonial period, the Hudson's Bay Company, blankets, beaver pelts, coats, hand tools, axes, traps, sleds, that thusly became something of a national legend in the country, like the Boston Tea Party in the States or like Stonehenge in England or the Eiffel Tower in France, but that no Canadian he had ever met had actually seen or visited or knew anything much about.

He thought about these points while he was reading the December 27 edition of the Toronto *Star.* Toronto was the premier city of Canada in a variety of ways, and when you walked through Toronto you could see the delineations of settlement and the inheritance of 19th century English history in the architecture of the city, and Scottish and Irish turns of phrase in the manners of the people or their way of making a gesture in a butcher store or on a streetcar or in a legal office while signing a small company charter; you could see the broad layout of the city and how it had developed from the docks at the foot of Bathurst Street north up the broad avenues of Bathurst and Spadina to the farm country south of Maple. The main east / west thoroughfares of Front and King and Queen streets, all very classical in an American sense and business-like and practical as well as hurly-burly, classical and reflecting a sense of space and propriety extant not only from the enormous available space of the area, place of meeting, but conduced also by a sense of space brought over from the cities of Great Britain and dumped here and allowed to take root and spread.

This was attractive and reasonable, but even though there were interesting things to do in Toronto, no bars but some half-decent restaurants, interesting streets, some history, dance places in the evening where you could go and pick up someone although he had no interest in doing that, he was comfortable with Hadley and when he thought of Hadley this morning he didn't think of sex so much as her eyes, her clean shining hair her mouth her breast(s) and the child, John Hadley Nicanor, he was definitely in love, like a great wave against the explosions in the north of Italy, and he was in love with the great Renoir painting of the child at the breast of its mother, but there were other places, not necessarily all that exciting but sort of interesting, where you could eat and drink, speakeasies and bootleggers' livingrooms, sports events and Winter Fairs, livestock and equipment, one opera house east along Queen, books and newspapers and silent films and burlesque shows, but despite all this there was a feeling of remove, not homesick for Michigan and not simply the feeling that he should be in Paris, but a feeling of remove from the world in general. Toronto was quiet and northern and slightly harsh and business-like, and the abstractness of it was quietly impenetrable.

The regular guys were very much like Americans. The restaurants were similar. Jimmy Frise and Greg Clark were terrific. The managerial types were a little different. They weren't stuffy Englishmen and they weren't outfront Americans. They were somewhere in between. Blunter than the English guys he'd met but more contained, more cautious, more limited than Chink Dorman-Smith. They were interesting, and sometimes more competent at what they did although they were rarely up on the latest developments in their given area; he thought the King streetcar drivers were terrific guys but they lacked flash; the woman who brought him his hot chocolate and cinnamon toast in the morning at Child's was terrific, but she didn't complain about her job as much as her Philadelphia counterpart probably would have; the plumber that he had a drink with one night at a speakeasy was a terrific guy, but he seemed licked into his job with no immediate general prospects of going east or west with it and not very much sympathy, oddly enough, with a recent strike that people had been talking about; Canadians were terrific, he reflected, but they were cautious and this modified their English wholeheartedness, or at least it seemed to for the managerial types, and the same sort of cautiousness limited their breadth except in simple forms like the enormous east / west Canadian Pacific Railway.

The physical nature of the country was English, American, but northern. There was a quality of abeyance, as if all the great national events were somehow being waited for or being thought about or expected from abroad. As if the government in Ottawa was a sort of holding pattern. There were a lot of imposing dark grey early 20th century Gothic public and business buildings, a mordantly shaded quality of public morality without real wrath or modesty, much great land, the lakes fantastic, small cities spread out westwards at a considerable distance from each other, Windsor, next door to Detroit, Winnipeg, north of Minnesota, Saskatoon, Regina, Edmonton, equipment depot and alleged gateway to the North, Calgary, cattle-town supreme but not a cowboy town, unlimited Rockies, Vancouver, north of Seattle, port city, inactive gateway to the Pacific. But the general overriding mood of the country, as set by the government and by the popular attitudes of the people, was one of restraint; the economy was an economy of abeyance. The government seemed to be a government of fools; the image of the country, despite its natural wealth and energy, felt from within, was one of abstractness: a broad country as naturally wealthy as the States but, especially Toronto, as northern and abstract as Hudson's famous and distant Bay-ba.

John Newlove

from *The Night the Dog Smiled*

The Perfect Colours of Flowers

... and as soon as he was alone in the room (except for me) he sliced the baby up; in such amazingly thin delicate slices. They folded and undulated like sheets of camera film too long soaked in water as he piled piece after piece of them over his bent forearm. Some of them were too slippery and they slid off his arm to fall on the floor and be trampled there. When he held them up to the light they were almost transparent, we could almost, not quite, see the world through them. What strange things they did to our view: how they distorted and disarranged and enriched everything, like some new paintings I have seen.

But I am not trying to be allegorical; when I say that we saw the world through a baby's flesh, I am not being allegorical. I would not want you to think that because of this strange modifier, panes of glass from a child's pain, that we saw new, wonderful things our eyes were not accustomed to, not that. Perhaps I should not have said the world. We only looked around the room and at each other; once, briefly, we looked out through the window at the grass and the trees, using the sheet of almost clear flesh we had in our hands at the moment, not any specially selected one. It did not really change things, nor did we look for changes, but there was something additional. We only used it as you would use a piece of dark glass or a black negative to observe an eclipse of the sun. But that sounds allegorical too. As if I were trying to make a point; I am not. It is only a manner of speaking. I am only trying to say that we looked at things through the flesh of a child to amuse ourselves, as it were, not to assume the vision, the viewpoint, not to assume the attitude and position of a child; only to amuse ourselves. We did not want to see the world as it really was, the room as it really was, ourselves as we really were, or to strip away the semblances, discover a master secret, the truth. None of that.

I told you that the sheets of flesh were nearly transparent. The blood was gone from them, yes. But they were not wholly transparent. I did not quite tell the truth. Apertures of the veins and arteries, sections of lungs and intestines, circles of bones – further up, the soft pink-grey discs of shell-encased brain, tiny – they all showed, they forestalled monotony, they were all beautiful. I have never quite seen paintings like them, though I hope to one day.

Perhaps, sometime, I shall make such a thing, piling and unpiling arabesques. He did a fine, lovely job.

And it was easier than you think, much easier. At first he thought that certainly the bones would give him trouble. So did I. But all in all it was only a matter of assembling the proper machinery; in some cases, I may as well tell you, even of inventing and building it, though vaguely similar things have been known before. He is a clever man that way. So neatly, so cleanly, so thinly and perfectly to slice a baby up, that was nothing to him. To us it seems a great deal of work to do such a thing properly, but he enjoys it. So would I, so would you, if we had his skill in making and operating machines, the most delicate, precise instruments imaginable; so would we all if we shared his delight in conceiving of, in inventing these marvellous techniques. This is not the only one he has made. Think of the ingenuity involved! We do not possess it, but him, he's a master of such things. Or a past master perhaps I should say, since he has died now, alas. As we all will die. It seemed a special shame that he should be removed from us.

I cannot speak more of it. He is not dead to me. He is still alive and I shall probably speak of him, if only out of sentiment, as if he really were alive. His work lives on. That is a trite thing to say, that is what everyone says, but I am sure of it.

Babies' bones are soft. That's reasonable. So soft. At first he had thought that the bones would give him trouble and he was troubled about it. It seemed a sensible worry. But as things happened they, the bones, gave him no difficulty at all. Or very little. Because they were so soft. Certainly he should have thought of that. I suppose it is always best to be prepared for the worst, though, never to take chances. I can agree with that.

What he finally devised did the job wonderfully, butchers would have loved it; of course the idea of fat smiling butchers, men with the raw entrails of sheep and cows draped about their shoulders, vendors of dead animals to eat, men with blood and feces and wipings of their own snot mixed on their aprons, using a device like this, a wonderful device, is too horrible to contemplate.

It was almost too powerful; almost, not quite. Only a few pieces were spoiled. Since he had forgotten to consider how soft babies' bones really are; since it was such a young child.

Very soft, very soft. Softer than, softer than what? Softer, I suppose, than swan's down? It is the same colour, I know; it is white, the swans are white as bones are white. But how soft is it? That is what we really want to know. I have seen swans myself, I have seen swans float, glide, skate on a pond or on a lake, a lagoon, skate like modelled figures of white wax sliding across the surface of a mirror. I have seen those swans; surely there must have been wires under the water, about their legs, to guide them. They moved with such precision, with such serenity, never making a mistake in their inevitable purposeless paths. But how soft is their down? I cannot answer, I don't know. But it is said to be soft, they tell me it is soft. I myself have never felt it.

Softer than what? Softer than a woman's shoulder? But some of them are angular. Softer than a fat woman's shoulder? Some of them have tough crusty pimples, mysterious and disturbing lumps. Were the bones, then, soft as a woman's breast, thin or fat? But some of them have cancer or hard repulsive nipples, they get hard when they are cold. I cannot find an image, an adequate image, to tell you how soft the baby's bones were. Of course, I have tried only one really, and half of another. But I can feel that there is nothing that will work, nothing worthy enough to describe that softness fittingly. You will have to take my word for it.

I forgot to tell you how when he first took the baby into the room he angled its chin into a coathanger and slung it from the top edge of the door. That part of it didn't interest him at all; it was merely part of the necessary preparation and anything would do. Always, no matter what you attempt, it seems that there are so many details to be looked after if things are to be right. But still, he did it with a certain flair. Another person, myself perhaps, I admit it, or even you, would have rudely noosed a rope, some rough-fibred hemp cord, whatever was at hand, about its neck and would have hung it from one of those parallel bars in the clothes closet. That would have been a foolish thing to do, I almost laugh when I think of the alternatives now, considering the merits of the various solutions. Of course, it's easy to be wise after the event. But better to be wise after the event than never to be wise at all, neither before nor after. That's what I say. A rope, you see, would have bruised the neck badly, it would have left a great red ugly burn about the neck; the wire of the coathanger made only the most pleasing of thin scarlet lines, a delicate contrast.

He slit the long deep vein in the sole of its foot and bled it into a basin. Perhaps it was an artery, not a vein, he slit. I don't know. I am sure it was in the sole of the foot, the right foot. Or along the side of the foot, of the instep. He used one of those old-fashioned straight razors you seldom see anymore. They may still be used in barber shops, but I don't go into them very often. Not at all. I shave every morning and in the early evening with an electric razor, a remarkable instrument really, but not a very interesting one. My hair is cut at home, too. That's why I don't know if barbers still use those old-fashioned straight razors. I believe they do. And perhaps a few old dying men here and there use them. With their wire beards, slack skin, their trembly hands and rheumy eyes, I wonder that they dare. I suppose there's a knack to it one acquires. But that was the sort of razor he used. And very efficient it was, too. I don't know where he got it.

It cried some when the razor went in first. That's reasonable; babies cry at surprises. But we did not expect that after it had been hanging there, a good hour on the door for people to admire. How fine it looked. But it cried all the same, that is one of the things one must put up with. With which one must put up. And it wailed and it wailed. Not very loudly, thank god. What would the landlord have thought? People would have said, There's a child on the second floor, I can hear it crying.

No, it didn't cry very loudly; only a thin choked reed of a sound that could not be heard very far, that disturbed no one. It reminded me of something or other, I don't know.

The blood running down the door.

After cutting the vein he had taped ankle and toe of the child in such a fashion, in such a position, that the blood ran right down the door, not spraying or spurting out at us. With what a deft movement he did it, how dexterously he did these things, all things manual and machine-like and not only them. I wish I were like that; so do you.

I keep thinking of him in the present tense, by mistake, and it is an effort to change, as if he were still alive; I keep forgetting that he is not. I told you I would do that, I always do.

But not for very long. The blood didn't run down the door for very long. After all, how much does a baby weigh, one so young as that? Not more than fifteen pounds, I'd say. Maybe sixteen. It's hard to judge. But it would weigh about fifteen or sixteen pounds or certainly not more than twenty; and how much blood could it have in it? Not very much. It would be unreasonable to expect very much blood from a child of that size and that age.

Children's blood is lovely. Not that it looks any different from the blood of a youth or an adult, of course not. Or even the blood of an ape, of a pig, a cow. Even the blood of fish and lizards, of birds. But it is lovely, simply because, as you look at it, you do not imagine all the passions, the cunning, the secret urges and lusts, the perversions, even drugs or alcohol or nicotine swimming in it, diseases polluting it. This is subjective, I know that, but you do not imagine, whether it is present or not, ugliness in the blood of very young children. You see them pure and delightful and somehow you are pleased and proud.

It cried a bit when the razor first went in. I told you that. But I was wondering if cried was really the right word to use; I want everything to be right. No doubt you do too. That is a human trait, to want everything to be right, almost a failing sometimes, but usually good. Perhaps cried was not quite the proper, the completely accurate word to use. I want you to to understand. It gave a long thin wail like the sound you would expect an adult, not a child, to make as it bled to death. A very knowing sound. Or as they say you may hear the hungry wolves howl on a winter's night in the north while they circle in their precarious, tortuous routes, devouring what rabbits, soft rabbits and other small things, small favours, may fall to them in their pathways; as the hungry and dangerous wolves howl, but far off, very far off. If the child had not been before my eyes I would have thought it was some starving wolf away across the snow, separated from me by a forest or two. Or another might have thought it the sound of some lost fantastic primitive man drifting far out at sea in a little boat, shaken, pushed and pulled, and swaying in the waves of unfamiliar waters, the currents of the sea, loosing and losing a desperate prayer to his dying gods; you might have imagined that it was him, heard on an alien shore by ignorant and frightened tribesmen of another nation, to hear that insolent child cry. It was like that and I cannot recall now what it was that it reminded me of; of these things, surely; yes, of these things. But they are only made-up fancies, inventions, conceits to explain that sound to you. They are not what I wanted to remember. They, the hungry circling wolves, the lost and crying man, they are not what evades me.

Then, as the baby bled, it seemed to grow very sleepy and its body stretched out long and white and limp against the dark brown door. And it looked fine there, it looked exactly right. Long, long is not the word for it; it was stretched out unbelievably, hanging there with its muscles all relaxed, the bones seeming to melt, to turn to fluid, dissolve.

Not all of them seemed that way, of course. The rib cage in particular stands out in my memory as in fact it stood out from the body, jutting out from the flesh, its skin pulled tight over it. How good it all looked, with the head angled far back and to one side, the eyes half-closed, the lower lip sagging fatly but the top one tugged up over the perfect pink gums, with the exquisite line of the throat, the smoothness of the chest; and then, suddenly, that wonderful protruding ridge of ribs to break the spell, break the monotony, and the rest of the body hanging without resistance, jelly-like, seeming to depend from it, how good, how good.

Its body was very white. Alabaster, plaster. Like those swans we were speaking of, or like snow in mid-winter far out in the country, away from smokestacks and kitchens, diesel engines, factories, mines; like snow then, when you catch it momentarily and one flake at a time with a gloved hand before it slips erratically onto the ground and is crushed underfoot there, the snow through which the wolves roam, white as the perfect paper, unspoiled by human words. And that white against the brown-stained door compared with the splash of blood in the enamelled basin on the floor below it, what dissonances these colours made, and what new harmonies I discovered in their relationship.

It is when you know where a thing comes from that it is most valuable to you. You would not have believed that anything could be so white. I would not have believed it, not even I. Startling, those three colours – the dark brown, the pure white, the violent liquid red – like the perfect colours of flowers, waiting to console you for whatever you cannot remember.

The perfect colours of flowers. The perfect colours of flowers are waiting to console you if you will only seek them out, seek them out and never hesitate to appropriate them and take them home.

Mary di Michele

To Inherit the Earth

("Everybody in Italy has a family!" from the film version of *The Garden of the Finzi-Contini*)

i. To Survive is not Success – A Foreward

Why do I remember it now, that line, from another time, another continent? How are the atrocities committed here in Chile mine? In transit, I view them. Victims of the military regime tell me their stories because *they* believe poetry tells the truth, because even the military believes in books enough to burn them, because the relatives, of the executed and of the disappeared, believe in charity and justice that lives elsewhere. They tell me their stories because they believe that the Good rule in Canada and rescue will come like the cavalry at the last minute, the cavalry in whose interest it is not to come. They think they are alone because the world does not read about the peasants buried in lime pits, countless bodies lost in loam, in silt, the slit throat of the teacher, the bodies bound up in the air field, the bodies beached in the Mapocho,the murder of the foreign news correspondent, the night raids, the technology of the torturer, the housing crisis in Santiago cemetery. The disappeared in the sea feed the *machas*, the razor back clam indigenous to Chile, render their colour, that peculiar and naked shade of pink. When these horrors are not *felt*. We eat them. Still the Chilean people do not see what stocks the shelves of our supermarkets. They think they are alone because if these horrors *are* known to the world, then something else is sinfully wrong. The horrors are not felt. They count on the poet, part angel, part animal, to be one who has not forgotten to feel. Whose words are secreted from the glands, words with the tincture of iodine, the shock of insulin, with the bite of adrenalin, the nuances of estrogen and testosterone. Words as given to us by DNA. So that what we are, and feel, and think, form grace\ful and inter\weaving spirals.

ii. Verdant Overtures

You know May as raffish green exploding. But as Canadian winter ends, Chile's begins. Though in that country of copper and irony green persists. Colder inside the house than out so your breath forms a shadow. Albeit white. Arboreal fog. Beautiful reminder of your mortality, of the moment when breathing feels miraculous. It escapes like dust swirling in sunlight.

Clara lights the salamander. You open your door to capture its warmth. The sound is near, wood spitting in fire. The sound without the heat. A light rain starts up. Leaves of some bush you can't name slapping against your window to the rain's rat-a-tat-tat. If it keeps on pouring the streets will overflow. That much you can forsee; your boots were not built for the flood.

You bunk down as in a nun's cell. The room is too narrow, it belongs to a child. Your friends try to set you up with a saxaphone player. Fertility rites are perennial. That much is assured. That much is good. Match-making even when the atmosphere is icy. In another life you would love the saxophone player, with his golden horn. In this one you fill a hot-water bottle, sip lemon-balm tea and pull on alpaca socks and a sweater.

Drinking pisco in the kitchen the others listen to a broadcast from Pinochet. Pinoshit. But his regime is more scatological than their language. Pinochet's high pitched proclamations spluttering like Donald Duck on fast forward. *Atrophied balls.* The men know such things about one another.

It's a dream this time. You're lost again in that suburb, accosted by the hedge in the shape of a large fist. Raised. So the hand, in a dictatorship, is pruned of tenderness. Some salute. Others bow to the sun. You sleep through the verdant dark. Bombs blast the hydro station.

iii. To Inherit the Earth

When she hears the shots she rushes down the stairs forgetting the broom in her hand. She finds her husband slumped against the front steps. As she touches his hand, before she can speak to him, she is dragged away by military police. At noon. One man takes her broom. He snaps it, like a pencil.

They keep their submachine guns cocked. With the butts of their guns pressed against her back, they push her into the armoured van. The muzzles feel hot. The men are fully armed. She still wears her apron.

The children are upstairs alone. Her son is six years old. Her daughter is two. The children are waiting for lunch. The buns harden in the oven. The tortilla burns in the pan.

In the hands of such men she can't imagine what will become of her children and this fear is greater than the pain from the beatings. You can believe this, when there is nothing left to believe. The way women give birth and instantly forget labour. Heh, because they keep on doing it.

Her captors thrust her head into a sack; they strip her body. For twenty days she is naked. She is given no blanket, not the slimmest sheet to sleep with. She does not remember sleeping. Her face is covered and she cannot see. But she can be *seen.* Examined. Interrogated.

She forgets the cold, the hunger, the pain, the things she will not tell to strangers. She remembers her children. The way the guards tell her they have her daughter and son tied up in the other room. *Listen to their cries. Listen to the cries your silence perpetuates.* And the wails are as children wail. And she does not know that they are not her children. This is the only way to experience a tragedy which is not truly your own. When you do not know whether it is not your own or not.

For a month she knows nothing. Before that, she thought she knew music. But after such darkness, she has to find it, the way the blind find colour. She learns the touch of sound, she learns to feel it in the body more than in the ear. To smell it. The skin is an organ of such sensitivity that it connects us to the world the way the umbilical cord binds a child to her mother. Love as knotted and as far reaching as the convolutions of the entrails, or of the brain.

After the "questioning", a trial of sorts, and a prison sentence for loving her husband. For two years they lock her away among hookers and drug peddlars. In that jail she finds warmth. The shawl of a Magdalen. Among whores more humanity than among generals.

Her children were cared for by neighbours. She comes back a stranger to strangers. To become a man her son has made of his body a billy, a blunt instrument. His fist rising to shake at the radio in a gesture of his father's. The same bullet from the same gun waits for the boy.

She needs to work, but every job is forbidden her. Her children are thrown out of school. Her family drinks tea which expands and warms the belly, a soft drug which fails to nourish. There is no food, no money to buy it. Her husband is the lucky one. And those like him, who have learned to eat earth.

iv. The Heart Like a Kite

After a night of rain, the survivors, bright leaves, cling to cobblestones. It's still cloudy but sunshine cuts through, razor thin. The architecture for a change of heart, a winter one. The school you enter is a former convent, veiled in ivy. And within its walls wind dim corridors, birth passages for more secular souls. Coffee steams from styrofoam. The incense of caffeine, white breath swirling around the rim. The eyes of the teacher, your guide, are the blue of bruises, the blue of chicory. Her smile moves on her face like a child hiding under her bedding.

You need a key even to go to the restroom. She accompanies you along such a convoluted passage that you wonder whether you are being led to the loo or the minotaur. Once you've locked yourselves in and the teacher is sure she has you alone, she blurts out her secret. It is spoken in a whisper, but seems loud, or her words are loud, but intoned like a whisper. An inside. A theatrical whisper. You think you recognize their pitch from the confessional.

"My husband has been missing since '76. I can't speak of it here. Not to my colleagues. Not to anyone." Tears with her words are as rain with wind. "He talked too much, you know. A psychoanalyst, he talked, then he disappeared. I have to keep my mouth shut about it. That life can pull such tricks!" She wears a brilliant scarf knotted at her throat. She tightens the knot. "My husband haunts me, but I can only keep teaching with my silence. I can't afford to mourn him publicly. They might conclude I am one with him in opinions! My husband. I want a funeral for him. I want pennies to shut his eyes, garlands to drape his grave, I want to take the ash I'll sprinkle on his coffin and trace a cross on my forehead. and then I want to make room for something more, to make room for my life I want to bury all the men's suits in my closet. And I want, for his body to rest in a graveyard bordered with trees, so that as long as there is wind calling through the eucalyptus there will never be silence. As his voice was silenced.

I am a teacher of literature. I know how in Greek tragedy it is the dead who cannot rest. But my husband has inherited this earth! I am the one to be pitied. And if I should protest I would bring down an avalanche of bones on my head and my house. If he still knows anything, he knows that. You must realize, you have children of your own! – I have family responsibilities. We cannot afford another sacrifice. You understand there is nothing more to be done." There's an icy draft wherever we turn. As she speaks she fingers the nap of her silk scarf.

When her hand drops away the restless air tugs at her tie as if at the tail of a kite she's just let go.

v. Trading in on the American Dream – An Afterword

Listen, whatever I write here, what you read, is safe. It's between us. In North America writers don't disappear. They are not tortured. They are ignored. People are not arrested. They are illiterate.

Entertainment has become an industry, hybrid or boardroom and circus. How can we be touched by what the video screen dissolves into snow? It's a cold country.

Sitting on the floor, writing in my notebook, I can see under the table the network of spiderwebs holding up my printer. Displacement is vision. How can we be touched? Two NASA planes from Punta Arenas, Chile, measure the damage to the ozone over Antarctica. There is a growing rent in the sky. The blue we will view as through O'Keeffe skulls. But not bovine, our own. Our skin and our children's will burn and fester. On the network the voice-over, with the gravity of an anchorman, urges the nation on. "To survive is not success!" it proclaims: images of executives, Wall Street gray suits, Rolex watches,, leather portfolios, men scrambling to work: "So America has been made **great**!"

Over the planet the ozone is thinning,
over the earth where to succeed is not to survive

Kim Maltman

Two Prose Poems

The Technology of History and Resentment

Already it is near sunset and the headstones cast, this time of year, enormous elongated shadows – soon the grounds will close. Only caretakers remain. One, arriving in a pick-up, moves among the graves removing from the ground the withered wreaths, handfuls of flowers, now unsightly. Moving with that practiced, deferential economy that does not offend. But in the older sections there is nothing to remove, and here one may still walk awhile, undisturbed, try to read the weathered stones. Agatha M. Colin *blank*. Beloved. Dearest wife *blank*. 1846-1883. *Blank*. A last phrase, probably "with god." And so on. This is the power of the headstones. That our imagination can be made to seem as if from something other than our time. Already the city has begun to darken. Soon I will call you and we will go walking, arm in arm, perhaps, among the crowds, and I will tell you of that economy and how it did not offend, though it is nonetheless part of the dissolution. At a distance one is apt to feel omniscient, neither sorrow nor embarrassment, but something in between. That both this time, and those beyond it, could have been such crucial points of focus for those lives when what remains bears no resemblance to the whole. Like the dried-out insect casing you mistook once for a twig and, having thrown down, horrified, returned to, laughing and incongruous, so that the fear was isolated, and then lost. That single startled gesture, like the headstones, now without connection, all custom and formality. Perhaps this seems a little comfort, yet it is. How much faith. Such desires become the true anachronisms.

Do not despise the body.

The Technology of the Hostility of Objects

Into his early seventies now, the man's sense of balance begun to fail and he feels this more keenly than the other losses – the poor eyesight or lack of breath, the way his joints creak as he walks – because it makes him feel helpless. Once the thought that there was a particular disease on which the unsteadiness could be blamed would have been a comfort, fixed it in time, made it seem something one might hope could be controlled or cured one day, but now such distinctions seem useless, and the sense of gradual degeneration he has alternately fought and feared for over thirty years wells up again inside him. In the morning, no doubt, he will wake and have to reprimand himself again for having overdone it, although he will have walked only the half block to and from an old friend's house for Christmas dinner.

As it is he's barely arrived and already he is bone-tired from the first half of the walk. Knowing he is too unsteady, in stockinged feet, to navigate the hardwood floor, he must ask one of the young men to help him to the table, explaining that the floor is slippery, and no more than that, as if the polished hardwood and the tremors of Parkinson's syndrome were one and the same. All during dinner this hostility of objects will continue. The knife that chatters suddenly and uselessly against the plate, a bowl set just out of reach, the wine, so easily spilled, which he takes in careful sips now, apprehensive, talking of his own son. In his mind there is that continuing equation, himself, his son, though, if one were to ask him, he would admit everything, the disabilities, each infirmity of age, minimizing nothing. No, it is not so much to fool himself as because he is ashamed. Ashamed that those things which once were to be played of used at will, his own body, this house, this street, have passed beyond his control, although, of course, it has always been so.

So – if after dinner, it being already rather dark and, depressed by the sudden gaiety, he decides to leave, do not imagine it is easy for him, realizing he cannot negotiate the steep stairs to the street alone, or that he has not thought of it before. And when he asks for help, at the last moment, having gathered together shoes and hat and coat, because no one has sensed or sought to ease the difficulty, if it seems the staircase is made to bear all the menace, do not imagine it is for himself that he speaks so, or wince if the words are phrased uneasily to hide the subterfuge. Do not. Because it is not true sorrow that you feel, and you have not earned the right to pity.

Judith Fitzgerald

from *Diary of Desire*

Letters

maudlin *a. & n.* 1. *a.* Weakly or tearfully sentimental, esp. of tearful and effusive stage of drunkenness. 2. *n.* Weak or mawkish sentiment. [a.f.n. (w. ref. to pictures of weeping Mary Magdalen), ME f. OF *Madelaine* f. eccl. L *Magdalena* MAGDALEN]

We know this. Thursday evening depression descends, a blanket of tiny scars and knives,
simply passive, adverbial at best. West, west: Why do you refuse me? My head aches,
my hands splinter, my heart consistently shatters in the frame of your reference, antecedent to

far too many years to reify, rectify. Hard times, hard music, each of us hardened against
the beautiful psychic vulnerability, the open note, the pure pitch of pain.

Yes, I confess, my friends know my name but you may call me *Maudlin.*
Hurt – no – stunned, I stumble through days and nights with the silence of self an interior exile.
Abdicant. Supplicant. My hair intuits your destiny. May I? I ought. Teach me
to transcend the fiasco, to learn penitence, patience, consciousness.

I always (all ways) love you. From the moment you stop me that brilliant spring day.
Confident. Dazzling. That summer, watching and catching glimpses of a yellow windbreaker
returning from Ireland; my heart a fragile bird, unnamed, opaque. I always love you
and you always disbelieve me. I always want you and you always want a sideshow.
My body a book of matches; my mind a vessel. Year by year I live without you here
in my hands, in my heart.

And these men. I want to erase you from my arms, remove all traces of your beautiful cunning.
Flesh a shroud of love these times. Some women forget; others do not fall; my spectacular
misfortune: Loving you until I forget me. The attempts to lose, not myself, but you, in other
men. The night on Belvedere? I remember motives; recollect actions; but memory draws
a blank when it comes to the act of sex. Amnesia in spite of itself. Love in spite of love.

You taught me to hurt with hard clarity. The ex-hypothesis of my existence – *If he was fire,*
then she must be wood – predicated on the futility of belief. We disappoint, grow old, discount.
I love you and hate you for loving you and hate myself for the same reason.

Let's leave these lovers wondering why
they cannot have each other ...

I ask too little: To open your hands and find love blossoming; to open your heart and discover
a raging need for calm, and silence, and safety; to open your eyes to the pathetic love in which
I wallow. I ask too much: Consume. Consummate.

I slash away at my hair and ribbons of blood bathe your feet.

Phones

Unrelenting, the elements and phonological puzzles coalesce in
these nightmares – skin a body's wrap and fragile against invasions
of sun, rain, tongue, palmetto. Winnipeg, you do not hear me, cannot save me
from the glare of this new frontier. And, if I turn to you for comfort
or reassurance, I also turn back time, time when you spoke love and I believed
your language. Now you echo the past through these long-distance strands.
You hold up your trophied/atrophied heart. Your inventive logic. Your mendacious
hands. I tear my fingers on these artificial borders. Nails splinter night.
The clock strikes one. Remember the dawn on Roncesvalles? I froze both
feet following your tracks. You loved me only after you knew you could not.

With the present too heavy, too tense, you made me past perfect. Your low voice
penetrates this room awash in liquid tyranny. Insects rub wings here; there, angels
make snow of your words. The clock strikes two. I move out of you, hear
the parasites in your inflections. Your heart defeats you, offers science an
example of symbiosis despite itself. I long for amniotic respite from our future,
return the receiver to its cradle. Love's autopsy performs itself. Re: birth.

A Shot of Morphemes

Abandon: I assume the logical adjective (abandoned),
the seductive argument (abandonment). Unattainable. Wanting
to continue wanting, needing in spite of, desire against
the sheer grief my heart silences.

And yes, I desire. Cool white space, heart lodged in its proper persective,
its home of hands. It hurts, desire. Its heart, desire. The need to need.
Not simple, not simply. Take my name (džudIΘ), my number (singular),
my kind (a bundle of isoglosses); ease this linguistic pain.

Christmas at the Casa Mañana

My heart regularly breaks in your presence, your absence of thought
fullness and the blue blue feeling nothing will always remain the same –
no space, no number, no open line to home. Not even the faith in
language I once possessed. I speak loss and loss, ever constant, speaks
back. Self-imposed exile. The demographics of love. What keeps me here
keeps me caught. I can walk up Duval but that would not create
departure.
I can book a flight but that would merely exacerbate this distance. I
sleep
in a Key West cocoon and wake to the upper hand, the lower keys, the
aching grace.

Here, in the sub-tropics, every thing saturates itself. We learn bones
and conchs and keys beyond heat-drenched glass on marguerittas and
Jose Cuervo
and *Cayo Hueso.* We cannot speak the language we believe we master
effortlessly.

Christmas here, the sun and sweat, the failure of headlines and dead-
lines. A long-distance call between war and warmth. Jingle bells and
resistance cells. Do this in memory of memory. The paper reads *armed
and dangerous.* Things rarely change.

Key West – a drug you do not use – fans out into your veins, makes som-
nambulent, pathetic. I sit planted here, a worthless Canadian flag in-
capable of leaving the last resort, this twentieth-century Dodge city-by-
the sea, by the searing and seductive sea. My skin asserts its own
eerie logic. My mind turns to descents past Cerberus. My hands dream

Magnum .357s and Derringers and .38 Specials. Post-modern insurance coverage (or courage). I learn the language of violence too well.

The Margaret-Truman Drop-Off Launderette

Every silver lining offers us clouds but we who understand
such cumulus configurations know also that beneath each silver
lining lurks a zipper, a serrated dream circumscribed by cirrus
perceptions. Here, at the Bloor Laundromat, I acutely think of Key West,
drag my brain cells into some semblance of remembrance of sun-
dusted days along North Roosevelt through the Cuban section
to White Street. On a corner, further into town, Margaret
and Truman intersect. We pass the corner. Each time I remember
Bill Percy's memory of the Margaret-Truman Drop-Off Launderette.
I want to get a shot of it. We never stop. Either the car or our accelerator
feet urge us on. [Who drives anyway?] That corner resembles this corner,
Bloor and Palmerston, but rhetoric and history intrude. I know the difference
between bleach and unbleachables. Bones bleach. *Cayo Hueso.* The drama
of this laundry drops me below sea level. I receive photographs from Bill and Vina.
We stand on the steps of The Moorings in Granville Ferry. I wear white.
I have you on my mind. I can see you in my eyes. Turning, my clothes
in the dryer spin and spin and the ice on my heart melts in the warmth
of this artificial paradise. First person critical. Fragile, vulnerable,
we drive and drive. Clothes spin. Island parade through steamy recollections:
Nova Scotia, Virgin, Canary, Cayman Brac, Key West. We do our laundry in public,
you see? At replicas of the Margaret-Truman Drop-Off Launderette
everywhere we find solace in linings and zippers, seek safety, ignore this insistent sign:
No Dying in the Dryers.

Douglas Glover

from *The Mad River*

Panther

The Jewish legend was that Jesus was the son of a Roman Centurion, Pantheras, the Panther. Christians argued that Panther was a corruption of the Greek parthenos which meant "virgin," though it is not easy to explain how the word migrated from Greek to Hebrew. I have seen itwritten that the German scholar Von Domaszeuski claimed to have found in England the gravestone of Panther which showed that his legion had been stationed in Judea about 4 B.C. Aulus Plautius led his troops across the channel in 43 A.D., ten years after the Crucifixion. For other forms of this tradition – first met with in the second century – see Origen contra Celsum, Palinurus, the Talmud, Sepher Toldoth Jeschu, quoted fragments of lost Apocryphl gospels, Craveri, Strauss, Haeckel, etc.

*

I was Mora, the lord's daughter, princess of the Cymri in my sixteenth year. One day I was with my lover Rhean Dhub in the forest when we were discovered by a party of Romans from their earth-walled camp by the sea. The grey one, their leader, fell upon Rhean Dhub and slew him with a blow that spattered his brains upon my face while we yet clung together. I was prepared to die for I saw a look of blood madness in his strange blue eyes. Lo, we had slaughtered scores of his men whom we trapped in the thickets.

But the grey one stayed his hand. Others dragged the smoking corpse of Rhean Dhub from me. The grey one saw my nakedness. He saw the woven plaits of a princess and the snake mark of a seer. He pierced my heart, knew that I would taste death like a wanton, and, in place of butchery, let the soldiers have me, one by one, by the body of my lover, while I shuddered, helpless, impaled upon his eyes.

When they had finished, when I stretched riven and gory on the bracken, the soldiers were sore afraid, and clutched together, whispering, for they had violated the lord's daughter in his forest and knew that vengeance lurked where the shadows lengthened. But the grey one was not afraid. O, he was practised in the ways of hate.

He sneered at the heroes, kicked and bullied them with his sword butt till their blood flowed, laughed until they were more afraid of him than oak and elm. Gathering my plaits in a paw-like fist, he scythed them off, ripping my scalp at a stroke. Arm out-flung, he taunted the four quarters with a trophy, challenging the Cymri to claim its get. Then he ordered ropes brought and my ankles tied, and they drew me naked, face in the path, to their camp.

There he bade them chain me like a dog to an iron peg anchored in rock by his tent. My plaits he had hung from a crossed pole, with the head of Rhean Dhub spiked above. And he commanded the soldiers to take me as they liked which they did often at night when darkness cloaked them from the world's eyes, and from my eyes and from the staring eyes of Rhean Dhub.

For a week I lay thus, dying, yet knowing I would not die that I might one day revenge myself upon the grey one. By day I watched the Romans march out in disciplined ranks; evenings they would return, fewer in number, supporting their wounded, exhausted, terrified, a beast at their backs. Each Roman death was life to me; each wound a balm for my wounds. Their blood refreshed me through the earth.

By night they snatched that semblance of comfort from my flesh, their mad hot breath warming me with its desperation. Only the grey one came not; only he watched and was not afraid. He was my keeper: He knew me through the eyes more intimately than the others with their brutal tenderness. This strange cat-like man they called Panther.

This man loved death, his body leathery with battle scars. This man loved war. Yet he never came to me as a warrior. His soldiers pricked me out of fear, their mail armour tearing my skin. Panther was beyond that, his soul driven by hate to a place where sorcery and madness met.

And I, Mora, saw this through his eyes when he looked into me in the morning and the night, by the sun and the flames of torches. Yea, he was one of us, though without the snake mark of the seer to identify him. Yea, he was one of us.

O this I saw by the sun and by the flames of torches, I, Mora, the lord's daughter, princess of the Cymri in my sixteenth year....

And the sun and the moon gorged on blood in the days of my captivity. Death struck lonely, swift and fierce in the thorn-choked paths of the wilderness. The main body of Romans had sailed north across the estuary; daily, sentinels scoured the cupping waves for ships. But none came. I watched fear slip from eye to eye like a little bird whenever a forage party set off for the forest. I exalted in the terror of the Romans. The dew was sometimes black with Roman blood, and it exalted me.

Then came a morning when I started awake to the crack of catapults, the screams of horses, harsh shouts and the ragged thunder of the maniples wheeling on the square. A red moon, a hanged god, squatted above the parapet, and other moons, globes of greek fire and barrels of pitch, howled overhead as engineers sweated at their wheels.

All round the forest glowed. Sparks darted like shoals of fingerlings in undergrowth and dead-fall, until whole trees burst into flame, tossing their blackened skeletons in the hot wind. The Romans nodded approval from the battlements. It was as though they had come to fear the shadowy brakes more than the lean dark men, daubed with woad, who stalked them.

After sunrise the troops marched gaily out to catch the Cymri as they fled. But they found the villages empty. And my kinsmen lay in streams while flames rolled over them, then rose like water sprites to slay the stragglers. By twilight soldiers came to murder me, but Panther drove them off.

A day later, the two Israelites, attracted by the column of smoke, brought their hide boat to the beaches below the wall and begged admittance. I watched them at the gate: one was elderly, yet robust, with a stiff beard down his bosom; the other, a cripple, wore a hood and leaned upon a staff. This cripple spoke little and only to his companion. But the old man was full of talk, questioning the sentries, folding his hands to listen, gesticulating, and cocking his head at times to catch the soft words of the other.

I know now of what they spoke though at the time I could only see that they peered often in the direction of my keeper's tent. It seems they were no ordinary wanderers, not traders or settlers following the legions, but seekers, hunting from port to port, from garrison town to bivouac, for the man called Panther. Yet now they had come to the end of this long journey, neither seemed relieved or eager. The old man's face was taut with a look of sad wisdom; I could not see the other.

Learning how that morning Panther had led a score of swords beyond the gate to harry my people, the cripple merely nodded to a sunny place against the wall where they could rest and watch the tent above which the loved head of Rhean Dhub glared. The old man unrolled a carpet and arrayed his apparatus: a bowl, a mortar, an oil lamp, a row of tiny jars and a glass philtre. He asked for water. And at first I thought it was some strange magic he wished to perform, some devilish revenge, that had brought these men so far; but I was wrong.

The vessels held rare medicines. The cripple instructed; the old man mixed the potion, bathed and bandaged his feet and hands and side. He did this patiently, like a man long used to the service, like a parent with a child. The invalid lay as in a trance, his arms tucked limply over his chest, his head propped against the packed earth as though he had not the strength to hold it upright.

Yet, when the gate opened for Panther, returned in triumph, he sat straight, forgetting his weakness, and followed the grey one intently with his eyes. And again I was reminded of magic by the directness of his gaze and the way Panther became aware of it and turned from his ascendancy to stare at the cripple by the wall. The grey one asked, was told, and looked again. I saw a queer expression of bafflement cross his face. He turned to his tent, then looked again. Then saw my eyes, observing him, and brought his sword hilt crashing against my brow.

Yes, all this I swear to by the eyes of Rhean Dhub whose head I guard in my pillow bag, I, Mora, the lord's daughter, princess of the Cymri, then in my sixteenth year....

I lay as dead, I know not how long. When I awoke the lame Israelite was kneeling beside me, his hand on my cheek. "Be still, princess, I am a physician." He seemed to say this though I know he did not speak. I felt it rather than heard, the way the tongues come when I listen to the old ones. "Be still, princess."

It was past nightfall; I could not see the rotted face of my lover upon his spike. Yet I saw the eyes of the cripple and was afraid, not of death, but of something more terrible than death. His eyes spoke to me. They spoke of power offered and accepted, of ghostly pride, of betrayal, of suffering beyond the grave, and of despair. Yet these eyes were troubled for me.

"Be still, Mora," they said. And I felt his hand grow hot like a hearth-stone on my forehead. The pain of it shot through my body, burst from the tips of my fingers, my toes; I felt it spout from my eyes like liquid fire. I wanted to struggle, to escape, but his eyes held me. And then it seemed as if his hand sucked back the pain it gave, and the other, the pain of my captivity, sucked it out of me like air from a bladder. I saw it cloud his eyes. I saw his eyelids quiver and droop with the pain of my suffering. I saw him falter, and yet his eyes said again, "Be healed, daughter." And I was.

I heard him gasp. And this was real, not magic. He fell across me; I caught the physician and held him. He seemed as dead. I held him to my nakedness as a mother a child, for all the pity of my womb went out to this man who was troubled for me. And I understood the manner of the old man toward him. I felt the bristles of his face hair against my nipples. I felt the bones of him against my breast.

Yet I knew that it was not death that took him thus. Yea, this was no man as other men. I felt not the heat of my bowels go out to him as a man. And his cheek was cold upon my heart. And I knew, I knew, that he was some weird thrust back from death, some unquiet soul come back of a purpose, a shade not at peace with his god. And for a proof, as he lay thus upon me, I unwound the bandages and lifted his tunic and saw there wounds the like of which I have not observed on living men. Dark rents that did not bleed, empurpled putrid flesh, yea, even as the flesh of the cheeks of my lover above, gashes that never healed.

I felt his flesh quiver against me. He awoke. When he saw what I had done, he smiled into my eyes. "Strange, is it not? A physician who cannot cure himself, a dead man who cannot die? It is God's fool you see before you. I am my father's son." He shook his head bitterly at his hands. "No, it was not man who betrayed me; it was God."

He shifted in my embrace, throwing his waxen arms around me and pulling himself against my bosom. "Warm me," he said. "Warm me, O daughter of Adam, for I am cold." And I held him close and would have warmed him with the breath of my life had I been able. But his face lay cool against me. And I felt cold tears upon my breast.

"I was called the son of God, but I heard them whisper in the marketplace that my mother was a Roman's whore. It was God's doing that it should happen thus on the road to Golgotha. I could not die with that terrible doubt in me, so that when Joseph the Arimathaean took from me the cross I was as I am now, waiting, seeking, doubting, cursing my father, whether God or man. I have followed this Roman across the face of the world, following the trail of death where he has gone like some restless Moloch feeding on the children of men, knowing ever more surely that I must be his son, knowing ever more surely that evil dwells within me as within him, that perhaps all the evil of the world dwells within me."

I stopped his bitter mouth with my hand for I could bear no more of his awful speech, that was not speech. My warm tears fell upon my breast and mingled with those of the physician, warming them as they trickled down my belly. But I had not stopped his eyes, and he gazed up at me, saying, "Be still, Mora. It is over now. This is the last suffering of all: to know that I never was God, nor ever will be with God, and that I have taken the sins of the world upon my shoulders, alone."

The last word came to me like the wind when it shrieks through the brakes in winter, like the shrieks of unwanted babes left in the thickets to die. It seemed as though the earth trembled and the whole camp must wake, yet all was quiet as though the soldiers were under some spell. One only heard and stirred.

Panther, the grey one, stood naked beneath my lover's head, clutching a short Spanish sword in his fist, his face distended with blood, his eyes and veins bulging with rage. He beheld us together by the iron peg. I saw death in his face. Not human, he was. His body was of stone. The cool wind feathered the grey hairs of his body.

The physician stood himself as though his wounds were nothing. His cloak slid from his body, so that it fell upon my shoulders; I know not if he meant it. His eyes were on Panther. He raised a horrid palm in greeting. Yet his soul spoke once more to me. "Be still, daughter of Adam. The chains of men no longer bind thee."

Then came the voice of the grey one: "What seekest thou here?"

"Thee, Father, I seek thee," said the physician.

"I am not thy father. Fool, thou art mistaken."

The physician felt at his girdle for a small leathern pouch which hung there. "I have brought thee a gift, O Panther."

"I am not thy father."

"You know me not. Yea, I am Jesus, son of Mary whom you knew in Nazareth in the days of your occupation under King Herod. Why didst you forsake us, Father?"

I saw the grey one's sword arm flex, his eyes flash. He stepped forward with the blade raised to strike. But the physician's hand stayed him. And I, Mora, felt the hairs of my head rise for the sorcery that was there.

"I am not thy father," came the terrible voice.

"This is the cup from which I ate before they took me to be crucified. In this cup, Joseph, my companion, caught my blood as I hung upon the cross. Take it, Panther. It is for thee."

And suddenly night became day as the camp was filled with a wondrous twinkling that shot up to heaven to humble the stars. From his skin pouch, the physician brought forth a cup, but no ordinary cup. It was of silver, bossed and figured, yet no ordinary silver. For the cup shone as if it were the sun itself. And we, Panther and I, must needs cover our eyes that ached from its brilliance.

"I am not thy father," roared the grey one like some beast that has been brought to bay. "As the gods witness, I have not lain with woman. Put thy cup away."

And in my heart I rejoiced for the poor physician for I knew that Panther spoke the truth.

And the physician understood as well. A look of surpassing joy came upon his face, a light shone therefrom, and he fell to his knees, raising his hands and eyes to heaven, crying: "O Lord, I have doubted thee."

I wist not what he meant, but the grey one, thinking he still addressed him as father, howled with rage and plunged his sword into the Israelite's breast. The man Jesus fell backward and was still.

This, too, I saw in the light of the silver cup, I, Mora, the lord's daughter, princess of the Cymri in my sixteenth year....

With the death of the physician, I seemed to wake as from a dream. Panther brooded over the corpse. I lay by my stake. The cup, partly hidden beneath the body, glowed less brightly. All around us was silence, the sleeping Romans, the forest going out to the sea, the sea going out to the stars. I waited, hardly knowing whether to expect my death, or my salvation.

The grey one stirred. His great paw-fists went to his eyes to rub them as a child in the morning. He looked slowly around, put his hand out as though to touch something. He seemed baffled again, as when he first saw the strangers against the wall. His eyes roved over me without seeing. I saw his eyes, and then I knew the beast was blind. And my heart beat in me for the punishment that had come to the slayer of Rhean Dhub.

He knelt and probed the body with his hands; I thought to find his sword that he might kill me at last. But his iron fingers closed on the cup, lifted it to his milky unseeing eyes, touched it wonderingly. As in a dream, he rose again and stumbled blindly to his tent, hiding the seething metal against his chest.

Remembering the words of the physician, I looked to my chains to see what wondrous thing he might have wrought with them. And, behold, I stood and the chains parted from my neck as water weed.

Wrapping myself in his cloak, I stole toward his body, felt the sword hilt in his bosom, and wrenched it out. So strange it was to find no blood upon the blade. I followed in the steps of the grey one and found him kneeling by his pallet, naked, clutching the cup before his eyes. He saw me not, nor any other thing. I drove his own short sword into his throat with all my might, felt skin tear, muscle rend, felt the breathing tubes crush.

I saw his blood spout like a fountain, black blood. I felt it rain upon me, knowing not at first what it was. I watched him fall, riven and bloody; I watched the black life of him bubble out onto the dry sepulchral earth. I caught the blood in my hands and drank of it, knowing the joy of vengeance, knowing that I, Mora, had slain the unholy Panther, death-bringer, world-roamer, the djinn who knew not woman.

Yea, this I saw....

George Payerle

The Shores of August

Yes. The white sand. The water curling in pale as glass. The palm trees. Green. Too much green. Under the plantain leaves, a man. In the green shadow, the gun. Or the eyes like a gun with tow names. Blue-black certainty of what he will tell you. The man says, "Swim there, that is a good place." If you swim there, you will drown.

In the hotel the tourists drink pina coladas, or black rum mixed with green fruit. They sit on the terrace or under big fans in the bar. They shine in the sun. They wait for the man to come out of the green shadows where the people who live here move like fish. They wait for young brown bodies to slip out of the night while they lie trying to sleep in the heat and their pink skin throbs with what they think is passion. They wait to go home. They wait to go swimming, and any who swim once do not swim again unless they are lucky.

A man crosses the terrace with a telegram in his hand. A beautiful blonde woman stands up and laughs – a sound you would expect to hear in the mansions of Boston. The telegram says, "The end of the world is nigh."

She goes to her room and steps out of her clothes. Her body in the white room stands among elegant furniture. Out the French doors she can see the pale green glass of the ocean beyond the dark green wall of the forest. Her body stands like a statue in its room, a moment in the Louvre when all things are seen as they might be forever. It is the hottest part of the day, and in that moment nothing calls her. In the visible world, nothing moves, by the hand of man or god. The fan in the ceiling turns the air around her as though it were a sculptor's hands finishing clay.

She steps into the bath. She smiles like one in victory. The froth of soap cradles her breasts and dimples her knees, in case she wishes to rise like Aphrodite from the ocean spume. She shakes out her shimmering hair and hums a cheerful tune. she thinks she might have liked Cole Porter, or Cary Grant, to step into the room, if she had been alive at the time, with a sponge in one hand and champagne in the other artfully held by the neck, long-stemmed glasses crossed between the fingers. Or both, for a lark.

So she is surprised when two black men step into the room, silent as Fred Astaire, or ghosts.

The two guns in their hands make holes in her glistening skin, pfwtt pfwtt because of the silencers. The two men vanish, as Cole Porter and Cary Grant and Fred Astaire had done before them.

The red soap darkens in the sunset.

When her lover finds her he loses his mind. Since he cannot put himself on an airplane without his mind he is arrested and left to occupy space with himself in a cell while his money changes hands and the process of international law exercises itself languidly.

By the time he is returned to Boston it is too late for the hosts of psychotheraps to succeed in laundering and retailoring the shreds of his mind that they find. Starched, pressed, and full of chlorpromazine, he re-enters the society in which her laughter echoes from the throats of young women whose slim shoulders rise from swaths of green satin.

He sits in the Waldorf Hotel among people who once were his friends, and sees green shadows in the air. A man plays Spanish guitar. The mind of the man whose lover died laughing moves like the mouth of a fish out of water. He laughs in the green shadows, a flat, stiff sound. His friends stare at him. "You always laugh like that," they say.

Colleen Thibaudeau

from *The Martha Landscapes*

In which I Become Confused, the End of the World Being Imminent

They say the world's near ending and this confuses me. I've a mad desire to try on everything in Eaton's. I rush there as fast as I can pick my way through the rubble; far away on another street the buses are still running. Eaton's has lost part of its roof, but the escalators still bear us upward. Passing me, going down, is the Wife of the President of the University. She nods encouragement to my smiling mouth (shaped into a "hats?"), to my two big Ohs of eyes. The staff is putting all to rights though a stiff breeze from the roof area nullifies their efforts; blouses move on the racks like sailing ships eager to leave port; in the Shoe Dept., a Clog Dance; – they are thinking in Promotions, thinking, and soon there will be a Special: the Super End of the World Special. I hope it won't get going till I finish my shopping.

Was that what I came for? Shopping? The pink-orange neon of a truly beautiful sunset pervades the Lingerie Dept. I feel we are part of an ad lay-out; I dart among the shoppers; we seem happy to be there.

"There's no coffee. They have no water," I hear a slightly familiar voice saying as I enter the cafeteria. "They have Coke." With coke and biscuits and cheese I too am quite contented. I puzzle about where the voice belongs in my past. Just trying to fit a face to the voice will keep me occupied for quite some time.

The Tomato Pickers Observed

Civic Holiday – 1981 – St. Thomas

The block between Ross and Moore is still torn up for the new drainage system so that the whole busload of us is disembarked in the wasteland at the rear of the Bus Depot. Charterways is not unkind – that's how it is:

The Queen Anne's Lace growing by the tracks droops a bit forlorn in the iron breeze. The gravel moves, shimmering illusion, just slightly in the humid air.

Despite the holiday, construction men are working, but slowly; moist and damp, the distinct smell of excavation and possible Legionnaire's Disease wafts over from Talbot St.

Naturally the Bus Depot is closed up – tight.
Tout ferme.
The Tomato Pickers have about an hour to wait for the Leamington Greyhound, but they don't know that, nor do they know where to wait.

Like a digger's load of fetid earth and gravel, the rattle of the Driver's parting instructions; the small stones of his staccato English, received full face, have now covered them.

They are still monuments sitting on their suitcases, smoking feverishly, red-sweatered the women. Man Statue leaps up, tries to get across the chasm of Talbot St. to the closed restaurant and the only visible comforts tombed away.

But even as I leave them, the Tomato Pickers have that slumbering energy of the temporarily entombed. They burn with avidity and fervour for the tomato, love apple, with a primitive instinct for dim-remembered fields.

As even after the holocaust, language unusable, stiff-boned, laughter and energies benumbed, the Tomato Pickers of the earth will rise, picking their way out of the rubble; small people, incomprehensible to most, battered suitcases clutched; enduring.

Marlene Nourbese Philip

She Tries Her Tongue; Her Silence Softly Breaks*

All Things are alter'd, nothing is destroyed
Ovid, *The Metamorphoses.* (tr. John Dryden)

the me and mine of parents
the we and us of brother and sister
the tribe of belongings small and separate,
when gone....
on these exact places of exacted grief
i placed mint-fresh grief coins
sealed the eyes with certain and final;
in such an equation of loss tears became
a quantity of minus.

with the fate of a slingshot stone
loosed from the catapult pronged double with history
and time on a trajectory of hurl and fling
to a state active with without and unknown
i came upon a future biblical with anticipation

* Ovid, *The Metamorphoses.* (tr. John Dryden)

It is important, when transplanting plants, that their roots not be exposed to the air longer than is necessary. Failure to observe this caution will result in the plant dying eventually, if not immediately. When transplanting, you may notice a gently ripping sound as the roots are torn away from the soil. This is to be expected: for the plant, transplanting is always a painful process.

The Practical Guide to Gardening

seek   search and   uproot
the forget and remember of root words
uncharged
            pathways electric with the exposed lie
circuits of dead
            currents of still
                        words
synapses of unuse and gone
                        words
wordless
                        in the eden of first sin

                                    and

naked

1. The limbic system along with the hypothalamus, hippocampus, amygdala, fornix and olfactory bulb rule the basic drives for food, sex and survival.

2. The limbic system or primitive cortex plays a significant role in emotions; it is indispensable in the formation of memory.

3. Human memory may be either immediate, short-term, or long-term.

4. The cerebral cortex is the storehouse of our memory – it makes us human.

5. What we choose to store in our long-term memory is closely linked to our emotions.

6. Memory is essential to human survival.

Facts to Live By and Die

without the begin of word
grist in a grind and pound of together
in the absence of a past mortared with
                                                            apart
the harsh husk of a future-present begins

... and the big bad wolf came and said,
"Little pig, little pig let me in."
"No, no, not by the hair of my chinny chin chin."
"Then I'll huff and I'll puff and I'll blow your house in."
The wolf huffed and puffed and he huffed and puffed and couldn't blow the house down.

The first pig built his house of straw; the second of wood. Did the third pig buy his bricks or was he given them, and why? Where did he get his money to buy his bricks with?

Straw, wood or brick. The moral of this tale is that the right choice of materials secures safety.

– How to Build Your House Safe and Right

oath   moan   mutter   chant
                time grieves the dimension of other
babble   curse   chortle   sing
                turns on its axis of silence
praise-song   poem   ululation   utterance
                one song would bridge the finite in silence
                syllable vocable vowel consonant
                one word erect the infinite in memory

... the day of Pentecost was fully come....

And suddenly there came a sound from heaven as of a rushing mighty wind, and it filled all the house where they were sitting.

And there appeared unto them cloven tongues like as of fire, and it sat upon each of them.

And they were all filled with the Holy Ghost, and began to speak with other tongues....

... every man heard them speak in his own language.

– The Acts of the Apostles 2. 1, 2, 3, 4, 6.

absencelosstears   laughter   grief
in   any   language
                        the same
only larger

for the silence

monstrosity
obscenity
tongueless wonder
blackened stump of a tongue
torn
out
withered
petrified

burnt
on the pyres of silence
a mother's child foreign
made
by a tongue that cursed
the absence
in loss
tears laughter grief
in the word

... and if a stranger were to touch her newborn child, the mother will have nothing to do with it. She can smell the stink of the stranger on her child and will refuse to suckle it, believing the spirit of her child to be taken by the stranger.

*De Matribus et Advenis**

* *On Mothers and Strangers.*

I do not presume to come to this thy table
father forgive
most merciful father, trusting in my own righteousness
foreign father forgive
but in thy manifold and great mercies.
forgive her me this foreigness
I am not worthy so much as to gather up the crumbs beneath thy table
forgive me this dumbness
but thou art the same Lord, whose property
this lack of tongue forgive
is always to have mercy

upon
this
thisthisand

disfigurement this
dis
memberment
this
verbal crippling
this
absence of voice
that
wouldnotcould not
sing

Kyrie eleison
Christos eleison
Kyrie eleison

Is it in the nature of God to forgive himself–
For his sin?

The Book of unCommon Prayer

Hold we to the centre of remembrance
that forgets the never that severs
word from the source
and never forgets the witness
of broken utterances that passed
before and now
breaks the culture of silence
in the ordeal of testimony;
in the history of circles
each point lies
along the circumference
diameter or radius
each word creates a centre
circumscribed by memory ....and history
waits at rest always

still at the centre

history, *n – L. historia, "narrative, story, narration, account," from Gk.... "learning by inquiry, knowledge obtained by inquiry; account of one's inquiries; narration, historical narrative; history....*
memory, *n -ME. mémoire, fr OF. memorie (F. Mémoire), fr. L. memoria, "memory," fr. memor, "mindful," which stands for *me-mor, and derives from I.-E. *mer-(s)mer-, reduplication of base *(s)mer-, to care for, be anxious*

about, think, remember. Cp. memoir, commemorate, consider, remember.... Cp. also martyr, mourn, smriti.

– Klein's Comprehensive Etymological Dictionary of the English Language.

Without memory can there be history?

That body should speak
When silence is,
Limbs dance
The grief sealed in memory;
That body might become tongue
Tempered to speech
And where the latter falters
Paper with it words
The crack of silence;
That skin become
Slur slide susurration
Polyphony and rhythm – the drum;
The emptied skull a gourd
filled
With the potions of determine
That compel the split in bridge
Between speech and magic
Force and word;
The harp of accompaniment the ribcage
Strung with the taut in gut;
Flute or drumstick the bones.
When silence is
Abdication of word tongue and lip
Ashes of once in what was
... Silence
Song word speech
Might I ... like Philomela ... sing
continue
over
into
...pure utterance

....and on the last day of the great salmon run, the first salmon caught is cooked and shared among the elders – men and women. The oldest women of the tribe, accompanied by the youngest girl-child, then goes down to the

waters and returns the skeleton whole to its watery home. This is the way the tribe ensures future gifts of winter food.

Of Women, Wisdom, Fishes and Men

Crad Kilodney

from *Malignant Humors*

Advanced Oboe Problems

1. The Enigma of Fatality

A death claim has reached the desk of Mr. Zwarun, age 26, of the Workers' Compensation Board. A worker in the research department of the Excelsior Oboe Company, Ltd., killed himself while testing a giant experimental oboe powered by an electric wind machine. Due to a miscalculation, the instrument emitted an infrasound wave of approximately 10 cycles per second at high amplitude. The worker fell dead instantly. His internal organs had been mashed into an amorphous jelly.

Mr. Zwarun must decide whether the company is liable for the worker's death, and, if so, to what extent. Did all the equipment used in the experiment belong to the company? Was the experiment done with the knowledge and approval of the company? Does the legal definition of "oboe" extend to giant-size models?

Mr. Zwarun is wondering whether to open a new file for a new type of accident, which would require the approval of his superior. Now he is looking out the window of his sixteenth-floor office and suddenly realizes that what he has really wanted to do with his life is become a bass guitarist. Do you believe this would be a wise decision, career-wise?

2. The Uncertainty of the Poet

The poet laureate of Radford, Virginia, looked over her typewriter out her window and saw the cows coming down from the mountains. A little shepherd boy was leading them, playing an oboe, which he had made himself from primitive materials according to gypsy traditions. His gentle melody inspired the poet, who began to write:

Try to give an oboe
That will be a lasting thing –
That will, through tomorrow,
Have a song to sing.

She tore it up and began over:

> *Try to give an oboe*
> *That memory and time will refine.*
> *It may not seem much today,*
> *But tomorrow the oboe will shine.*

The poet left her typewriter and went into the bathroom.

Which of the following kinds of lines occur in the above texts: amphibrach, choriambic, dactylic, anapestic, trochaic, iambic, detersive?

How would you compare the poet's style to that of Homer, Robert Lowell, or Edgar Guest?

How are we to interpret the poet's belief that the oboe will shine tomorrow?

3. The Conquest of the Philosopher

A philosopher answers the following ad in *True Men's Guts:*

> "HEY GUYS! Tired of missing out on hot action? Now GET GIRLS by playing the oboe! Only $19.95 brings you easy instructions by the colored dot method plus song sheets of favorite oboe hits girls like!"

The philosopher buys a second-hand oboe and applies himself to the course diligently. Within two weeks he can play Schubert's *Die Forelle.* He then invites a freshman girl from his Logic 101 course home for dinner. Thereafter he seduces her.

Taking the seduction as the result, identify the efficient cause, formal cause, material cause, and final cause in the sequence of events. Are Aristotelian assumptions of causality "true to life"?

4. The Nostalgia of the Infinite

Pinky Lee came into the kitchen, but he knew already there would be nothing to eat but ketchup and Ritz Crackers. His three children, all in their thirties, sat passively at the table with little bibs tucked under their chins. Mrs. Lee looked at him sadly and said, "Pinky, there is no food, and we have no money left in the bank. If only you had saved more money from the show ..."

"Please, let's not go into that again." Pinky put on his checked jacket and funny little hat and walked out into the evening air. Through the years Pinky had become closer to God and when pressed by doubts or exalted states of mind, he would try to get as close to God as possible. Since the completion of the World Trade Center, he had gotten very close indeed.

On his way up the elevator, Pinky thought of his birth in St. Paul, his early devotion to the oboe, and his success in the school band. Later when he contemplated a career in show business, he had an operation on his eyelids to modify his Chinese features so as to look Caucasian and not frighten children's television audiences of the mid-50's. He remembered all the times he sang, *Yo ho! It's me. My name is Pinky Lee!*, and how the smiling faces before him made it all worth while, despite the fact that the after-effects of the eyelid operation had turned him into a heroin addict, which cost him most of his earnings from the show.

Was Pinky dreaming, or was the speaker in the elevator emitting the poignant melody of Milhaud's *Oboe Concerto?* Wafted into the Infinite by his reverie, Pinky found himself sitting at the edge of the building, from which he could see the sun setting upon New Jersey. Or was it St. Paul? His body seemed filled with music, and he was at peace, and it was without a second thought that Pinky sang and danced his little dance right off the edge of the World Trade Center.

Will Pinky's family collect on his $100,000 life insurance policy? If a witness can be found to establish that Milhaud's *Oboe Concerto* was playing in the elevator and if medical evidence can be adduced to show its likely effect on Pinky's state of mind, can a case be made for accidental death? How would you argue the suit for the beneficiary? For the insurer? Is there a basis for *mens sana in corpore sano? Mens sibi conscia recti? Ars longa, vita brevis? Ex mero motu? Joci causa?* Does the oboe have a different effect on Chinese children than on Caucasian children?

5. The Mysterious Baths

A dead body is found wrapped in a sheet in a Turkish bath, with an oboe next to it. Explain.

6. The Archaeologists

Oboes have been found in Egyptian tombs dating back to the First Dynasty. Have your group act out a psychodrama called *The Archaeologists,* in which two archaeologists find the world's oldest oboe and must decide on its proprietorship. Roles to be assigned: two archaeologists (one male and one female), mummy, and high priest. Time limit: 15 minutes. Group discussion to follow.

7. The Enigma of a Day

The following is an extract from a book by a man who has devised a means of receiving messages from God by deducing code words or phrases from the events of the day:

Thursday, May 5th. 1970. Code phrase: *Requirements of a Vice President.*

Fixed rod in toilet to make it shut off. (Needs to be able to fix things out of adjustment.)

Woolworth – Got rubber stick-on soles for use on tennis shoes and other shoes. (Needs to be in good physical condition.)

Dentist – To get teeth cleaned. Assistant commented that I have a long upper lip from playing the oboe, which tends to stop one discolored tooth from showing. (Needs to have good personal appearance.)

Mail – a medical insurance ad. (Needs medical coverage.)

TV – Boy played the oboe in a youth talent show. (Needs to be talented.)

Life magazine with cover picture of Vice President. "Spiro Agnew Knows Best," "Stern voice of the silent majority." (Needs to be able to protect the interests of the majority.)

Puppy got head stuck in Marge's oboe. (Needs to be curious.)

Outside 7-11, blind man playing oboe asked for money. Gave him ten cents. (Needs to be charitable.)

Evaluate this extract from the viewpoints of: religion, psychiatry, general semantics.

Is the author's belief supernaturalistic, rationalistic or merely intuitive?

Do you agree with his choice of code phrase in this case?

8. Autumnal Melancholy

K. is poor and unknown and lives in a basement in a large North American city. He wishes to write something that will have sufficient impact on the world to change his life and lift him out of his misery. He has chosen the subject of oboes, but not for any particular reason. K. does not even play the oboe and had to look it up in a book to remember what it looked like. Assuming that K. is competent in the English language and has a great deal of time at his disposal, what should he write to accomplish his objective? Set up an equation expressing the probability of his success. Your equation should include factors relating to the social value of oboes, the number of persons likely to read K.'s work, and any assumptions you care to make about the forms of gratitude likely to be manifested by readers. Show all work and be neat. Send your solution to the author, who, in the meantime, is sitting patiently before a blank wall in a basement with a small window overhead, through which he can see red maple leaves falling from the trees.

Ron Smith

from *A Buddha Named Baudelaire*

To live divinely is to embrace simple joys; to partner the holy grace of moonlight. To live out of time, beyond the brief darkness of dreams, is to court demons.

Listen, walk the streets through this city as if the jackal snapped at your heels.

> What we heard was not the vision.
> What we saw was not the trumpet of Jericho.
> What we tasted was not the fragrance of the morning sun, an open orange blossom.
> What we smelled was not the salt of your thighs, the song on your red lips.
> What we felt was not the end.

> ... a Buddha named Baudelaire reflects in the mirror
> ... which reflects in the window ...

Your hand reaches for mine; you wait until the last of the music is silenced by the click of the record player. I rise. You lead me from the kitchen. It is cooler now. We crawl into the white tangle of sheets. I no longer think of snow. Is it safe to touch ... to love? Can it be, as the bird soars where it might have been, in the fullness of a blue sky, that you have entered my soul? I stare at the walls. White sheets, white bodies, white paper.

Stan Dragland

from *Journeys through Bookland*

Beth Gêlert

The point of the story was that the master had made a tragic but understandable mistake in killing the dog, acting on the evidence of the moment which suggested that the dog had killed the child.

The father returns home from a long journey to find in tatters the richly embroidered hangings, the tasselled canopy of the bed, in his son's room.

From the bed the silken sheets have been torn and lie, slimy with blood, in confusion on the floor. The only live thing in evidence is Beth Gêlert. His welcoming doggy grin, his wagging tail express a terrible indifference to the gore, particularly to the blood in his own teeth. Between the blood and the dog there is a leap of association that blows up to the size of the father's mind. In the next instant he has drawn his sword and killed the dog.

And an instant later the cry of his son issues from the tangled mass of bedclothes under which he has lain in terror. Throwing the covers back, the father gathers his son into his arms. Though blood-bespattered, terrified, the child is unhurt. Then who ... ? Still cradling his son, the father kicks the sheets away. He reveals two fierce wolves, clearly slain by Beth Gêlert, the gore in whose mouth is now explained. Defence of his friend, son and heir to the lord of this castle. The father is filled with grief. He kneels beside the corpse of the dog, and weeps.

The man who remembers this story, over thirty years, is a son and a father. Now he asks himself what is missing from the tale. Not a sense of fair play to wolves, who haven't earned their bad reputation. No, what is absent is the nurse, nanny, governess. Somehow the mother is entirely out of the picture. Who leaves a child alone with ravening wolves about? On whom did the child call in his terror? Who is he now holding on to, cause of terror past? Once the tale of an heroic dog, now an abandoned child. Who left the child's protector out of the tale?

Three Wishes

Seven years we lived
    in the Peace River Country
        Land of Twelve-Foot Davis

and only once
    one morning like
        some consequence

of a broken mirror appeared
    a faded fourth-rate midway at the edge
        of town by the NAR tracks

where the crocuses pushed up
    out of the black spring
        burnt-off grass

A cheap sort of magic maybe
    such a sink of lost chances
        as would depress me now

but I was a boy of ten
    enthralled
        when a High Dark Lady

collared me: "Boy
    you ask your mother
        she wash my clothes

I pay her well"
    Of course the laundry
        was an excuse

The Lady was in search
    through all the land
        of a faithful servant

one gold among the many
    souls of brass and
        I aimed to please but

all I got to trade
    for three wishes was "Tell her
        I don't wash clothes for gypsies"

Journeys through Bookland

The story of a man's mistaken murder of the dog who saved his son from wolves was current all over Europe when the folk tradition was strong. How much of the story is myth? Might wolves actually have found their way into a castle through a door left ajar, up a broad stone staircase to the second-floor bed chamber and its helpless occupant? Not unless the whole household had absconded, or been frightened or enchanted away; while something savoury turned on a spit in the kitchen, while fires still burned cheerily in the fireplaces.

A different sort of story might conduct us carefully to the moment during famine when wolves are drawn to settlements out of a hinterland just a stone's throw away. Crossing open ground to the undefended castle not from evil bloodlust, though deliberately, but goaded by hunger. The story might explain everything, and still the horror persist.

With or without details, accurate or fanciful, the story was once known all over Europe. William R. Spencer wrote it down in his ballad entitled "Beth Gêlert," and Charles A. Sylvester, the editor of *Journeys Through Bookland* (ten illustrated volumes), gathered it into volume three of his hardbound "plan for reading applied to the world's best literature for children." The volumes are graduated in difficulty so that a child might grow up with the series, as I did (but randomly) from nursery rhymes to Shakespeare.

I don't remember my mother reading to me from *Journeys Through Bookland,* though she was the one who bought the set. With her head full of nursery rhymes and fairy tales, she could do without the lavishly illustrated volume one, and early on I could read some of the others for myself. She had taught me the alphabet with the help of a little easel-blackboard, well before I went to school, in the new kitchen of the National Grain house in the Peace River Country town of Grimshaw.

I spent my twenty-five cent weekly allowance on comics at Martin's Drugstore. Fifteen cents for a Classics comic, like *Ivanhoe* or *The Iron Mask* or *The Hunchback of Notre Dame,* and ten cents for a *Scrooge McDuck* or *Red Ryder.* I traded comics with the Stuart boys and Aubrey Tingle. When Bernice Palmer babysat, older boys suddenly remembered their abandoned stacks of comics, brought them over to trade and didn't care what kind of deal they made. Bonanza! There were Mercer Boys books, Nancy Drew books, especially Hardy Boys books. I had some of my own, but I remember borrowing them from other kids too. There were library books from school, but not from the Women's Institute town library, which closed during the war and didn't open again until 1953. So I am told in *Land of Hope and Glory: A History of Grimshaw and District,* which also says that Dr. Grimshaw, the town's namesake, was born in Kingston, Ontario. And that Matt Wilcox, who cut my hair, and Mike Miller, who ran the Esso garage, had pioneered in the district. So the Grimshaw that seemed to me to have existed forever during the seven years we lived there was just over twenty years old when we arrived.

There were other books, then, but I remember having no permanent library beyond *Journeys Through Bookland.* When I recently bought a second hand set for my boys (bound in blue rather than the red of my own, which disappeared) I was surprised to find in it introductions and study questions supplied by the editor. I had also forgotten the pictures of authors, though I greeted the one of Robert Louis Stevenson like an old friend. Who could have helped liking this young man, with his shoulder-length hair and his warm, open face smiling directly into the camera?

I didn't need to be reminded of certain illustrations. I had pored over them much more than I read the stories and poems, and they've stayed with me over thirty years. There was a detailed realistic salmon leaping from a mountain stream, and that was Loki in one of the shapes he took to flee punishment for his betrayal of Balder. There was Robinson Crusoe, heavily bearded and dressed in animal skins, kneeling on the beach of his island to examine the print of a bare foot in the sand. His story was crossed in my mind with the more delicious one about The Swiss Family Robinson, whose tree house

Falconhurst I loved. All the Tenniel illustrations for *Alice in Wonderland* were sharply reproduced, brightened with the odd greens and reds that appear throughout the ten volumes. I believe I was an adult before I read Alice, but the story was familiar. I had absorbed the text through the pictures. There was a man writing at a desk, lit by a lantern that had a window in it and a ring at the top to lift it with. While he wrote, a spider let himself down from the gloom of the ceiling as if to watch. The story was called "The Gold-Bug," though I associated the spider with the one who had something important to show Robert Bruce.

I couldn't understand some of the pictures, like the simple line drawing of a naked man with webbed feet squatting on the single branch of a tree, while someone below tried to hand him a garment. This had something to do with *A Midsummer Night's Dream.* But more often an illustration implied a whole story: Roland sitting under a tree in exhaustion and dejection, straining to wind his horn one last time. Or the slain dog and the wolves in the bedchamber, all in black and white except for the red blood that graphically poured from their mouths. Did I read "Beth Gêlert?" Perhaps; the poem is not very long. whether the poem or the picture is responsible, those wolves still haunt me.

There is no way to separate the incompletely conquered fears I felt as a child, in a family anchored firmly by my mother, from those I find in my own boys, in a family Penny and I have both tried to make loving and secure. The same fears travelled all over Europe in the story that crystallized as "Beth Gêlert." They went into the lonely lament of the solitaire whose world has crumbled at the end of *Beowulf.* They cry out in Grettir, the outlaw of Icelandic saga, holed up and beleaguered in some rocks, the only habitation left for his misery. The same fears thrummed between the calm words of the man speaking by telephone from his Beirut basement to Barbara Frum in Toronto. Upstairs, outside, they were blowing apart his beautiful ancient city. Feeding a communal nightmare.

I lived these perilous stories in Alberta, and my boys live them in Ontario, both in their dreams and their lives. The family cat swells to wolf-size and lunges out of a closet, a ferocious dogfish lurks in First Depot Lake. The elder cringes amid a chaos of older kids in a school bus carrying him to a stepmotherish kindergarten teacher, the younger slips off a wooden footbridge into the cold March water of Depot Creek. Wearing his snowsuit. The faces of the story blur change and sharpen again and again, as we recognize but never quite grasp, like the one we love, the thing that scares us.

Fraser Sutherland

from *In the Village of Alias*

The Sacred Glow: A Novel

Chapter One

Are successful journalists – even successful business journalists – frustrated artists? Jim Vickers had stopped asking himself that question. Indeed, if Jim had kept his college friends the 29 years since his graduation, they might have laughed at him, the editor-publisher of *Plastics Today*, for he'd been part of a writing circle at the University of Toronto, reading poetry as devoutly as some people devoured their morning *Globe and Mail*. He recalled the cosy pipe-smoking sessions, friends gathered round – U. of T. out of Oxford – and the endless talk about poetics. He edited a poetry sheet put out by the group. *Rudiments*. Yes, they'd laugh at him. But they'd be laughing at themselves. Just the other day he'd spotted an appointment notice in the *Globe and Mail* "Report on Business." The group's most rapturous poet had been named general supervisor in the Montreal office of he Prudential Life Insurance Company.

Chapter Two

Alec Carson, whom Jim knew slightly in college, was a bulky, rumpled, broad-shouldered man who wore heavy tartan shirts and often stank. Alec did not like arguing about cadences but once, over some girl, had gotten in a fight on Jarvis Street and been thrown in jail. Jim published one of his poems but after Alec quit school, heard no more of him for five years. In those years Jim graduated, got a job with a newspaper, then switched to a company which published trade magazines. It was short-term, he told his friends, until he had enough money saved to be a poet full-time. He was being practical. Once he had a stash, he'd go to Scorpios or Hydra. The flame still burned within him, and the Muse hovered, waiting, ever watchful.

Chapter Three

In the early '50s he founded the little magazine *Soliloquy*. He'd married and Vivienne had a bit of money. They got along well in bed; he was sure she believed in his talent; she paid the printing bills. It was a good combination. One day, warmed by successful domesticity and the pride he felt in helping to shape, even create a Canadian literature, he got a handful of poems in the mail from Alec Carson. At first, Jim was not sure they were the kind of poems he wanted for his magazine. He wanted contemporary poetry, but Wallace

Stevens contemporary poetry. Yet he admired Alec's muscular images, the hard taut tensions. He wrote him a short, pleasant note of acceptance.

Chapter Four

Soliloquy went through six issues and several more of Alec's – and Jim's – poems before Jim reluctantly closed it down. He'd started payments on a house in Etobicoke, a borough for the prosperous, or those who hoped to be so. Appropriately, Jim's lot was near the bank of the Credit River. He put Greece aside – temporarily, he said.

Chapter Five

But he kept up with the writing that was going on in Canada, and filed the little magazines neatly away in his den, on one wall of which was mounted the Meerschaum he'd ceremoniously puffed during those halcyon college days.

Chapter Six

As the years passed, Jim went the trade magazine career route from editorial assistant to assistant editor to managing editor. He worked for *Office Furnishings & Equipment*, *Canadian Food Processor*, and even for a few months on a fortnightly distributed to plumbing suppliers, *The Gasket*. The bald title looked almost as bad on the cover as that of the British trade journal, *Chicken*. With some relief he found himself appointed editor of *Plastics Today*.

Chapter Seven

The day his appointment came through, Jim had lunch with a friend of his, a junior editor at a trade publisher. Harvey Mossbaum told him about a book of poems and stories he had just read and unavailingly recommended. The editorial board had decided there was too much risk involved in putting Alec Carson's book on the market. But it was great stuff, Harvey told Jim, and he believed in it so much he was willing to put up his own money to launch it. Provided he could find another backer. Jim agreed to join him. Liaison Press was formed and even made a small profit on Alec's book. Encouraged, Harvey quit his job and begged Jim to become a full-time partner in the new venture. Jim thought it was the hardest decision of his life when he turned down the offer.

Chapter Eight

Tempted as he'd been by Harvey's proposal, Jim now had an orderly, comfortable life. He could no longer be sure of Vivienne's moral or financial support, the Vivienne who, a small-town girl catching up, increasingly acted out a *New Yorker* advertisement. As well, there were mortgage payments to meet; they were worth it because Etobicoke land values had gone skyward. As for his job, it was a bore, but the routine was undemanding, almost automatic. He could spend long lunch hours looking at paintings. There were few, if any, in his firm who could read Baudelaire fluently in the original, or who slowly savoured the work of Wallace Stevens. This was a source of undemonstrative pride to him.

Chapter Nine

On a whim, he invited Alec to lunch at a restaurant with a fine Italian buffet. Vivienne, who'd been shopping, came along and the tree of them sat and ate the marinated beef and the good salad. Alex was bearded now, but still wore a heavy tartan shirt. He looked like a lumberjack sitting there with the shirt bulging out the corduroy sports coat. Vivienne sat opposite, in her neat navy blazer and grey wool skirt. Jim enjoyed the contrast, admiring anew the restrained good taste his wife had dedicatedly acquired, her slim legs and model's waist. Pugnacious Alec, known for his fierce rows with reviewers, was cordial and unexpectedly modest.

Chapter Ten

For the next few months, Vivienne became something of a stranger to Etobicoke, her Volvo station wagon seldom gracing the driveway when Jim arrived home at six o'clock. She'd become a busy volunteer for the March of Dimes. This was a new development, and Jim was glad she was getting involved. Still, when one evening she told him that she'd grown tired of good works, he was a little relieved.

Chapter Eleven

About this time Alec's first novel appeared; "brawling" and "lusty" were the reviewers' adjectives. Some added "Rabelaisian." Book-of-the-Month took it, and his bearded, scowling face became a feature of the television screen: among the bland professional liberals he looked real, to be counted on for combativeness and energy. He travelled a lot and drank a lot, took up women and dropped them. Newspapermen, scrambling for comparisons, called him a latter-day Jack London, a Canadian Norman Mailer. The critics said that only his poetry was valuable, and Jim agreed.

Chapter Twelve

The phone rang on Jim's desk. The editor of *Municipalities* suggested lunch. Jim said, "I'm up to my neck in work." After he hung up, though, he pushed the stack of paper back and, using his favourite escape route, went out to lunch alone. In the restaurant with the lavish Italian buffet he sipped Dubonnet, half-reclining in the chair. He liked the restaurant's downy carpet, the walnut panelling, the four-square window frames, he liked the food, the drink; when it was time to settle he liked the colourful array of credit cards from which he chose. Going to the buffet for beef, he concluded, was not such a bad life. But those were not especially poetic thoughts.

Chapter Thirteen

The newspapers were full of it the next day. Alec Carson had been fatally stabbed in a downtown bar after a brawl over the bill. His drinking companion had been arraigned. One report even mentioned that the tab came to $163.50. Disturbed, Jim was unable to work. He went home early but when he tried to talk to Vivienne about Alec's end, she was non-committal.

Chapter Fourteen

Alec became even more a success in death than in life. That Saturday's edition of the Star carried a full-page feature on the "racy, turbulent life of Alec Carson." The CBC gave a radio hour to him, and a half-hour special on TV. At first, Jim wondered if he would be interviewed about his connection with him. But there were so many people in Alec's crowded life, so many explosive episodes.

Chapter Fifteen

The promotion came through. He was to become group publisher, six trade journals under his control. There was also a large jump in salary. He was now an executive. That same day he read that Alec's literary efforts were to be auctioned later in the month. Alec's papers, his notebooks, even his hash pipe were up for sale.

Chapter Sixteen

Jim sat in a middle row in the auctioneer's showroom, not sure why he was there to watch the bidding. Alec's holograph manuscripts were on the block. The leading bidder was a university archives, betting on posterity. Suddenly, Jim found his hand in mid-air. The auctioneer nodded, and the bidding climbed, Jim's arm still paralyzed in mid-air, like an Olympic runner holding aloft a torch. Then he won. The whole wine-stained, pencil-smudged portfolio was his. The library had only limited funds for posterity. Jim Vickers walked back to his office with the bundle under his arm. Hurrying up the street he saw at the end of it, near an intersection, a sheet of ice that caught the sun. There in the middle of the street it became a warm golden patch that glowed and glowed, and for an instant became a flame of pure light. Jim was happy with the moment.

John Riddell

Criss Cross

ONE NIGHT, AS OZ WORKED ON HIS NOVEL...
OMEN
MEMO
GAD! THIS IS SENSATIONAL STUFF...

OZ decided th
one way the forms mi
run might be might be ag
he thought perhaps one way th
forms might run might be the other
way. Hmmm. Had any run that way before? He
really didn't know. From where he was he tried to
AWRK!

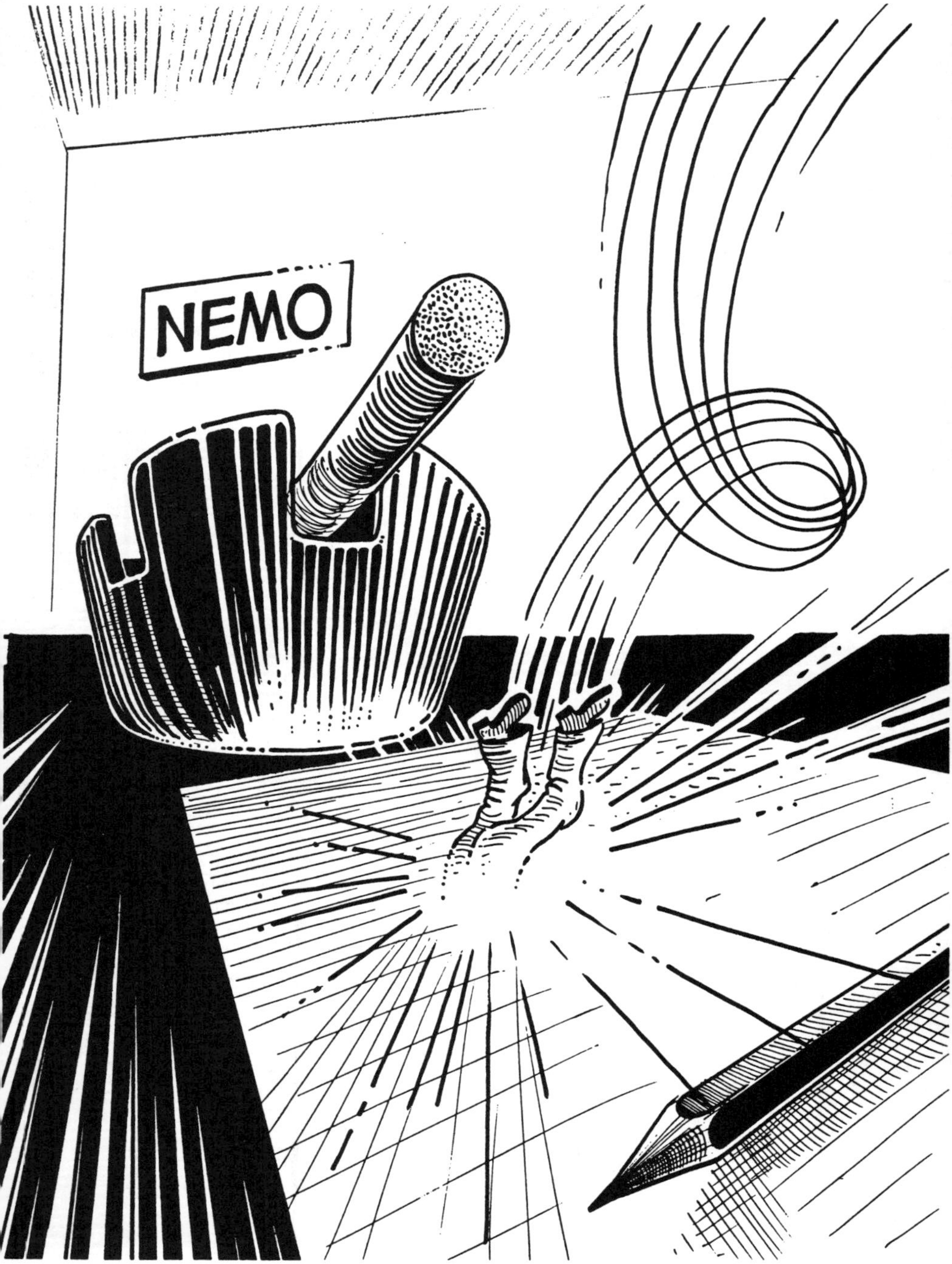
NEMO

HM-M-M... WHERE AM I?
OH NO!.... TRAPPED
BEHIND MY OWN PROSE!
A PRISONER OF
THE TEXT!

GAD! WHAT A MESS...

WHEW!!
AH!
A CLEARING
SPACE ...

HM-M-M,...
WHAT'S THIS ?

GAWD!
IT'S A GIANT H!

OH NO.... DON'T!
AGH!
IT'S GONNA FALL!!

AH-H-H-H

WHEW!
ONLY A DREAM!

Geoff Hancock

Singularities: fragments, parafictions, prose poems
New Directions in Fiction & Physics

A Parafictional Truth

Something new has happened to Canadian Writing.

Let's call it a break with the Cartesian order of continuity.

True, I've been rereading recent fiction in the light of recent insights in quantum mechanics. Quarks. Spinors. Twisters. Spin Networks. Calibi-Yao space. Orbifolds. Or my favourite, tachyons, faster than light particles. All fictions, all hypothetical insight.

Some people like simple pictures. Objective. External reality. Not me. I experience a different despair.

This book for example. Another anthology. A book of fragments. Prose poems. Parafictions. Surreal objects. Word constructions.

Parafiction, now there's a word you don't hear much. It's a slippery little bugger of a word that refers to the thin line between autobiography, fiction, and non-fiction essays which incorporates some of the elements of narrative.

I experience this book of fragments as an integrated whole. All the images impose a pattern, a form, on formless material.

Yet, each blank space is different.

Each space carries a different meaning. I'm a child of the sixties. I know what Jim Morrison and the Doors meant by "Break on through to the other side."

I would like to make a bold assertion: *The singularity presents the biggest challenge of contemporary fiction and physics.*

Andre Breton reminded us in another context the surrealist act is not aesthetic. Realism is juxtaposed with abstraction. Creation is always a magical act. Get that thought into your thick head, as my Dad would say.

The Big Shift

I want to be reckless, return to Sam Roddan's grade 12 English class. Join the Writer's Club. I had uncertain direction. I should have been in the Science Club. The Chess Club. The Parliamentary Debating Club. Someplace with nuance, vision, order, and theorem. My glasses never fit properly; I filled Hilroy notebooks with shifty assertions. I wrote, "a change of perception contains a desire to change the world."

The biggest shift in art is a new interpretation of realism. I knew this in grade 12. The 1990s bring new and different attitudes towards the problem of mimesis, or representation. In physics, its epicentre is in the new science of chaos or disorder. James Gleick's *Chaos* and Stephen Hawking's *A Brief History of Time* are two years on the *New York Times* best seller list. Yoichiro Nambo invents the term "postmodern physics," and contemplates the string theory. In the Writer's Club, I was in the same situation. My theories, ideas, and concepts were abstract, far ahead of any written experiment.

Instead of experiment and observation, my investigations were always in the realm of formal language structures. I wanted to expand the theory, admire it, make it consistent and related to other theories. I knew the structure of mind and the structure of nature were reflections of each other.

I loved molecules, the space between myself and the night sky, the shape of galaxies, star atlases. I would watch the stars until my hands and feet froze, too amazed to go indoors.

I wanted to reproduce in print how I felt about all of this. But I knew Canadians did not like manifestoes, theories, independent scholars, social revolutionaries, pure ideological speculators, surrealists, or esoteric spiritualists. I knew I needed my own magazine.

But I always came back to literature. Anguish, Denial, Revenge. The sharing of wisdom. Insight. The synaptic connections of the brain and its neural networks. In literature and literary theory, deconstruction theory and practice questions all that we take for granted about language, experience, literary practice, philosophy, and "natural" systems of human communication. It was so obvious in the Grade 12 Writers Club.

Language was only a surface, with depths, and then more depths. Not the sign, the signifier, or the signified. But the periphrasis. The gap between sign and meaning. The phase transition.

Prose that appeared marginal and isolated was the true centre of Canadian writing.

I thought, even then, about cultural shifts. Borderblur. Blurred genres. Fragments, prose poems, broken narratives. Not as poetic ambiguity, but as the collapse of tradition into another tradition. A big shift.

Singularities

Stephen Hawking's best-selling *A Brief History of Time* describes the Theory of Singularities. This special instant, Hawking suggests, may be the origin of the universe, or the end of it. Yet, we cannot describe what lies before or after it. When a super star collapses, space vanishes and time comes to an end as a Black Hole. A black hole consists of two parts. Its surface is called an "event horizon," a frontier beyond which everything is hidden. (Coach House Press published a book of art essays by that title.) Within the event horizon is a single outlandish point of infinite density at one moment of time called a singularity. Here the known laws of physics break down.

The known laws of physics break down.

How closely that echoes the Second Surrealist Manifesto. That the artist strives to attain "a mental vantage point (point de l'esprit) from which life and death, the real and the imaginary, past and future, communicable and incommunicable, high and low, will no longer be perceived as contradictories."

In music, previously forbidden intervals emerged as the basis of a new harmony.

For surrealists, the contradiction should not be obliterated or ignored, but stood upon as the highest artistic ground. "Reality is the apparent absence of the contradiction. The marvellous is the eruption of the contradiction within the real," Louis Aragon writes.

The discoveries of modern astro-physics – black holes, white holes, wormhole bridges – are so astounding that I'm surprised fiction hasn't erupted everywhere, in the same blinding flash as the Big Bang.

Modern physics developed a new way of perceiving reality, the "field of theory" view. Impossible questions had to be solved to force us into a new understanding. The ideas of Einstein, Plank, Bohr, Heisenberg, Margeneau, Penrose and Hawking challenged us.

Black holes are strange warped places. All that can be seen at the event horizon is a distorted region of x-ray energy, with bent space and dragged time, proof of the power of gravity as suggested by Einstein's General Theory of Relativity. Gravity can bend light rays if enough matter accumulates in a region. A strong gravitation field can create a "Trapped Surface" from which light cannot escape. A traveller would have a "singular experience" if he followed a beam of light into a singularity. Space and time would come to an abrupt end. Poof, he would disappear.

I've recently become a student of meditation. Once, at the end of the three and a half day meditation, my body disappeared. A spiral of energy swirled up my spine, my head felt like it unravelled in a diamond bright blaze of light, and "I" no longer existed. Buddhist and Hindu monks know this experience as "the enlightenment," the displacement of the ego. In the Kundalini experience, I saw the thousand petalled lotus. As a tai chi chuan student, I saw my origin, the mysterious light from which my chi or life force energy arises.

How to understand this, how to explain that my personality did not fragment, but became more coherent and organised, like those wonderful statues by Rodin where the uniqueness of a subject becomes unfinished stone, part of the raw material of the planet. As the Yang body in tai chi becomes part of the Yin space.

The Greatest Singularity of all might be that primordial seed which expanded fifteen billion years ago out of quantum foam to produce our universe. Atomic particles may themselves be "tiny singularities." Who knows? The new fictions and physics deal in the Concept of Uncertainty. This fringe area is unknown, maybe unknowable. Astrophysicists call this Cosmic

Censorship. The truth within a black hole may be forever denied us. For me, the fundamental question is revelation, not of the divine order, but of the dimly perceived human one – how to describe what is real through fiction.

The vast problem of representation is an ancient debate. From Plato's "Phaedo" to Locke's Essay Concerning Human Understanding, Diderot's Encyclopedia, Nietzsche's proclamation of the textual nature of truth, to Derrida's aesthetic credo "there is nothing outside of the text," all demonstrated repeatedly unresolved problems. How to describe the undescribable? By the 20th century Albert Einstein argues "A singularity brings so much arbitrariness into its theory it actually mollifies its own laws." If the centre of the universe is not a singularity, what might it be? Hawking muses on the Big Bubble, the Edgeless Universe, that self contained union of space and time with no boundary or edge, no beginning no end, a place for a Creator.

Just like these fictions.

Fiction is an imitation of a reality, Aristotle wrote. These fictions present the new reality, a dynamic web of interrelated connections. Ideas, concepts, observations, a ceaseless process of transformations and clarifications unfolding to find deeper interconnections. Cross grain slices of fiction. The discoveries of space / time singularities proved that time and space are not rigid, but changing.

I am fascinated by difficulties of literary thought. Prefer sketches to finished works. Sketches, journals, diaries reveal something of the experience of writing, about beginnings, about how books come into being. Prose poems and fragments are intense, brief, self-contained, concentrated, concerned with material objects, and hard to write. Fragments have a will of their own. Erin Mouré suggests, the writer "has to imagine the shape of the poem before it occurs."

Mind Over Matter

The front line of theoretical physics, post-relativistic concepts, and new insights of quantum theory and logic indicate a new kind of reality. Here, matter is subservient to, and contingent upon, the concept of "mind." These fictions imitate that contingent reality. Space and time are mind constructs. To accept them in this century means a radical shift in perception. In zen, yoga, or tai chi meditations, my brain accepts and rejects details until a satisfactory picture emerges. To reveal reality, I must go beyond its surfaces. I need to explore my introspection, the directions I dream, the unknowns to which I aspire. The awareness that my personality is an expression of the cosmos. My mind is full of tunnels. Small awarenesses. Not quite paths, gates, doors, or openings. But pathways of some kind, that lead back to some place in my mind where I want to go. Nothing I can imagine, no place definite. Alan Watts calls this the unrecognised self.

The surrealists saw Man everywhere in Nature; the stars beckon, the Tarot cards speak, all Nature awaits our glance. A picture book of galaxies is, with a little effort, a book of the stars within ourselves. Galaxies are magical signs, a means of achieving our desires. Magnetic fields connect us to the universe. Such images seem hallucinating, monstrous, the very fabric of our mental life. Itzhak Bentov's experiments proved pulsing magnetic fields develop around the hemispheres of the brain during kundalini yoga meditation. He suggested such magnetic antenna will bring information about our extended sun and solar system and interpret other geophysical phenomena to better advantage. The mystery of life, as Alan Watts says, is not a problem to be solved, but a reality to be experienced.

About ten years ago, I became interested in shiatsu, acupuncture, and Taoist yoga. A friend said I could meditate without needles, directly on the energy meridians. This was my first insight into a new concept of character. An agate slab, the kind you can buy in any rock shop for about five bucks, is a microcosmic map of the universe. (Look at the universe maps in Eric Chiasson's book, *Relatively Speaking:* a study of black holes, relativity, and the emerging universe.) The slab's colours roughly approximate the lights in the mind during the middle stages of meditation.

Such an agate slab is a natural mandala. From the DNA molecule, the shape of the human skeleton, the postures of the tai chi set, the electromagnetic energy surrounding the body, everything I do is a mandala. During meditation, I spiral the light of the stars into my crown point and inhale cosmic dust through my third eye. In the pa kua meditation, I create a crystal of energy into my abdomen, and send a pearl of light into my spirit and energy bodies. In this magical dictation lies proof that the laws of Kepler, Newton, Carl Sagan, and the Great Code of Northrop Frye do not always suffice.

Fiction About Everything

These fictions represent developments in multi-disciplinarity, fragmentation, the disappearance of linearity, and the transformation of the art object. These pieces are hybrid, mutant, and evocative. Unclassifiable. I'd guess their intellectual roots are in the modern art theories of Duchamp, Schwitters, Dada, Kaprow, Kenholz, Beuys, De Maria, Aybock, Jonas as well as contemporary thoughts in science, pop art, and math. Ideas "in the air."

My reading of the new fiction draws from new age mysticism, shamanism, and Taoism. Fiction with ideas first put forward in a non-literary context. Beauty and Symmetry in physics may be the key ideas that unify all elementary forces and particles. In his *Letters from the Equator,* "what matters is symmetry ... the order of the universe," C.H. Gervais writes. Or perhaps, what matters is not Cosmos, the order of the universe, but Chaos, its turbulence and disorder. In such unity, fiction and physics draw together.

Our human destiny seems linked with contemporary narrative forms. Beyond a certain point, conventional methods of analysis don't work, be they generic, thematic, or rhetorical to explain what happens in some new writers. *Singularities* includes many registers of writing: condensed writing, spacious writing, compact writing, free writing, ironic writing, liberated writing, writing taken with a deep breath, writing that is concise. Writing based on the drama of competing textual codes, such as poems and prose. Yet these pieces are about humanness, about existence, about glimpsing spiritual dimensions beyond any literary abstractions.

One of the unexpected developments of particle physics in the 1980s was that theories became entwined with astrophysics and cosmology. Many of the selections in *Singularities* entangle science, language, metaphysics, and literary speculation, including reader response theory. Ed Witten, famed for his Theory of Superstrings – fundamental ten dimensional particles viewed as one dimensional curves – calls these unexpected developments "topologies."

A topology is concerned with boundaries, intersection, and containment. Primitive, yet powerful relationships might link explicit forms with an underlying implicit, or enfolded form. For example, a pair of scissors is topologically the same as a tea kettle because both have two holes. Distant events may be directly connected through this new order of understanding. Ed Witten's new Theory of Nothing deals with minimal connections, what he calls "phase transitions." The "essence" of water is the same whether it's ice, liquid, or steam. A "phase transition" occurs when one form changes to another. Perhaps the contributions to this anthology are in a genre phase transition.

Topology is usually applies to the study of geometric figures as they are distorted or deformed in various dimensions. But ordered relationships within different categories turn out to be compatible in subatomic processes. Physics connects, perhaps, with cosmic strings infinitely thin, astronomically long, to become fiction.

Following my natural instinct, I find a resonance – a topology – between the New Age, New Physics, and New Fiction. For centuries, our assumptions about the nature of reality have been determined by the theories of science. Yet, I'll go back further than this. Taoists, in their insistence on yin and yang, have known for 5,000 years that bright stars (yang, or male) must be accompanied by dark stars (yin, or female). Yet the black holes were only determined in the 1960s, and the first identified as recently as 1979. Quasars – the most distant objects on the edge of the universe – have their light bent by the gravity of dark, or "missing" matter. An amazing correlation exists between Stephen Hawking's description of the universe as an expanding and contracting sphere with no boundaries, the Taoist Yin-Yang circle, and the opening and closing of a book.

Ninety to ninety-nine percent of the universe is "dark," "not visible" as radio astronomers proved with the 1960s discovery of pulsating radio sources, or "pulsars." Quasi-steller objects, or "quasars" emit enormous amounts of energy at X-ray, radio, or infrared wavelenths. The observed structures of galaxies and superclusters give way to the theoretical structures of superstrings, cosmic voids, and the background radio wave echo of the Big Bang.The first black hole was discovered in the 1970s in the constellation Cygnus; the second in the Large Magellenic cloud. Now cosmologists speculate that the centre of the Milky Way galaxy may be a supermassive black hole. Some even say the universe itself is an enormous black hole.

It follows, and is proven by Kirilian photography, PET and CAT scans, auras, and acupuncture – not to mention chakras, astral, and ethereal envelopes – that ninety percent of the human body is invisible. From a Taoist viewpoint, such energy fields raise the question at what point do I end, and you begin? Thus, a fiction might also be ninety percent invisible, in the gaps, the spaces, the margins, what Gerard Genette calls the paratext where reader-response and criticism occurs. Genette writes about zones of transition between text and space, zones of transaction between text and implied reader, and intentions or thresholds which direct the reader. Physicists speak of resonance when elementary particles react, interact, and remain together. A resonance occurs in a tiny region of space, its energy temporarily bound, a fiction.

This is where I meet you, words leaping across some power line between page and eye. The brain scientists call these K lines, or knowledge lines. Beyond the conventional boundaries of fiction, logical reasoning, and intellectual analysis, lies a correspondingly larger sense of our identities.

The Art of Discontinuity

As Patrick O'Donnell, author of *Passionate Doubt: Designs of Interpretation in Contemporary American fiction,* writes, "The reader is a participant in an unfolding language or sign system of the book being read – at once its witness, its mediator, and one of its referents." Stephan Jay Gould, a popular science writer, calls the rapid change of a narrative tradition a "punctured equilibrium." Somehow I get the feeling the modernist period is over. These fictions represent a change in attitude. Perhaps they describe a hope or fear. Perhaps they focus attention on the nature of literary modernism and post-modernism. Perhaps we should concentrate our attention exclusively on the nature of change itself.

In the early vestiges of Canadian post-modern, the fictions, as Richard Pearce says, are conspirators, accomplices, agents in the "demolitions" of linearity. These fictions, "by denying us the security of a frame as well as the stability of a centre ... compel us to take full responsibility for our perceptions, sensations, and judgements." What is a definition of modern fiction? What is our pre-eminent literary construction? What is the nature of literary form? Which forms are unnecessary? Which historical styles are the losers?

When fiction changes, we are naturally afraid of what might replace it, as we fear our ego death when it approaches enlightenment – the source of our being – during the rising and spiralling of prana or ch'i. We have an uncertainty of remodelling. We might develop a taste for hybrids. To call these fictions post-modern raises the question of what was modern. These fictions are post-modern because they reflect or create the confusions of mass society. Modernist culture has broken up, we're on the verge of some new realm, and these fictions spill out.

These fictions, or "literary spills," are from the edge. The fringe. Marginal writing. Abstractions which correspond to some deeply felt need of our culture. As Michael Dean searches for the perfect lawn, he takes care of patterns, of fictions, of edges, of dreams, of grass. "I was the pattern in the lawn." He adds, "for the truth you don't always have to look beneath the surface." Cutting the grass offers contemporary challenges to coherence and continuity. Can you cut it?

The story itself is a "particle." It's connected to that basic desire of a writer to shape random events into a pleasing order or design. My human need for order is itself a fiction-making process. Virginia Woolf said she wanted to record the atoms falling on the mind as they fell, and then trace the pattern each insight or incident scored upon consciousness. Gay Allison's "The Slow Gathering Of" details such a process in an interconnected collage of meaning. What is the decisive encounter that transforms? What new pattern might rearrange our understanding of history, say, from a feminist viewpoint? What delight is to be found in a permanent altered state of consciousness?

American fabulist Robert Coover said, "Life is so complicated that we have to live by fiction, we cannot handle all the input, so we isolate little bits and make reasonable stories out of them." When a static and linear method of presenting the world is replaced with multi-layered responses of uncertainty and relativity, then fiction and physics have come together, with the fictions as playful as atoms clattering in my hand like marbles. As Eugene McNamara suggests, everything falls into place despite the lines of dramatic action coming from several different directions. Ch'i is a dynamic energy pattern of relationships that follows a certain direction and defines that falling into place.

Zen and the Art of Fiction

Each of our minds evolves its own internal universe. It's usually orderly, but sometimes all the rules break. What is the zen of these texts? Zen, New

Physics, and Mysticism: the less individualistic explorations of science and non-Western philosophies have prompted many literary investigations, especially in the freewheeling on the road dharma bum days of literary improvisation. bp Nichol ponders toes and questions the narrative of the body within. He perceives a split not only between the mind and the body, but between "pre-atomic feet" and "post-atomic poet feet." The internal message of the body may be that somebody, something, speaks from the other side of language.

The third eye is totally overlooked by IQ tests. Michael Bullock ponders some of these questions in his perceptive story, *Jonathan Weltseele Enters the Garden.* The Divine Serpent, or Kundalini Experience, travels up his seven chakras and illuminates the crown. But "it's an incomplete enlightenment ... a pointer towards the possible that had not yet been realised."

The Paradigm Shift

Many of these stories are departures. Meaning is not stable, final, and fixed. The collection vibrates in many dimensions. Certain meanings in criticism are not final, a univocal meaning. These ideas may only just be beginning to challenge gender, genre, closure and fixity, the idea of the saluatory wholeness of the self.

A modernist writer, like Virginia Woolf, believes in a transcendental world. The fragments of language are shored up against the ruins of our civilisation. Yet Transcendence is possible. Over *there* is the ultimate realm of truth, or eventual coherence that helps define, articulate, unify, make intelligible what's *here.* Joyce believed language could order existence. Hemingway had his Code. Wallace Stevens his Supreme Fiction. T.S. Eliot believed in the Great Tradition, W.B. Yeats had Byzantium. And us? We have Robert Kroetsch deconstructing the transcendental. He builds a house of bones, sends horses through department stores, gives us excerpts from the real world.

"Canadian writing takes place between the vastness of (closed) cosmologies and the fragments found in the (open) field of the archeological site. It is a literature of dangerous middles. It is a literature, that, compulsively seeking its own story (and to be prophetic after all: this will still be the case a century from now) comes compulsively to a genealogy that refuses origin, to a genealogy that speaks instead, and anxiously, and with a generous reticence, the nightmare and the welcome dream of Babel," Robert Kroetsch writes in *Beyond Nationalism: a prologue.* "That's why CanLit is on the threshold of the incredible."

Canada: A Borderline Nation

These stories are not about representation, but a reassessment of representation. Maybe even a new order of representation. I'm on the side of disorderly Canada, the alive Canada,the consciousness of its subatomic particles. Question: how is this book structured? Answer: around the competing themes of separation and reconciliation. This book is a giant net: what's caught in the mesh is what I've offered you to read. The Dravadians would call it interweaving psychic energies.

Singularities is about the loss of boundaries, experimentation, exploration, and multiple identities that is short fiction. Fred Wah notes in his moving "Elite," "I see only your singularity ... " We see in words, facts are unreal, and so are photos, memories, and dream noises. The reader must respond to the gaps. Gaps are all in the family. CanLit is preoccupied with intervals and discovered fragments. The white stuff on the page is our ignorance which makes us Canadian.

The breakdown also occurs in the way in which the fictions are told. John Parks writes in *Human Destiny and Contemporary Narrative Form,* "The abandonment of plot and character in favour of episode and voice, and an often fragmented and discontinuous narrative, reflect a radical questioning, if not outright disbelief in, a notion of human destiny and a sense of relatedness to any overarching theological and cultural narrative paradigm."

For many writers, a central story doesn't explain and give value to human experience. Conflicting realities find expression in competing literary dimensions, and previously unknown forms of linguistic experience and energy. Writing Against the Grain. Antagonist and Aesthetic conflict between genres. Except that in these fictions, emptiness is also a state of activity. The spaces between these fictions is nothing but the post modern condition. Doubt triumphs over absolute certainty.

Entropy

But as always, I prefer the surrealists. Their favourite metaphors were part of physics. Interference was the cancelling out that results from crossing different wavelengths; the short circuit was a dangerous and dramatic breaching of a current of energy, and communicating vessels registered barely visible or magnified responses among tenuously connected containers. All the forces of life intermingle and interlink.

Entropy is the link between black holes, relativity, quantum mechanics, and literature. Einstein's equation $E=mc^2$ proved matter and energy are interchangeable.

Formally speaking, I address my class thus: The increasing disorder in the universe is called entropy. These fictions challenge a sense of an ending, of traditional closure, with the concept of entropy. As a root metaphor, Entropy represents a central image, understood as literal truth, a world view of unlimited scope. Entropy represents disorder, pessimism, vagueness, ubiquitous change, a talismanic law of nature beyond our control, and even contradictory applications of the metaphor. I accept all this information, I tell them.

No one here remembers the Aristotelian idea of the proper balance of beginning, middle, and end. Fragments develop aesthetic variance in defiance of traditional genres. Why should a piece be instantly understandable? The reader of *Singularities* needs to be completely receptive on many levels. Interiorize the piece. Decode the various messages.

Oppositions

The pieces in this book tend to cast off the oppositions between poetry and fiction. *Singularities* is about the fundamental conditions of perception. Data is synthesized and united to become a complete experience. How do we remember fiction? Bits and pieces, fragments, scenes, narrative cells. Fiction is about breaks and a multiplicity of interruptions. Fiction is basically a discontinuous process.

"Short fiction and narrative fragments are the theme indicators of our changing consciousness. We understand the form, content, thought, and motifs of fiction by understanding an author's attitude towards time and space. Understanding how time operates in narrative has led to changes in the art of fiction. Late modernism blurs into post-modernism as theory blends into technique. The whiteness and silence of the page leads the mind into a dialogue with itself," I wrote in a CFM editorial, No. 56.

I continued: "Lately, I've been obsessed with time, physics, particles, fragments, and as Thomas Pynchon might say, the contours of ignorance which must surely exist though we ourselves remain ignorant of them. What exactly is the short story in Canada at the end of the twentieth century?"

I questioned: What's this about the fragmentation of language, the destruction of genre, the breakdown of formal behaviour and works that resist classification? What exactly is realism, and how do changes in our notions of what the world is inaugurate new methods of presenting, or more exactly, imagining this world?

Particle Theory

The idea of Particle Theory comes from three main sources. First, of course, is particle physics. The 19th century discoveries of X-rays, radioactivity, and the electron, led to the twentieth century science of nuclear physics. The first great find of the twentieth century was relativity. Einstein instructed us that gravity, the weakest of nature's forces, is best described as a geometric effect, a curvature or warp in space and time.

The second great find was in the microcosmic. Quantum mechanics replaced certainty with uncertainty. In the realm of the minuscule, changes are abrupt and discontinuous, nature becomes chance and probability. Gauge particles carry the forces between the interacting hundreds of subatomic particles, many still undiscovered. *The Particle Explosion,* by Frank Close, Michael Martin, and Christine Sutton, (Oxford) depicts a spectacular illustrated world of the subatomic. What was the connection between the macro and the micro? The search for Beauty (Symmetry) became an accurate description of nature. Science became an Art; the search for pure aesthetics.

In Quantum Theory, everything results from the interaction of fields of energy. The subatomic world of pions, kaons, omegas, psis, "strange" particles, and charmed particles are categorised as quarks, leptons, and gauge bosons to form a world deep within the contours of our ignorance. "Intertwined universes inhabit each of our bodies," Kroetsch said.

In 1988, mysterious particles were detected from a star in the Hercules constellation. In 1990, mysterious particles emanated from a fiction collection.

Fiction and Physics

From this perspective fiction has nothing in common with the calculated trajectory of classical narration. Yet aren't we told that fiction is an imitation of a reality? If this new world is the reality, a new model of fiction is demanded. How does a writer describe a labyrinth that grows and feeds on their efforts to advance through its ever more complex structure. Ed Witten's Superstring theory suggests the universe is built of "closed" strings, tiny loops in space that vibrate invisible in the three spational dimensions, one of time, and six others. I tie a string around my finger, to remember this.

Jean-Francois Lyotard has a concept of "Meta-Narrative." He means the Great Narrative of which all stories are merely tracings of an absolute that cannot be defined. Stéphane Mallarme's had the same idea of The Great Book. Such a narrative, Lyotard argues, cannot be approached by traditional critical or creative writing methods. It has to be analysed in terms of "language particles" *(particules langagieres).*

Reader response critics say the meaning of the fiction emerges according to how the reader's imagination plays or moves with the pieces. Samuel Beckett writes we communicate as we can, in dribs and drabs. The Physicists search for the Origins of the Big Bang; and writers search for the Big Book. A connection. Neils Bohr, father of Quantum mechanics says, "When it comes to atoms, language can only be used as in poetry. The poet, too, is not really as concerned with describing facts as creating images."

What makes this collection post-modern? Lyotard would say the narrative functions have lost their functors, their great heros, their great dangers, their great voyages, their great goals. A modernist meta-narrative would hold its universe together; but these post-modernist fictions lack a unifying force. Micro-narratives, multiple meanings, and prose poem bits strive against a unified meaning in the post-modernist universe.

Bits

Fragments are the ideal expression for the disasters of our time, since the major disasters are not historical events. They are disasters to our being, our essence, our system, and history. Works that resist genre also resist signifying meanings in advance; as models of description, my selections might resist meaning. In an era of diminished interest in writing by the 1990s, these borderblurs speak to the loss of identity which genre once provided.

"Des-astre" is the image of being separated from the stars, from Copernicus and Galileo and the discoveries of the Renaissance and beyond that abolished our centrality in the universe. Today, the possibility of precipitation is 60 percent. The mathematics of doubt. Our disaster is our non-relationship with the stars. (In Toronto, the newspapers are named after a globe, a sun, and a star. Hardly a cosmic affiliation.)

Euclidean and Non Euclidean Narrative

Let's look at the contrast between Euclidean and non-Euclidean geometry. Francis Ponge has lectured on non-Euclidean Rhethoric as a means of understanding Manet, Lautremont, Baudelaire, Rimbaud, and Mallarmé:

"Why? Because the figures of the old rhetoric, the ellipses, the hyperboles, the parabolas, were equally figures of the old geometry, of Euclidean geometry. The two are the same. However, everyone knows that we are no longer in Euclidean physics. That fact is significant. As a result, it became impossible to account for the window or read the daily paper. We are no longer in Euclidean space."

The role of rhetoric in communicating meaning has changed since Plato and Aristotle. Rhetoric is usually connected to social history, political institutions, and daily life. The western cultural tradition usually organises figures in space (writing a certain way) that affects the character, and hence meaning, of language. Social process affects literary form at the level of genre.

Non-Euclidean writing (fragments) is connected to a crisis of transcendental culture and the historical emergence of new literary meaning. Here, the individual is against the collective, aesthetics versus literary politics. These stories represent a buried class struggle among the genres.

Fiction, then, is no longer continuous. A figure in a ground. The old fictions assumed you could take a stance outside them, know in a sweeping glance what governs the whole process, assumes that narrative is determined from a standardised beginning to a stereotyped end.

Such deterministic narrations are now impossible. Bye bye Aristotle, and his proper balance of the beginning, middle and end. Now that physicists have dematerialised matter, fiction knows its beginning is nowhere are everywhere. Its true starting point emerges from an undetermined moment from within a multi-dimensional space-time. Someplace foggy, undetermined, common, but with a strong sensation, a pulsation, an urge to begin ...

Fractals, Chaos, and Fiction

If the space is no longer Euclidean, with lines, cones, spheres, circles, and triangles, then what might it be? Late in 1987, I attended a lecture at the Ontario Science Centre on "Fractals and the concept of Chaos." How is order found in the chaos that surrounds us? Chaos: the study of turbulence and disorder, is a new science. The guest speaker was world famous mathematician, Benoit Mandelbrot. By the end of the evening, our view of physics, philosophy, mathematics, computer science, and art could never be the same. We gave him a standing ovation for altering our perceptions.

From the right perspective, both the real and the unreal can be seen clearly. Mandelbrot's theory actualises the marvellous, "the wonderland of revelation and dream" that is our human potential, as the surrealists hoped. His math is not mysterious and obscure, but lucid and convincing.

Mandelbrot's world of new mathematics is so strange that new terms have been devised to name its citizens. Benoit Mandelbrot calls his math, fractals, from the Latin *frangere*, "to break, or to create irregular patterns." His book *The Fractal Geometry of Nature*, challenges Euclidean geometry. His figures are irregular, fragmented, jagged, broken up shapes. They include coinages such as dust, curd, whey, grainy structures, hydra-like structures, ramified structures, tiled and pertiled surfaces, self-squared dragons, monkey's trees, Minkowski sausages, flattened flowers, skewed webs, random slices of Swiss cheese, and chains and squigs.

Banished forever from the fractal world is the notion that nature is a collection of things seen from a middle distance. This is a surface world seen up close. These are the likenesses of nature, not nature. The figments of your imagination offer proof that maybe nature is a partially subjective concept. The abstract problems of a new geometry are seen as vivid, recognisable shapes. Visual. Spatial. Mandelbrot would call his mathematical creations fictions. As Baudelaire suggested, we should "dive to the depths of the abyss ... in our never-ending search for something new."

Mandelbrott both discovered a world and invented a world. Einstein said "physical concepts are free creations of the human mind." Poet Muriel Rukeyser said, "The universe is made of stories, not atoms." What exactly is real here, in the language of the writer, or the fractal mathematician, or the quark physicist? Is reality material or spiritual? Which of the many vocabularies shall we adopt? The fractal world is a disruptive beauty.

What is more amazing, as Mandelbrot's slideshow of computer generated images suggests, is the uncanny relationship of fractal geometry to fields as diverse as painting, architecture, surrealistic fiction. That point where art and science again unite. In the fractal world of non-Euclidean geometry, clouds, snowflakes, riverbanks, coastlines, tree branches, air passages in the lungs, natural drainage systems, commodity process (a hint that Darwin was equally influenced by the rise and fall of stocks), tree bark, the stars in the sky, and galaxy clusters are all fractal.

As he ponders the Mandelbrot set, the most complex object in mathematics, he wonders if the set exists. If he exists. If we exist. Fractals describe the way things cluster in space and time. They describe the way things meld, branch, bifurcate. Mandelbrot offers insight into the organising structure hidden within complex shapes. Such shapes, such fictions, carry meaning. Fractals are the key to the essence of a thing.

As fiction seems to be real, a computer generating fractals seems to generate somthing like nature. Necessary shapes. A math professor becomes as much creator as observer. He creates the things portrayed, but not the things themselves. How long is the coastline of Canada, Mandelbrot might ask? It depends on the length of the ruler you're using. The coastline can be measured without limit, from kilometres to inches, from millimetres to microns, down to molecular scales. *Singularities* is an unfinished fractal portrait of Canada.

The Mystery of Schroedinger's Fiction

Traditionally, geometry is presented as the discipline of the ideal. Classical geometry is a powerful abstraction of reality. It created an important philosophy, Platonic harmony. An exact description of physical objects determines their position in space. Platonic harmony does not apply to pitted, pocked, broken, twisted, tangled, intertwined objects. Fractals fracture rhetoric; each object (fiction) determines its own rhetorical form. Each writer establishes his or her own rhetoric.

As a reader, I can adopt one of two basic perspectives to view either elementary particles or textual meanings. I can be ontological or objective, looking at basic properties, relations and structures to come to a theory of the object. Or I can be epistemological, looking at various modes of perceptions. Which one to choose? Traditional philosophy and literary theory offers three metaphysical postulates, according to U of Alberta Comp Lit professor Uri Margolin. First, I can assume the textual meanings are constant, stable, and independent of the observer and of any specific mode of knowing that may precede them.

Or I can assume the object may exist independently, but with its properties accessible only through the mediation of consciousness. And finally, I might assume the properties of the object are a function of the knowing subject and are constituted by him. *Singularities* is an anthology of alternate choices, the mystery of Schroedinger's cat. The animal is alive and dead at the same time in this famous math paradox.

Math and Physics and Fiction. What connects them? Each had to invent a language to talk about the world. In the precision of language what we learn about the world is a result of the way we write about the world. The role of language is important in shaping our experience. As Einstein said, "To him who is a discoverer in this field, the products of his imagination appear so necessary and natural that he regards them, and would like to have them regarded by others, not as creations of thought but as given realities." Einstein, a closet surrealist. Fiction creates new relations between various domains, new ways of organising and understanding the actual and non-actual world.

Einstein said, "It seems that the human mind has first to construct forms independently before we can find them in things. Kepler's marvellous achievement (on deducing the orbits of planets) is a particularly fine example of the truths that knowledge cannot spring from experience alone, but only from the comparison of the inventions of the mind with observed facts."

Fragments push up against boundaries. Where literature, culture, art, and philosophy stop, the fragment begins.

Non-Linear Dynamics

If beginnings are indeterminate, insignificant events can be amplified. The fate of these fictions hinges on the condition that a singular event takes place. What was micro becomes macro. Fiction depends on these improbable deviations. Something unknown takes shape through the cloud of unknowing. Fractals involve non-linear dynamics, as do many of these fictions. Chaos is a metaphor. Physics is for poets. The structures are complex. Patterns appear in leaps and discontinuities. A beginning is a discontinuity. An abruption of knowing. To read Karl Jirgen's "Strappado," for example, is to participate in the Periodic Table. The story included is "uranium," and the fiction dramatises various levels of narrative mutation.

As a Canadian, I think about space and interface, separations between things. Marshall McLuhan's famous essay on Canada as a borderline case is of enormous importance in the imaginative life of any Canadian, marking out, as it does, the interface of two major cultural identities, historical definition, literary distinction. These fictions then, are the point at which new intersections can occur. Our Canada in a blasted, fragmented, landscape cosmos which by the action of our presence we try to unite, writes Andrew

Stubbs. The writer goes for a synthesis, not only of what is "there" but what is hidden. In these fragments, we experience a freedom found nowhere else. The infinite possibilities of these broken texts require an active conception of the works. Again, as in tai chi, find the centre, the balance point.

In the interaction of these bits and pieces of narrative fragments across a textual field, I see the atomic particles of the Canadian imagination. These varying styles are the remnants of a "Canadian subject" we are so afraid of losing. What a heroic effort for the fragmentary writer forever exiled from the land of non-writing. Gwendolyn MacEwen is not jesting when she quotes from "obscure Kanadian poets." Grey Owl must write Kanada down, "the magnificent indifference of Nature, its broken silences."

Contorted Middles

What exactly are middles? What are natural developments? If the beginning can't be located, then the middle must be contorted. "It will look like a system that must reconcile discontinuity with organisation, breaks with repetitions, bifurcations with progress," one critic wrote. If beginnings are the first item of change in modern fiction, then middles are the second. These fictions contain few middles, only indefinitely entertwined networks.

N. Kathleen Hayles says in *The Cosmic Web* the biggest problem of reality is the problem of articulation. What language to use? The binary sequence of computer programs? The "wave packet" equations of quantum mechanics? The syntactically linearnatural languages of scientists attempting to come to terms with their models? "Because the task of articulation requires that a vision of a dynamic, mutually interacting field be represented through a medium that is inherently linear, fragments, and uni-directional, the novelist's concern with language will have much in common with these scientific concerns ... the authors ... have their own perspective and insights to bring to this problem. Whereas the scientific theories are created through the attempt to express the field view in rigorously exact models, the literary strategies are forged by the desire to find a form, and a language, adequate to express its human meaning."

What happens in the gaps? Where is the communion? Narrative interrupts itself, is threatened. Words meet blank space in the singularity. The centre of Canada is everywhere and nowhere, an absence. The centre of art is absent. Are Canadian writers even capable of "literature" in an absent country? The break, or rupture, represented by these fictions demands a separation from traditional thought.

In literary terms, these pieces do not respect "genre." But they do raise questions about culture and anarchy, including the question of whether there is any need for literature and art in a technological society that trivialised ideas and marginalises, if not outright exiles, most forms of creative activity. These short pieces call attention to the limits of other genres: poems, stories, novels. The professors would say these fictions foreground genre tensions, conflicts, and attempted resolutions. The prose poems especially raise a few oppositions, like those between capital L literature and ordinary language, especially in their concern with everyday objects and prosaic reality.

If prose poems have a political concern at their roots – to challenge genre, the fragment does not. Philip Beitchman writes in *SubStance*, "The fragment doesn't contend with or try to modify the dominant disciplines and ideas. It lets them gradually exhaust themselves with their increasingly obvious futility." The fragment is all that remains. Institutional logic creates its own barriers to the unfinished work. Outside such logic, these fictions might even be inexpressible, ungrammatical, nonsensical, unpatriotic, not part of the old Can Lit at all.

Maurice Blanchot demonstrates convincingly that what matters is not the works in themselves but the themes they invent and provoke, the experiences they originate in, and the times they point the way to. Blanchot doesn't care all that much for the written word, "the important thing is not exactly what the author said, but what he meant." For Blanchot, there is a strict analogy between revolution and *ars nova*, because both imply a radical break with the past. These fictions are at once "norm-breaking" and threatened with popular acceptance.

Behind many of these fictions lies a political hope for the disintegration of Canadian society and the power structures which comprise it. Too long, in Canada, literature has been dominated by elitist elements in society. The end of a traditional art and culture. Lola LeMire Tostevin's "A Weekend at the Semiotics of Eroticism Colloquium held at Victoria College" suggests male and female understanding, let alone survival, depends upon new perceptions. As Einstein says, it's the theory that decides what we can observe.

The Arts of Disorder

Fiction begins abruptly with a chance opening. Middles aren't possible. Events aren't always connected. Once set in motion, fiction proceeds to improbable ends. A fiction is an improbable, unstable, self-organising event. A story, a maze of stories, or even no story, is a reflection on the laws that govern its own production. The same as in any dynamic system. Fiction has its own language, as does science and mysticism. But the arts of disorder are the same in fiction, science, and nature.

These fictions reject hierarchy, teleology, or patterns. The heart of most literary, scientific, and philosophical conceptions of the world. Some resist closure, or a single clearly defined ending. This is fiction from the margins, the border, the oddity, the curiosity, the once only, the eccentric. Some of these fictions are without characters, plot, theme, setting, and even words. Martin Vaughn-James' "The General's Weekend" presupposes that fiction is either the residue of events that have already happened, or the ingredients in the artwork are the preparations for events that will happen in the margins. The drama is in the mind (yours, the author's) confronting the page.

I have to break a book open to get at what's inside. A harsh act. Subversive. Breaking the norm. Point to the weakness of literary conventions. The fictions in this collection are also a critique of traditional novels and short stories. Why must literature always include thoughts of unity? These fictions are forms of language that free thought from such unity. Thought images slip and slide. Language is an alien tool, Chris Dewdney notes, and is alive, malignant. The only way to survive language is to keep reading on. Only in this way, as he writes in the excerpts from *The Immaculate Perception,* can consciousness embrace its own materiality.

Magnificent Fragments

The French critic, novelist, and prophet Maurice Blanchot has a theory of "magnificent fragments" where he says the work of Kafka, Musil, and Nietzche challenges the concept of "finished art," say of Flaubert or Balzac. The particle, fragment, mini-fiction, and prose poem, challenge the idea of any kind of complete system. The purest fragment raises the idea that such ideal fictions can only exist in the realm of pure anticipation. The ideal; a genreless genre in a classless society.

The Body Chaotic

Chaos, or non-linear dynamics, may be the best way to comprehend the body's processes. Mathematical chaos is simply a hidden order. Turbulence, unpredictability, wobbles in planetary orbits, and the unpredictability of weather are larger chaotic patterns. Yet these unpredictable and random patterns may have, at higher levels of abstraction, simple patterns of organisation.

Which brings us to fiction. Human behaviour is rarely predictable day by day or minute by minute. But behaviour hovers around a strange attractor called character. Actions may seem random, but dig deep enough, it usually is not. Unpredictable, erratic behaviour, and fictions, can be chaotic, but not random.

The Process of Reading

A book is fragmented by the process of reading it. We read in fragments. A phrase or two, an emotion, a moment of encounter. Each erases the previous gesture. At the end of a book, we make our own book. How do we know which phrase is most important?

Am I looking for some secret law that leads to writing? Richard Pearce has a theory based on literary motion, not movement. Movement in fiction, he writes, is traditionally logical, purposeful, and clear. Motion, on the other hand, is alogical, unpurposeful, and confusing. David Donnell's "The Abstract of Hudson's Bay" develops its logic through associations. A reminder that Canada's most obvious natural feature is itself a meteor crater, a gift from space. (The mines of Sudbury, Ontario are also the result of an impact crater; every nickel in Canada is extra-terrestrial.) Such fictions of motion develop through a series of unpredictable transformations.

The art of short fiction in the 1990s seems to consist of small localised narratives which create a state of destablisation, an unsettling challenge to the concept of order. The author's imagination in recreating fiction particles and fragments has replaced our reliance on traditional stories. In the small narrative, as in pieces by Michael Kenyon and others in *Singularities,* is the greatest invention. The disorder of words and events never leads to dispersion, but to the production of open, growing, and unpredictable structures. Ordered structures from disorder.

Fiction Without Form

The Marxist critic Walter Benjamin suggested the fragment is an adequate expression of what an artist tries to say. Benjamin argues the fragment, then, is much better than a finished work that has been forced by necessity and society to be completed. The fragment might be a catastrophe for the History of Art, but is a crucial part of the process of creation. More than this, writing means nothing less than freedom. Hence, the profound power of writing. We think about this for a moment; the background noise indicates the state of our minds. (Mandelbrot's study of fractals emerged from "noise," interference in electronic transmission which could not be explained.)

The Art of the Fragment

Stories submitted to me at *Canadian Fiction Magazine* seem longer and more traditional these days. A response to a conservative time, a fostering of a traditional canon, a neglect of avant garde thought? I sadly ponder the neglected possibilities. Short fiction encompasses aphoristic and epigrammatic writings, (which the fragment opposes because these forms represent a historical often political need for unity and coherence, closed and finished fragments, made useful and quotable socially).

Short fiction appears as prose poems, Sarraute's tropisms, unfinished works, designed fragments, abandoned works, failed narratives, and texts that defy genre, all unexplored areas of short fiction in Canada. These fragments, poised in that tortured space between logos and silence. Fragments challenge anything that is stylistically and thematically stationary. Including the notion of representation.

Is not the purpose of art its capacity to challenge an audience to question their lives? Is not reality composed mostly of interruptions best conveyed by fragments? Is not the most potent element in a work of art its silences, so claims Susan Sontag in Against Interpretation? Does not failure make possible the continuation of narrative?

Some Latin American writers saw the fragment as part of a text drawn from an ideal, though invisible, order. For Latin American writers, literature is political. Literature asks questions, including the very possibility of art in societies increasingly dangerous, cold, and violent. Post modern fiction implies a distrust of History. We all know there are two histories, that which is recorded, and that which is not. The three pieces of Mary di Michele's "To Inherit the Earth" show the political promise, the anger, the anxiety of short narratives.

Roland Barthes suggests a fragment presents a writer's universe in brief bursts. A fragment does not move towards a conclusion, but maintains a tension, built into the text and felt in the reading. Shorter narratives also refute the assumption of what makes a text important.

Film, of course, is the art of the fragment and the dislocation of time, as shown in the fiction of David Halliday. The *bande dessinée* has been a major influence on Martin Vaughn-James. These stories depend upon a Narrative Eye as well as a Narrative Voice.

Michael Bullock's and Gwendolyn MacEwen's fiction brings together fragments that reveal the formal design of a life. Letters, tapes, celluloid, and numbers may well be the basic and we ourselves are those ruptures, constantly editing. We read in small bits. One page calls to another. We flip back and forth, gather a phrase here, an idea there. Consult the *I Ching Kanada* of Dave Godfrey. Or the Tarot cards. Or have a Kundalini experience.

Absence Makes the Heart Grow Fictional

Blanchot writes of Joseph Joubert, who spent his whole life preparing to put himself into a condition to start writing; only his journals remain, proof he "was willing to sacrifice the results of art to a discovery of the conditions that make art possible." Robert Kroetsch says it's all in the absence, all in the failure, all in the star crossed "I" and "you" of his shifty narrative in "The Dream of Leather is Softly to Enfold." How many characters? How many authors? How many dreams? Whose shoes dream? Heidigger considered Socrates, whose works do not exist, as the Ultimate Writer.

Italo Calvino has shown that fragments are assembled to tell a story that can never be complete. A fiction is an assemblage of fragments (names, characters, theme) that find (through some literary Kibbs-Hibble particle? The character as the genetic code of fiction?) a relationship. Or do they? I like the fictions of disconnected fragments that challenge the idea of "reader" and "character." With this comes the idea of fiction as a game with pieces to move, language and anti-language, the juxtaposition and interpenetration of myth and reality, fantasy and real life, and the fiction of recombination: magic realism, with its marvellous in a real place, or other cross breedings of myth and genre as the particles in fiction combine to make new forms.

Karl Marx, Sigmund Freud, Stéphane Mallarmé, all demonstrated the basic truth of the twentieth century as an escape from the formal signs of the 19th. The world of the 20th century was no longer marked out, pre-organised, geometrical. Heisenberg used new points of departure to understand the modern science of nature. Forms and thoughts were deconstructed to set up new schemes and models of perception. Monet proved with his cathedral paintings that a picture is only a document of the fragmentary nature of our vision at a certain moment of our history. Mallarme saw that a book was made up not of words, but of relationships, when he suggested all of earthly existence must be contained in a book.

In the 1990s, the fiction writer too has to deal with atomistic effects. After Dostoevsky, after Breton, after Cortuzar and Borges, after the literary explosion in Canadian Literature in a twenty-five year period, the writer's skill lay not in Great Answers, but in Great Questions. After *Singularities,* the writers must connect the strands of invisible webs.

Singularities is an accident, a piece of the 21st century that fell backwards into the 20th century.

Biographical Notes

jwcurry lives in Toronto, where he publishes dozens of pamphlets and broadsides from his Curvd H&dz press.

Dave Godfrey is the publisher of Press Porcepic in Victoria, B.C. He won the Governor-General's Award for his novel, *The New Ancestors.* He is a professor of Creative Writing at the University of Victoria, and a pioneer in computer literacy.

Gwendolyn MacEwen won the Governor-General's Poetry Award for The *Shadow-Maker.* Besides several volumes of poetry, her fiction includes two novels, and two story collections, *Noman* and *Noman's Land.* She died in 1987.

Erin Mouré won the Governor-General's Award for poetry in 1988 for *Furious.* She lives in Montreal, and works for the railroad. Her other titles include *Domestic Fuel, Wanted Alive, Whiskey Vigil,* and *Empire, York Street.*

Joe Rosenblatt won the Governor-General's Award for poetry in 1976 for his book, *Top Soil.* Along with several volumes of poetry, including *Brides of the Stream,* he has published prose poems, ink drawings, and two volumes of an autobiography, *Escape from the Glue Factory* and *The Kissing Goldfish of Siam.*

Michael Dean has been doing lawn research since 1976, for his book, *In Search of the Perfect Lawn.* He is a world renowned sound poet, and performance artist with the text / sound ensemble, Owen Sound, and a co-founder of Underwich Editions.

sean o huigin, who lives in Ireland and Toronto and works as a highly successful children's writer, has written *The Nightmare Alphabet* and *The Granny Poems.* His most successful children's book is *Scary Poems for Rotten Kids.* He was winner of the Canada Council Children's Literature Award in 1983.

Anne Szumigalski was born in England and came to Canada in 1951. She now lives in Saskatoon. Her most recent books include *Doctrine of Signatures, Dogstones,* and *Journey / Journee,* co-authored with Terrence Heath. She has twice been nominated for the Governor-General's poetry award, in 1984, and 1986.

Karl Jirgens is editor-in-chief of the foot long post-modernist and pataphysical magazine, *Rampike.* His first story collection was *Strappado.*

Lola LeMire Tostevin is Director of the Creative Writing Program at York University in Toronto. Feminist critic, poet, and translator, her books include *Colour of Her Speech, Gyno-Text, Double Standards,* and *'sophie.*

Smaro Kambourelli was born in Greece, and came to live in Winnipeg in 1978. She now teaches at the University of Victoria, B.C. Her books include *in the second person,* and *A Mazing Space: Writing Canadian Women Writing,* co-edited with Shirley Neuman.

George McWhirter is head of the Creative Writing Department at the University of British Columbia. Winner of the Commonwealth Prize for his poetry, his short fiction has been collected as *Bodyworks, Coming to Grips with Lucy,* and *God's Eye.* He has also published two novels, *Paula Lake* and *Cage.*

Michael Bullock is Professor Emeritus of Creative Writing at the University of British Columbia. Translator of over 150 books from French, German and Italian, he is best known as Canada's leading surrealist poet and fiction maker. Recent books include *Vancouver Moods, Poems on Green Paper,* and *Randolph Cranstone and the Veil of Maya.*

Claire Harris is a writer and teacher who has studied in Ireland, Jamaica, and Nigeria, and now lives in Calgary, Alberta. She won the Commonwealth Poetry Prize for *Fables From The Women's Quarters,* and the Writers Guild of Alberta Award for her poetry collection, *Travelling to Find a Remedy.* Her most recent book of poetry is *The Conception of Winter.*

Patrick Lane lives in Saskatoon. Winner of the Governor-General's Award for poetry for *Poems: New and Selected* in 1979, he has since turned to fiction. In 1989-90, with his companion Lorna Crozier, he was writer-in-residence at the University of Toronto.

Gay Allison is a poet, editor, and English teacher who was born in Saskatchewan. Her recent books include *Life: Still, The Unravelling,* and *In the Valley of the Butterflies.*

Eugene McNamara lives in Windsor, Ontario, where he is a professor of English at the University of Windsor. His short fiction is collected in *Salt, The Search for Sarah Grace,* and *Spectral Evidence.*

bpNichol was one of Canada's most remarkable performance, sound and concrete poets. His prose, poems, and fictions appeared in dozens of booklets and pamphlets, as well as more formal book presentations, including his six volume *The Martrology, Craft Dinner, A Bunch of Proses, The True Eventual Story of Billy the Kid* and the unfinished *Organ Music.* He won a Governor-General's Award in 1970. bp died in 1988.

Rod Willmot is poetry editor of Black Moss Press. His work includes *Ribs of the Dragonfly.*

Paul Dutton lives in Toronto where he works as a poet and editor at Underwich Editions. A member of the sound poetry ensemble, the Four Horsemen, he published many books, including *The Book of Numbers.*

Fred Wah has written several books of poetry including *Among, Loki is Buried at Smokey Creek, Breathin' My Name with A Sigh, Music is at the Heart of Thinking,* and *Waiting for Saskatchewan,* which won a Governor-General's Award in 1985. A founding editor of TISH and co-editor of the electronic journal *Swift Current,* he lives in B.C.

Daphne Marlatt has published over a dozen books of poetry and / or prose, most recently *Touch to My Tongue, How to Hug a Stone, What Matters, Steveston,* and a novel, *Ana Historic.* She lives on one of B.C.'s Gulf Islands.

Betsy Warland is a writer and editor whose books include *A Gathering Instinct, open is broken, serpent (w)rite,* and with Daphne Marlatt, *double negative.* She most recently co-edited *(f.)lip,* a newsletter of feminist innovative writing. She lives on one of B.C.'s Gulf islands where she is writing a play.

Michael Kenyon lives in Victoria. A member of the editorial board of *The Malahat Review,* he is a frequent contributor to *Canadian Fiction Magazine* and other leading periodicals.

C.H. Gervais lives in Windsor, where he edits the book and religion pages of the *Windsor Star,* and publishes the prize-winning titles of Black Moss Press. His own book titles include *The Rumrunners, Into A Blue Morning, Letters from the Equator,* and *Autobiographies.*

Paul Savoie is a man of many talents, who writes in both French and English, and who is also a musician and lyricist. Some of his titles which have received high praise include *A la façon d'un charpentier, Acrobats,* and *Nahanni. The Meaning of Gardens* was his first book with Black Moss Press. He lives in Toronto.

Leon Rooke lives in Eden Mills, Ontario. He has published hundreds of short stories which have been collected as *Death Suite, Cry Evil, A Bolt of White Cloth, The Birth Control King of the Upper Volta,* and *The Magician in Love.* He won the Governor-General's award for fiction for *Shakespeare's Dog* in 1983.

David Halliday lives in Islington, Ontario, where he is a devotee of film. He has published four books, including *The Black Bird,* and *Making Movies: the Films of Samuel Bremmer.*

Susan Musgrave lives in Sydney, B.C. Author of nine books of poetry, and two novels, *The Charcoal Burners* and *The Dancing Chicken,* she is a literary columnist for the Toronto Star.

Martin Vaughn-James lives in Paris. His books include *The Park, The Cage,* and *After "The Cage,"* a special issue of *Canadian Fiction Magazine.*

Christopher Dewdney is from London, and lives in Toronto. His books include *Predators of the Adoration* and *The Immaculate Perception.* Dewdney's work closes the gap between literature and science, between reality and irreality.

Robert Kroetsch is a professor of English at the University of Victoria. Winner of the Governor-General's Award for fiction in 1969 for *The Studhorse Man,* he has become a major theorist of post-modernist fiction and poetry in such novels as *Badlands, What the Crow Said,* and *Alibi,* and poetry or prose in *The Stone Hammer Poems, The Ledger, Seed Catalogue, Field Notes, Advice to My Friends,* and *Excerpts from the Real World.*

David McFadden lives in Toronto. He has published more than twenty-five books of poetry and fiction. Among his fiction are the comic novels,

A Trip Around Lake Erie, A Trip Around Lake Huron, A Trip Around Lake Ontario, Canadian Sunset, and *Animal Spirits: stories to live by.* His most recent book is *Gypsy Guitar: one hundred love poems.*

David Donnell is from St. Mary's, Ontario. Winner of the Governor-General's Award for his poetry collection *Settlements* in 1983, he now lives in Toronto. His prose works include *Hemingway in Toronto, The Blue Ontario Hemingway Boat Race,* and *Water Street Days.*

John Newlove lives in Ottawa. His poems and prose include *Grave sirs, Elephants, mothers, and others, Black Night Window, The Cave, The Fatman,* and *The Night the Dog Smiled.*

Mary di Michele lives in Toronto. Her books include *Necessary Sugar, Immune From Gravity,* and *Bread and Chocolate.*

Kim Maltman was born in Medicine Hat, Alberta. He is currently a particle physicist. His books include *The Country of the Map Makers, The Sickness of Hats, Branch Lines, Softened Violence* and *The Transparence of November Snow* (with Roo Borson).

Judith Fitzgerald lives in Toronto. Author of thirteen books of poetry, she also edited two important poetry anthologies, *Undozen: Thirteen Canadian Poets,* and *Sp / elles: poetry by Canadian Women / Poesie de femmes canadiennes.* She is a prolific contributor to national and international publications, which won her the 1983 Fiona Mee Award for Outstanding Literary Journalism.

Douglas Glover lives on a tobacco farm in southern Ontario. His short fiction has been collected in *The Mad River* and *Dog Attempts to Drown Man in Saskatoon.* His novels include *Precious, The South Will Rise at Noon,* and in-progress, *The Life and Times of Captain N.*

George Payerle lives in Vancouver, where he works as poet, editor, and typographer. His fiction includes *The Afterpeople and Unknown Soldier.*

Colleen Thibaudeau was born in Toronto and is married to the playwright / poet James Reaney. Her publications include *Ten Letters, My Granddaughters are Combing Out Their Long Hair* and *The Martha Landscapes.*

Marlene Nourbese Philip is a "New World" writer who has lived in Canada since 1968. Her poetry includes *Thorns, Salmon Courage,* and *She Tries Her Tongue; Her Silence Softly Breaks,* for which she won the prestigious Casa de las Americas Poetry Prize in 1988. She has also published a novel, *Harriet's Daughter.*

Crad Kilodney is a one man book operation, writing, editing and selling most of his books on Yonge Street, usually published by his own imprint, Charnel House. Other titles have appeared with other presses, most notable, *Lightning Struck My Dick, Malignant Humors* and *The Girl on the Subway.*

Ron Smith lives in Lantzville, B.C., where he teaches in the English Department at Malaspina College. He is a frequent contributor to Canada's finest literary magazines. His latest book is *A Buddha Named Baudelaire.*

Stan Dragland lives in London, Ontario. Founding publisher of Brick Books, his own titles include *Wilson MacDonald's Western Tour, Simon Jesse's Journey, Peckertracks,* and *Journeys Through Bookland.*

Fraser Sutherland lives in Nova Scotia. Founding editor of the poetry magazine *Northern Journey,* his most recent prose collection is *In the Village of Alias.*

John Riddell lives in Toronto. His first collection of stories was *Criss-Cross.* Long associated with the small press movement, he has published with grOnk, Aya, Phenomenon Press, and Konkakte.

Geoff Hancock lives in Stratford, Ontario. Editor-in-chief of *Canadian Fiction Magazine,* he has edited several anthologies devoted to challenging traditional models of perception. Surrealism, magic realism, metafictions, scatology, quantum mechanics, cosmology, and new research in narratology has informed his unique vision of Canadian prose.